Dedicated to

InterVarsity Christian Fellowship

CONTENTS

ACKNOWLEDGMENTS

This book is based on lectures given at the following conferences and institutions: Christian Theological Seminary, Indianapolis, Indiana (April 28, 1982); Trinity Reformed Church, Fulton, Illinois (October 5, 1984); Nazarene Theological Seminary, Kansas City, Missouri (April 21-24, 1987); Southeastern Baptist Seminary, Wake Forest, North Carolina (September 29-30, 1987); Southwestern Baptist Seminary, Fort Worth, Texas (February 14-17, 1989); Renewal Conference at Sheraton Hotel, Hamilton, Ontario, Canada (March 23-25, 1990); Evangelical Presbyterian Pastors' Conference, Kansas City, Missouri (April 23-26, 1990); Earlham School of Religion, Richmond, Indiana (April 8-9, 1991); Renewal Conference at Old Dominion Church, Ottawa, Canada (July 1-5, 1991); Ontario Theological Seminary, Toronto, Canada (August 26, 1992); Illinois Wesleyan University, Bloomington, Illinois (March 10, 1993); Southern Baptist Seminary, Louisville, Kentucky (October 26-29, 1993); Trinity University, Deerfield, Illinois (March 24, 1999); Word and Spirit Conference, University of Dubuque Theological Seminary, Dubuque, Iowa (June 10-12, 1999).

I acknowledge the help given to me by Paul Waelchli, Jaimie Shaffer, David and Debra Lovett, and especially by my wife, Brenda, apart from which this book could not have been completed.

ABBREVIATIONS OF
BIBLE TRANSLATIONS

GNB	Good News Bible
LB	Living Bible
NASB	New American Standard Bible
NEB	New English Bible
NIV	New International Version
NJB	New Jerusalem Bible
NKJV	New King James Version
NLT	New Living Translation
REB	Revised English Bible
RSV	Revised Standard Version

Note: Bible references not otherwise indicated are from the Revised Standard Version.

PREFACE

Within the past several decades the focus of the church has shifted to spirituality. Most often this has been understood as a technology of the Spirit by which we ascend to a higher spiritual realm in order to satisfy the longings of the human heart. My intention in this book is to differentiate between an authentically Christian spirituality and one that has been compromised by an amalgamation with purely cultural values and goals.

Spirituality is inseparable from theology. Indeed, it could be defined as the living out of theology. A critique of spirituality will necessarily include a critique of theology. A restatement of spirituality will involve a restatement of the meaning of the gospel, the nature of God, the person and work of Jesus Christ, the work of the Holy Spirit in the appropriation of the fruits of Christ's sacrifice and the role of the church in our salvation.

A spirituality anchored in Scripture will also endeavor to speak to the plight of humanity and the redemption of humanity by the living Christ. Spirituality is much more than therapy, though it will involve the healing of the tormented soul. True spirituality is service to the most high and holy God through service to our fellow human beings.

The church today is beset by a false irenicism that effectively blurs the differences between denominations and religions in order to meet the spiritual needs of the individual. We do not advance the cause of Christianity by promoting doctrinal indifferentism. Nor do we do so by altering the language in liturgy. I stand forthrightly opposed to William Johnson Everett's recommendation that we cease referring to Jesus as Lord because of its association with monarchy and patriarchy and instead refer to Jesus as President, thereby helping to democratize the faith.[1] I also take exception to those authors who reject the designation of God as Father for similar reasons.

A spirituality that can contribute to the renewal of the church will be

solidly trinitarian, as opposed to a mystical monism in which diversity in
God is sacrificed to simplicity. It will also be historically oriented—rooted
in concrete human history and directed to the transformation of history
into eternity.

A spirituality that can ignite the church will furthermore be churchly.
It will seek not the elevation of believers to a higher spiritual plane but
their empowering by the Holy Spirit in order to bear witness to the in-
breaking of the kingdom of God in human history. A churchly spirituality
will celebrate the redemption of the people of God and not merely the
beatitude of the individual soul. It will not counsel flight from the world
but hold out the hope of transforming the world into the kingdom of
God. This transformation will be effected not by an elitist class of Neo-
Brahmins who have discovered the secrets of self-mastery (as in the New
Age guru Gerald Heard) but by the company of the faithful empowered
and illuminated by the Spirit of God and acting in obedience to the living
Christ.

Spirituality in the Christian sense is not so much an upward progression nor an inward possession. Instead, it is an outward succession—following Christ into the darkness of the world, letting the light of the gospel
shine in our words and in our actions. Our goal is not flight from the
world but the overcoming of the powers of the world by testifying to the
mighty deeds of God and bearing the cross of discipleship. Spirituality
can be a means of evading the harsh realities of life. But it can also be a
means of coping with these realities by bringing the light of the Word of
God to bear upon them.

This book should be understood as a delineation of competing types
of spirituality and a warning against an injudicious blending of these
types in order to achieve a supposedly higher unity. The current move
toward eclecticism is especially damaging to the Christian understanding,
since the latter is founded on a divine revelation in a particular history.
At the same time, I do not deny that there are things of value in the older
mysticism and even in the new spirituality, which stands at marked variance with biblical claims. There is dross as well as gold in the mystical
heritage of the church (Wesley), a heritage that goes back to the synthesis
with Hellenism, which accounts for the enduring tension between the old

spirituality and the new mysticism of the earth. I see promise as well as threat in both the old and the new mysticism. But I am convinced that these are not the only options for the church of today. We must recognize that biblical faith creates its own form of spirituality, which resists any accommodation to cultural ideology and religion.

I do not deny the mystical or nonrational element in biblical religion but insist that faith needs to employ reason in its quest for greater understanding. Faith has a nonrational dimension, but it does not take flight from rationality. Reason is not the basis of faith (as in rationalism), nor is faith a substitute for reason (as in an aberrant mysticism); instead reason is the servant of faith—the position of a significant number of eminent theologians through the ages.

1

INTRODUCTION

Faith is not a naked and frigid awareness of Christ,
but a living and real experience of his power, which produces confidence.
JOHN CALVIN

Prayer is able to prevail with Heaven and bend omnipotence to its desires.
CHARLES H. SPURGEON

Faith is an antithesis to every mysticism of head, stomach, and heart,
to all critical mystical idealism.
KARL BARTH

In God there is no hunger that needs to be filled,
only plenteousness that desires to give.
C. S. LEWIS

The spiritual situation in the West today is similar to that of ancient Rome with its pluralistic milieu. We see a diversity of spiritual manifestations but a lack of spiritual direction in the culture as a whole. We are also confronted by a mounting secularism, though this is not devoid of religious content, despite Bonhoeffer's allegations that we are entering a nonreligious age.[1] Reinhold Niebuhr astutely perceived that secularism is a covert religion. Secularism indeed goes hand in hand with a new paganism. The problem is not that God is dead but that the gods are being reborn. Polytheism and henotheism are replacing the strict monotheism endemic to both historical Christianity and Judaism.

Perduring Types

In this book I shall be investigating three perduring types of spirituality: the biblical, the mystical and the secular. In the past it was commonplace to distinguish between biblical spirituality and mysticism. What makes my study different is that I give equal attention to the new spirituality, which locates the sacred in nature or in culture.[2]

Mysticism in the classical sense has constituted a major alternative to biblical religion, though many scholars have tried to make a case that these two types of religion actually have much in common. I am close to scholars like Friedrich Heiler,[3] Anders Nygren[4] and Emil Brunner,[5] all of whom see mysticism in many respects as contrary to biblical faith. Brunner in particular argues that mysticism signifies a clear departure from biblical norms and that much of the confusion in spiritual theology today lies in an unwillingness to recognize the cleavage that exists between these types of spirituality.[6] Those who stand in the ethos of the Protestant Reformation are much more open to this kind of typology than Catholics and Orthodox, but there are scholars in these traditions who make similar distinctions. The eminent Orthodox theologian Vladimir Lossky observes that "the Hellenistic world enters the Church with Clement and Origen, bringing with it elements alien to the Christian tradition."[7] According to Catholic theologian Hans Küng, biblical prayer, unlike mystical prayer, contains "no talk of methods, systems, a psychological technique of prayer;—no stages of prayer to be gone through, no uniformity of religious experience;—no psychological reflection on prayer . . . no self-examinations and ascetic efforts to achieve particular states of the soul."[8] The Dominican Simon Tugwell makes this candid admission: "Our spirituality has for a very long time been heavily conditioned by a mystical theology centered on God's eternal being. . . . Some writers have even encouraged us to leave behind all consideration of the Incarnate Christ, let alone prayer of petition."[9]

Kenneth Kirk tries to counter Heiler's critique of the mystical tradition of the church, though this is not the main purpose of his book.[10] At the same time he acknowledges the abiding Platonic bent in Augustine's thought and regards Heiler's distinction between mystical and prophetic prayer as accurate. Against a hyper-Protestantism Kirk argues that the ideal of seeing God, a motif in mysticism, is "neither selfish, unworthy, nor meaningless."[11] He concludes that the self-denial characteristic of mystical spirituality constitutes an underlying principle of true Christianity.[12] Moreover, "the emergence of monasticism in the fourth century . . . finds no explanation except in the genius of Christianity itself."[13]

A much more negative appraisal of mysticism is given by Henry Trevor Hughes, who was markedly influenced by Heiler: "Mysticism is in reality an escape from the world and a retreat into the soul. It is passive and inactive and seeks in resignation and contemplation its highest good."[14] Emil Brunner's critique is equally severe: "Pure spirituality is a pure fiction of philosophy, and purely spiritual life is a false dream of mysticism."[15]

David Steinmetz typifies a mediating position, which acknowledges mysticism as belonging to the historical unfolding of Christianity though standing in tension with the spirituality of the Reformation. In comparing Luther and Loyola, Steinmetz contends that the former was distrustful of dreams and visions as authoritative for faith and appealed to Scripture alone as the norm for Christian understanding. Loyola, on the other hand, confessed that he was willing to die for the evidences of faith that he had seen even "if there were no Scriptures to teach us." Both appealed to the human imagination "as an instrument of spiritual nurture and reform." Both sought the reform of the church, but Loyola found the key to reform in the recovery of spiritual disciplines, whereas Luther sounded the call to the discovery of the gospel of free grace.[16]

R. H. Coats in his *Types of English Piety* distinguishes between the sacerdotal, the evangelical and the mystical patterns of spirituality.[17] The first corresponds to what Heiler calls ritual prayer and the second to prophetic prayer. In this book I shall not be giving a separate treatment of sacerdotal spirituality, though in Catholicism and Eastern Orthodoxy it has long coexisted with mysticism. But ritual prayer has also infiltrated prophetic or biblical religion. It has always posed a significant threat to biblical faith because its emphasis has been on outward performance rather than on inward conversion.

Besides Heiler's celebrated book *Prayer*, the most telling critique of mystical intrusion into the piety of the church is Anders Nygren's *Agape and Eros*, in which he draws a sharp distinction between two types of love.[18] To transpose this into Heiler's language, agape love proceeds out of self-sacrifice. Eros love, to the contrary, seeks the perfection and fulfillment of the self in union with God. It is indeed this love that belongs to the ethos of mysticism.

P. T. Forsyth was also profoundly alert to the disparity between biblical and mystical religion. With some perspicuity he saw Ralph Waldo Emerson as representative of mysticism and Kierkegaard of evangelical spirituality:

> There is no greater division within religion than that between Emerson and Kierkegaard, between a religion that but consecrates the optimism of clean youth, and that which hallows the tragic note, and deals with a world sick unto death.[19]

Mentors and Teachers

My mentors in this study include John Calvin, Martin Luther, Karl Barth, Emil Brunner, Regin Prenter, Dietrich Bonhoeffer, Friedrich Heiler, Anders Nygren, P. T. Forsyth and Søren Kierkegaard. Whereas evangelical piety upholds a theology of Word and Spirit, mysticism elevates Spirit over Word and ends in the morass of subjectivism. Emil Brunner succinctly expresses my own thoughts on this subject:

> Bible without Spirit is orthodoxy; Spirit without Bible is mysticism or rationalism. Scripture and the Holy Spirit as one—this was the conception of true revelation which was held by the Reformers.[20]

I have also learned from such towering theological figures as Augustine and Pascal, both of whom maintained a significant evangelical thrust. Augustine's evangelical side was prominent in his debate with Pelagius, whose spirituality was moralistic and legalistic rather than authentically biblical. Augustine tried to combine aspects of biblical and mystical spirituality, and this accounts for the inconsistencies and enigmas in his theology. Pascal was much more consciously biblical and evangelical, emphasizing the need for a theology based solidly on Holy Scripture and celebrating the sovereignty of divine grace. To be sure, Pascal practiced a rigorous asceticism, but not as a condition or even a preparation for salvation. Pascal's asceticism was "a form of thanksgiving for benefits received."[21]

An evangelical bent can also be detected in the Eastern Orthodox theologian Tikhon of Zadonsk, who was palpably influenced by the Pietists Johann Arndt and Joseph Hall.[22] Tikhon was adamant that faith is not a work of human merit but a free gift of God: "the comforting perception of the gospels produced in the heart by the Holy Ghost."[23] Tikhon's concern was not with rubrics or rituals but with the conformity of the soul to the living word of God. "No utilitarian or even moral consideration, no effort of will, can produce what only grace can generate in man, which alone enables him to 'keep the wholeness of love towards our Bridegroom without return to the unchaste love of the world.'"[24] He confessed that our justification rests only on "faith in the Son of God who died for us and rose again . . . without regard to our works."[25] He also emphasized the crucial importance of preaching the gospel and deplored the decline of the preaching of God's Word in the Orthodox churches of his time. Tikhon gave equal weight to God's descent to us in Christ and the believer's ascent to God by the Spirit. This is a balance we should all aim at. Yet not surprisingly an enduring Platonic element infused his theology and spirituality, leading him to contend, for example, that our souls seek union with God because spirit desires unity with spirit.[26]

The Legacy of Pietism

A convergence between mysticism and biblical faith is clearly discernible in Pietism, a movement of renewal within Lutheran and Reformed churches in Europe beginning in the seventeenth century and continuing to our own day. An analogous movement grew up in Britain: Puritanism. Evangelicalism in the eighteenth century built upon both Pietism and Puritanism. Albrecht Ritschl tried to make a case that Roman Catholic motifs infiltrated Pietism, thereby rendering it a reactionary movement—returning to the vision of the church before the Reformation. Karl Barth was highly critical of the subjectivistic bent in Pietism, but he displayed a surprising openness to such luminaries of Pietism as Johann Albrecht Bengel, Count Nikolaus Zinzendorf, Friedrich Tholuck, Johann Christoph Blumhardt, Christoph Blumhardt and Kierkegaard.[27]

Pietism like mysticism assigns an important role to experience in Christian faith, but it is not really the same experience. The mystical experience is a sense of unity with the All, and this experience is accessible to non-Christians as well as to Christians. The evangelical experience is a sense of personal sin and assurance of pardon by a merciful and holy God. This kind of distinction must not be pressed, however, since those mystics closer to the center of Christian faith also acknowledge the need for conviction of sin and divine forgiveness through the merits of Jesus Christ.

A more crucial difference is that the Pietists stressed the personal nature of God whereas the mystics envisioned a God beyond the personal. In Pietism the God who is worshiped stands beside us. He is the God who walks with us and talks with us. In mysticism this God is a Spiritual Presence resident within us. Moreover, the goal in mysticism is the perfection and fulfillment of the self in union with God. The Pietists put the emphasis on mission to the world. For Teresa of Ávila, mystical sage and doctor of the church, it is by descending into ourselves in solitude that we find God, the animating source of our being.[28] The Pietists stressed finding God in the *koinonia,* the fellowship of faith. Ralph Waldo Emerson, representative of the new mysticism, defined prayer as "the soliloquy of a beholding and jubilant soul."[29] The Pietists, like the Reformers, conceived of prayer in terms of a dialogue between the living God and the regenerated sinner, though among the so-called radical Pietists mystical themes resurfaced, such as the loss of self in union with God. The goal in Pietism was the service of God in ministry to the world as opposed to being taken up in the grandeur and glory of God. William Perkins voiced the dominant mood in both Pietism and Puritanism: "The true end of our lives is to do service to God in serving of man."[30]

Continuing Questions

This book should be viewed as both an examination of spirituality and an advocacy of a particular kind of spirituality. But this does not mean that I regard any of the major types of spirituality as wholly bereft of Christian influence. My goal will be to assess the areas of strength and weakness in each of these types, always upholding Holy Scripture as the infallible norm for faith and practice.

One question I will address is whether these three spiritual traditions exclude each other completely or whether they can be enriched by some kind of assimilation of one to the other. According to noted church historian Arthur Cushman McGiffert, "it was in his conception of the Christian life . . . that Luther broke most completely with Catholic tradition."[31] I believe the evidence supports this controversial thesis, but this does not imply that the mystical element is altogether missing in Luther's mature theology, nor does it negate the possibility of learning from Catholic and Orthodox mystics in forging a thoroughly evangelical spirituality.

Another question concerns the extent to which the early church departed from its biblical moorings in order to embrace a mystical ideal. Owen Chadwick, who was committed to the vision of ecumenicity, nevertheless finds problems in correlating biblical and mystical religions.

> Eastern and Western spirituality as a whole conceives the ascetic life as a slow progress upward toward God, a climb of the hill by spiritual exercise—prayer, mortification of the carnal lusts, growth in the knowledge of God—until the soul has become Christ-like, God-like. The characteristically ascetic view sees the Christian life as an ascent of a ladder. The concept of the *scala perfectionis,* of the "ascent of Mount Carmel," underlies Catholic spirituality in both east and west. Dominated by this Hellenistic notion of life as an upward progression, some scholars have sought to show the lines of primitive and New Testament spirituality in terms of a ladder towards a goal, a ladder with one or two rungs instead of several. But in Scripture and the apostolic age the idea of an ascent is not found. The whole concept of "spirituality," of "ascetical theology" is foreign to the New Testament and the earliest Christian writers. The reason is plain: St. Paul or St. John, Hermas or even Irenaeus, could not conceive the Christian life in terms of progress towards a goal because they believed that the goal had already through God's acts been reached. The kingdom had come; the eschatological event, though its consummation was in the future, was also a present fact.[32]

The Reformation doctrine of *sola fide* was not original with Luther and Calvin but is found in the early church as well. The apostolic father Clement of Rome claimed that the patriarchs

> were honored and glorified, not through themselves or their works or their righteous behaviour, but through God's will. And we also, who have been called in Christ Jesus through his will, are not justified through ourselves or

through our own wisdom or understanding or piety, or our actions done in holiness of heart, but through faith, for it is through faith that Almighty God has justified all men that have been from the beginning of time: to whom be glory for ever and ever.[33]

Another critical question in this area of study is whether Christian love (agape) is motivated by a desire for self-fulfillment or is a spontaneous act of compassion in which self-regard is wholly transcended. Closely related is the question, does God himself demonstrate passion in realizing his objectives in the world or is he solely self-sacrificing in imparting undeserved grace?

Still another pertinent issue is whether spiritual methods and formulas can be employed by Christians in order to elevate themselves to a higher level of spirituality. In the original Reformed perspective "the Holy Spirit is free, and . . . acts according to his own choosing. For this reason John Calvin was always skeptical of methods and exercises of the Christian life. It is doubtful if he would be very pleased with the contemporary emphasis upon spiritual formation."[34] The Pietists and Puritans on the other hand perceived a need for Christian people to be guided in their life of faith by principles and formulas that keep them on the straight and narrow path.

Finally we must ask ourselves whether the denigration of the world (found in the classical mystics) is a subversion of biblical spirituality or whether it has the sanction of biblical and apostolic faith. Are we to give up our zest for life, as the quasi-Pietist Kierkegaard recommended, or can we affirm life in its fullness so long as this affirmation is subordinate to our commitment to the kingdom of God, which is not of this world?[35]

One of the pivotal ecumenical issues in this discussion is the relationship of church tradition and the Scripture principle. It is the thesis of this book that tradition is clearly subordinate to Scripture, but at the same time tradition can bring out or uncover truths that are only hinted at or implied in Scripture. We are obliged to remember that the Holy Spirit works through the church as well as through Scripture, but there are also other spirits at work in sacred tradition. This is why we need a norm higher than tradition, as many of the church fathers also acknowledged.

IN QUEST OF SPIRITUALITY

Whatever one looks for and seeks is altogether vain, because one seeks only himself,
i.e., his own glory, delight, and advantage.

MARTIN LUTHER

God can well hear the sighs of everyone, even the foolish;
yet, in reality, only those can pray who listen to God.

CHRISTOPH BLUMHARDT

We can develop our spiritual personality at last only by thinking about it less,
and being preoccupied with the realization and confession of God's holy personality.

P. T. FORSYTH

No sooner do we believe that God loves us than there is an impulse to believe
that He does so, not because He is love, but because we are intrinsically lovable.

C. S. LEWIS

Are we now in a spiritual renaissance, given the growing interest in the spiritual roots of our cultural heritage? Spiritual formation is high on the agenda of many churches and seminaries. *Spirituality* is now an "in" word and is definitely more palatable than orthodoxy and doctrinal purity, even for many of those on the conservative side of the theological spectrum. The key to ecumenical renewal is increasingly regarded as lying in worship and prayer.

Yet there is a disturbing ambiguity in spirituality. The paradox is that the growing fascination with things that are spiritual may highlight the death of true spirituality. Kierkegaard adamantly contended that the mark of true religion is suffering, not enjoyment. If this is so, most of us today are indeed far from the hope and vision of biblical faith.

We are living in an age marked by the rebirth of the gods. Secularism is giving way to paganism, modernity to postmodernity. The worship of the true God more and more lacks public visibility. Religious experience is valued over faith in the traditional sense of trusting in a God who is hidden even in his revelation.

It is well for us to keep in mind that spirituality is neither the field of revelation nor its focus: it is a very human response to revelation and therefore necessarily partakes of the relative and fallible. We must not be too hasty in celebrating the supposed spiritual renaissance. It contains more peril than promise. Our task as Christians today is not to abandon spirituality but to clarify it. This mandate places us under the obligation to discriminate between different types of spirituality.

Faith and Spirituality

The respected Jewish philosopher Martin Buber observed that modernity is hostile to faith but open to religion.[1] He might have said open to spirituality. The exclusive claims of Christianity are disputed in modern culture, but the Christian forms of religion are widely appreciated for the social cohesion and emotional reinforcement they bring.

In this discussion it is important to consider the signal contribution of Søren Kierkegaard, the nineteenth-century Danish prophet to the modern church, who had an enduring impact on Karl Barth and the whole movement of dialectical theology. Kierkegaard maintained that there is a decisive difference between what he called religiousness A and religiousness B.[2] The first is a religion of immanence, the second a religion of revelation. The first emphasizes the identity of God and humanity, the second their discontinuity. Socrates is the paradigm for religiousness A, Jesus for religiousness B. The hallmark of the latter is the consciousness of sin. In Kierkegaard's view the Teacher is at the same time the Savior.[3] He brings not only the message of faith but also the power to believe in this message. In the Christian scenario those committed to faithful discipleship know that in themselves they are nothing.

Kierkegaard also clearly identified three stages on life's journey.[4] The lowest stage, the aesthetic life, is characterized by detachment and enjoyment. The next stage, the ethical life, focuses on struggle and decision. Its supreme virtue is courage—the willingness to risk. The final stage, the religious life, is marked by passion, inwardness and suffering.[5]

Karl Barth's diagnosis of the situation was remarkably similar. Barth pointed to the abyss between religion and true faith, between the creative spirituality of a searching humanity and the venture of obedience that characterized the prophets and apostles. Indeed, "No human demeanor is more open to criticism, more doubtful, or more dangerous, than religious demeanor. No understanding subjects men to so severe a judgement as the understanding of religion."[6] Yet Barth allowed for a "true religion"—one purified and reformed by the Word of God. In his view, "Biblical *piety* is conscious of its own limits, of its relativity. In its essence it is humility, fear of the Lord. It points beyond the world and points at the same time and above all beyond itself."[7] Barth drew a sharp distinction between *geistlich* (spiritual) and *geistig* (religious). The spiritual person walks by faith alone, the religious person seeks experiential confirmation of the truth of faith.

Another modern-day prophet is the French lay theologian Jacques Ellul, whose insights were grounded in a probing biblical faith. Ellul distinguished between *manifestation,* which appeals to sight, and *proclamation,* which finds the origin of faith in the spoken word.[8] Ellul pointed to the Greek mystery religions as exemplifying the religion of manifestation. In the mystery cults there was a showing of the sacred, a "silent spectacle . . . imposed on language" rather than an effort at language and interpretation.[9] According to Ellul, religion is based on covetousness, on the desire to possess. When we see a thing, we possess it. Faith by contrast demands obedience. Religion involves ritual, liturgy, "staged worship in which the visual aspect tries to drown out the word" (Alphonse Maillot).[10] Ellul's insights on this matter were best developed in his brilliant but regrettably little-known book *The Humiliation of the Word.*[11]

We inevitably come to the question: does the Bible itself support spirituality? Barth was fond of underscoring the fact that the polemic of the Bible is directed against religion.[12] It is well to be reminded that the prophets were called to "preach against the holy places" (Ezek 21:2 NKJV). They were also united in their conviction that sacrifices offered for atonement are of no avail (Mic 6:6-8). What is pleasing to God are sacrifices of praise and thanksgiving. In Jeremiah we read, "I did not speak to your fathers or command them concerning burnt offerings and sacrifices. But this command I gave them, 'Obey my voice, and I will be your God, and you shall be my people; and walk in all the way that I command you, that it may be well with you'" (Jer 7:22-23). This same theme appears in the book of Hosea: "I desire steadfast love and not sacrifice, the knowledge of God, rather than burnt offerings" (Hos 6:6; cf. Ps 51:16). Paul the apostle gives a similar witness: "I appeal to you therefore, brethren, by the mercies of God, to present your bodies as a living sacrifice, holy and acceptable to God, which is your spiritual worship" (Rom 12:1).

The striking contrast between religion and faith is brought to light by comparing the tower of Babel and the cross of Christ. The first epitomizes humanity's search for God, the second God's search for a lost humanity. Religion is the prodigious attempt to make oneself acceptable before God. Faith is the earnest effort to be true to the commandment of God, irrespective of whether this brings benefits to the believer.

In the perspective of the Bible spirituality is not simply negated but converted to the service of the true God. Faith does not necessarily overthrow the rites and ceremonies of the believing community but transforms them. Spirituality in the biblical context signifies the demonstration of a life liberated by grace as opposed to an attempt to appease a wrathful God or make reparation for sin. There is one faith but various kinds of spirituality—diverse ways by which we seek to live out our lives in relation to the ultimate. Many styles of life can give evidence of a genuine religious commitment, but some exclude the possibility of faith altogether.

The breadth of the meaning of spirituality can also be partly grasped when we see it in its ineradicable relationship with theology. Spirituality is the way we live out our religious commitment. Theology is the way we reflect on God and on life in the light of the knowledge of God. Theology is oriented about *logos,* spirituality about *praxis.* The focus in theology is on the truth of faith and the confession of faith. The focus in spirituality is on the life and experience of faith. The hallmark of theology is the endeavor to know the truth. The hallmark of spirituality is striving for holiness. Theology's task is to maintain the integrity of faith in the midst of an unbelieving world. Spirituality consists in making our faith concrete in deeds of love. Dogma and praxis are inseparable; one leads into the other.

True Spirituality

Obviously there can be true and false spiritualities just as there can be true and false religions. Spirituality or religion can be destructive and enervating as well as salutary and uplifting. It can be a cause for anxiety rather than a balm for peace. It can be a means of escape from facing ourselves, even God. Religion can be a flight from God, not a quest for God. Karl Marx put his finger on part of the truth when he described religion as the "opiate of the people." Sigmund Freud was not entirely wrong when he referred to religion as "the obsessional neurosis of humanity." Yet these harbingers of atheism missed the possibility that there can be a true spirituality, one that fulfills humanity's deepest longings and motivates earnest believers to work for peace and justice for all.

By a true religion or a true spirituality I mean one that is anchored in a vital faith in the God and Father of our Lord Jesus Christ (2 Cor 1:3) and leads us into a caring concern for the welfare of our neighbor, even above the perfecting of our own souls. The focus of true spirituality is on God's holy love, not on humanity's spiritual fulfillment. But this divine love is celebrated not as a transcendent ideal but as a gracious act of God on behalf of a lost human race. The love of God is a love poured out for sinners, and this love can become a working principle in our own lives through faith (cf. Mt 9:12-13).

True spirituality entails the sacrifice of the self for the good of our neighbor and for the glory of God. It means serving the despised and forsaken of the world for the sake of Jesus Christ, who died on the cross and rose again so that all might live. It entails letting the light of God's glory as we see this in Jesus Christ shine in every aspect of our existence. Francis Schaeffer put it well when he defined true spirituality as the Lordship of Christ over the totality of life.[13] It implies not flight from the world but instead bringing the world into submission to Jesus Christ.

True spirituality involves living in the midst of the world's afflictions for the greater glory of God. It means taking up the cross and following Christ into the darkness of the world as a sign of the dawning of the new eon. Truly spiritual people live not unto themselves, not for their own glory and happiness, but for the glory of God alone *(soli Deo gloria)*. The glory of God is revealed when we die to self and live for the renewal and liberation of the world. True spirituality is not reducing the self to nothingness but elevating humanity to fellowship with the living God. It involves the crucifixion and resurrection of the self to a life of victory over sin, death and the devil. I firmly oppose the existentialist motto that "man is a zero." In the biblical view human beings are a little less than the angels, but they have fallen into sin and therefore stand in need of deliverance from their bondage to sin.

True spirituality calls for the restoration of true humanity. But biblical faith has in mind something more than a new creation. Our goal is sanctified service in the name of Christ. We should strive not only for authentic humanity but also for holiness—not just individual holiness but social holiness (John Wesley). Holiness in the biblical view means not moral faultlessness but transparency to the divine. To be holy is to reflect the glory of God in our thoughts and actions.

Holiness involves discipleship under the cross, bearing witness through our words and deeds to what God has done for us in Christ. It is not wholeness of personality but the fear of God that characterizes those who pursue biblical holiness. Holiness in its perfection belongs to God alone, but we can reflect and testify to this holiness in the witness of consecrated lives.

True spirituality rests on a holy optimism that God is in control of all of history and that he has acted to redeem the human race in Jesus Christ. It is kindled by the hope that God will remain true to his promises to set up the kingdom that shall have no end, a kingdom that will emerge out of the dissolution of the kingdoms of this world. True spirituality is life affirming because Christ came to give us life in abundance (Jn 10:10). It is confident, moreover, that the future belongs to God, that the millennial glory is still before us in the coming of the new heaven and the new earth.

The Crisis in Spirituality

Spirituality is in crisis today because the church is ignominiously accommodating itself to new winds of doctrine that contradict traditional Christian values and teachings. The cultural climate today is not Christian but post-Christian. Words that accurately describe the current spiritual situation are pluralism, syncretism, inclusivism, relativism and multiculturalism. It is commonly said that many roads lead to God. Martin Marty sagaciously describes the current religious situation as henotheistic over monotheistic. This is to say, people are ready to acknowledge one God—Creator of humanity—but allow for other gods as well.

It is increasingly evident that we are living in an age of theological erosion. We have spirituality without doctrinal substance. When spirituality is divorced from theology it speedily deteriorates into sentimentality. Biblical, evangelical spirituality is now in eclipse. Most current books on spirituality reflect either Neoplatonic mysticism or the new innerworldly mysticism. The high church movement calls us to return to the past, but this strategy can end by making us prisoners of the past. Ritualism and sacramentalism are dead-end roads, but the church still needs rituals and sacraments that enable it to retain continuity with its past history. With the Reformers I contend that sacraments derive their power from the Word of God written and proclaimed, not vice versa.

The new spirituality has various expressions. One of these is the electronic church movement with its emphasis on the aggrandizement of the individual over self-denial and self-sacrifice. The New Thought movement, another salient manifestation of the new spirituality, invites us to explore the power of the mind as opposed to bringing the mind into conformity with Jesus Christ.[14] A closely related spiritual aberration is the New Age movement, which has been described by some critics as the recrudescence of gnosticism. Harold Bloom, in his best-selling *The American Religion,* makes the astounding but credible claim that gnosticism is the real religion of America with its individualism and quest for esoteric knowledge.[15] He describes himself as a "gnostic without hope." The charismatic movement within the churches is a more promising development; yet too often this proves to be a fusion of the new spirituality and biblical spirituality. Some Pentecostals reflect this compromise when they elevate

praise over petition and even cast aspersions on prayer for material
things.[16] The positive confession movement within Pentecostal and charismatic churches with its emphasis on health, wealth and prosperity sig-
nals a major deviation from Christian teaching.[17] Feminist spirituality also
by and large represents a rebirth of gnosticism in which the key to personal and spiritual renewal lies in developing a higher form of consciousness. A more recent manifestation of the growing spiritual revolution is
the Emerging Church, reflecting again the drift toward an amorphous
mysticism and relativism.[18]

From my perspective the recovery of true spirituality lies in the resurgence of a catholic, evangelical theology that draws upon both the Protestant Reformation and the great tradition of the church universal. Today
we are besieged by many voices—some true and some false. More than
ever we should pray for the gift of discerning of spirits to guide us in our
spiritual pilgrimage. Among the truly prophetic voices of the modern era
are Søren Kierkegaard, P. T. Forsyth, Karl Barth, Emil Brunner, Dietrich
Bonhoeffer, T. F. Torrance and Jacques Ellul. These spiritual guides are
dependable, though because they are fallible humans they still need to
be corrected by the tradition of the church catholic as well as judged in
the light of Holy Scripture. Among seminal thinkers who bring a message
that stands at marked variance with biblical and apostolic faith and who
can therefore be regarded as untrustworthy guides are William Blake,
Ralph Waldo Emerson, Friedrich Nietzsche, Carl Jung, Teilhard de Chardin, Alan Watts, D. H. Lawrence, Nikos Kazantzakis, Gerald Heard, Morton Kelsey, Matthew Fox and Joseph Campbell. Jung reflects the new
mood when he says, "No matter what the world thinks about religious
experience, the one who has it possesses the great treasure . . . that has
provided him with a source of life, meaning and beauty, and that has
given a new splendor to the world and to mankind."[19]

The haunting words of the prophet Isaiah prove to be as relevant today as in times past: "It's useless to bring your offerings. I am disgusted
with the smell of the incense you burn. I cannot stand your New Moon
Festivals, your Sabbaths, and your religious gatherings; they are all corrupted by your sins" (Is 1:13 GNB). Let us become more critical of religion
but at the same time more open to the gospel. Let us pursue the holiness

that takes us deeper into the world of tribulation with a message of hope that has its basis not in human potential or in "secret doctrine" but in God's decisive intervention into biblical history culminating in the life, death and resurrection of our glorious Savior, Jesus Christ.

3

TYPES OF SPIRITUALITY

Such conduct may have an air of wisdom, with its forced piety,
its self-mortification, and its severity to the body;
but it is of no use at all in combating sensuality.
COLOSSIANS 2:23 REB

There are those who seek to penetrate the immensities and to see God.
One ought rather to sink into the depths to find God among the
suffering, erring, and the downtrodden.
MARTIN LUTHER

The key is not in process, and not in ideals, nor in their evolution,
but in crisis, in an intervention, an invasion,
a miracle of fundamental and final and holy grace.
P. T. FORSYTH

The Greek way of thinking was a kind of seeing,
whereas the Hebrew, Biblical and Reformation way of learning and knowing was
through "listening and responding, serving and obeying."
THOMAS F. TORRANCE

The term *spirituality* in today's world contains ambivalent meanings partly because its theological underpinnings are too often not visible. Spirituality as celebrated in the acculturized church readily proves to be a seedbed of heresy rather than a promise of renewal. The crisis in spirituality has its source in a collision of worldviews. It is incumbent on us to examine the major types of spirituality in order to understand the spiritual crisis that engulfs the church in our time.

As I have already made clear, I shall be focusing on three competing types of spirituality: classical mysticism, biblical personalism and the new spirituality. The first two represent traditional spiritualities, whereas the last constitutes a profound challenge to the Christian spiritual tradition. In this chapter I intend to give a brief synopsis of these three manifestations of spirituality, and in subsequent chapters I shall explore them in greater depth.

It should be recognized that these types do not exhaust the phenomenon of spirituality. There are others: gnostic (which I shall examine in an appendix), animist, Islamic, Judaic, even Marxist. My contention is that the three types mentioned above have all made a significant impact upon the thinking and practice of the church and therefore deserve special attention.

Mystical Religion

Whenever I refer to mystical religion in this context, I have in mind classical or traditional mysticism—that which constitutes the mystical heritage of the church. Like all mysticism it is typified by an immediate or direct experience of God that may well bypass the ordinary channels of redemption, such as the Word and the sacraments. Its focus is on a participatory knowledge of God rather than one that is purely intellectual or cerebral.[1] It looks to Christ as providing the occasion for the mystical experience of God. It fosters a Spirit-Christology rather than a Logos-Christology. Salvation is not simply something that happened in past history: it is being confronted by the ground of all being here and now.

Despite its inroads in Catholic spirituality, mysticism has always been resisted in the Roman church, mainly because of its devaluation of the rites and dogmas of the church. Cardinal John Henry Newman sardonically observed that mysticism begins in mist and ends in heresy. Yet he retained a deep appreciation for the great saints of the church, who were also its greatest mystics.

Christian mysticism, which is the subject of this discussion, represents a synthesis of biblical religion and Platonic and Neoplatonic philosophy.

Not only Plato but also Plotinus, Porphyry and Proclus helped shape the contours of patristic and medieval spirituality.[2] In addition, Christian mysticism drew upon the mystery religions, Stoicism and even Gnosticism, though it often treated the last with deep suspicion. It should also be kept in mind that the mystical tradition of the church has always maintained a tenuous connection with the East, especially India. We know that the Orphic mysteries were influenced by Hinduism and that Plotinus made at least one journey to the East.

Classical or Christian mysticism should be sharply differentiated from the new mysticism, which is basically post-Christian as well as postmodern. At the same time mysticism constitutes an ethos that transcends the particularities of religious dogma. Mystics throughout the world—in every culture and religion—have noted how much they have in common with one another despite the barriers of doctrine. This is what led Aldous Huxley to describe mysticism as "the perennial philosophy," since it appears under many different names and accommodates to many different allegiances.[3]

In all forms of mysticism there is an attempt to resymbolize God so that particularities are dissolved into universalities. Mystics, including Christian mystics, are gripped by a desire to rise above the personal to the suprapersonal ground of being. This sometimes takes the form of penetrating beyond the Trinity to the "God above God," the God beyond all distinctions and diversifications. The mystical God is an all-inclusive God as opposed to the God of prophetic tradition, who is militantly exclusive.

In the mystical ethos, words are inadequate to communicate the reality of the God who remains enshrouded in mystery. The highest knowledge is to admit that we do not know. The pathway to knowledge of God is through the "cloud of unknowing."[4] The content of our knowledge of God is the sense of the numinous rather than propositional truth.[5] There is also a move to get beyond anthropomorphisms in describing God. Among the new names for God in the tradition of Christian mysticism are the Divine Darkness, the Absolute Good, the One, Absolute Existence, the Infinite Abyss, Being-itself, the Eternal Now, the Undifferentiated Unity, the Infinite Unity, the Ground of Being, the Interior Silence and the Silent Desert.

Mysticism is generally both anthropocentric and theocentric. Its goal is the perfection of the soul, the satisfaction of desire, but the means toward this goal is faith in the God of revelation. We find our eternal happiness not in the pleasures of the world but in union with God, the all-enveloping Spiritual Presence. Mysticism is likewise very much inclined to be introspective, for it believes that God is discovered in the interior depths of the self. It speaks of a journey to the center of the soul and a descent into the "cave of the heart."

In its Christian as well as non-Christian forms mysticism is characterized by an eros spirituality—the love that is acquisitive, unitive and self-regarding.[6] It upholds the love that seeks possession of the supreme good. Augustine illustrates the mystical worldview when he remarks, "To love oneself rightly is to love God." This principle is not rescinded by the "love of God for his own sake," for in mysticism this kind of love is prized as the means for the perfecting and satisfaction of the soul.

The mystical heritage of the church did not question the traditional understandings of sin and salvation, but it supplemented these understandings with a vision more in keeping with the legacy of Neoplatonism. Sin becomes a fall from unity into multiplicity. The problem of humanity is time more than sin. Salvation becomes identified with enlightenment or gnosis. The goal is reunion with the ground and source of being, the return of the soul to its divine origin.

Mysticism paradoxically upholds both world-denial and self-fulfillment. We realize our divinely appointed destiny precisely in the denial of world and self. Mysticism espouses an otherworldly asceticism, which is indeed quite foreign to the Bible. The goal is the liberation of the soul from the entanglements of the flesh. While biblical faith makes a place for the subduing of the flesh, the meaning of flesh in this context is wider and deeper than bodily appetite (cf. Rom 8:1-11; 13:11-14; Gal 5:16-24; Eph 2:3; Col 2:11).

In this kind of spirituality prayer becomes meditation on the ground of the self and of the world. The aim is to rise above words and rationality. The story is told that after one of his lectures on God at the Harvard University Divinity School, Paul Tillich was asked by one of his students, "Professor, do you ever pray?" After reflecting for a few moments he re-

plied, "No, I do not. I meditate." Whether this story is historical or apocryphal, it conveys the truth that a thoroughgoing mysticism leads ultimately to the dissolution of realistic or naive prayer.

The two kingdoms in the mystical world vision are the temporal and
the eternal; the material and the spiritual; diversity and unity. Augustine
broke through the mystical understanding when he conceived of the city
of God as the advance of the forces of righteousness within history rather
than simply an inner condition of the soul.

Among the great mystics of the Eastern and Western churches are Evagrius Ponticus, John Climacus, Dionysius the Pseudo-Areopagite, Maxi-
mus the Confessor, John Cassian, Augustine, Bernard of Clairvaux,
Bonaventure, Gregory Palamas, Meister Eckhart, John Tauler, Henry
Suso, Richard Rolle, the anonymous author of *The Cloud of Unknowing,*
Walter Hilton, Catherine of Siena, Catherine of Genoa, Hildegaard of Bin-
gen, Teresa of Ávila and John of the Cross. More recently, persons who
reflect the motifs of classical mysticism include Simone Weil, Evelyn Underhill, Carlo Carretto, Thomas Merton, George Maloney and Benedict
Ashley.[7] Mystics like Friedrich Schleiermacher, Paul Tillich, Rufus Jones
and Gerald Heard are transitional figures, since they follow basically a
postmodern rather than a specifically Christian vision.[8]

Biblical Religion

Another strand of spirituality that has become part of the Christian tradition is what Heiler calls prophetic religion and what I prefer to call biblical personalism or simply biblical spirituality.[9] This kind of personalism
is not to be confused with philosophical personalism, which regards personality as the supreme value or the key to the meaning of reality.[10] The
biblical view finds the source of our knowledge of God in an encounter
between the divine person and the human person. God is not subordinated to the general category of person, but personhood is illumined by
God's self-revelation in Jesus Christ.

Biblical spirituality belongs to the ethos of the Old Testament prophets
and the New Testament prophets and apostles. It reappeared in Augustine, but it was partially eclipsed by his openness to mysticism. The biblical understanding of life in the Spirit was rediscovered in the Protestant

Reformation and kept alive in Puritanism, Pietism and to a lesser degree in Protestant orthodoxy. It was given special emphasis in Kierkegaard, Johann Christoph Blumhardt, Christoph Blumhardt, P. T. Forsyth, H. R. Mackintosh and James Denney. In more recent times it has found expression in the writings of Karl Barth, Emil Brunner, Philip S. Watson, Dietrich Bonhoeffer, Jacques Ellul, J. I. Packer, T. F. Torrance and this author. Biblical personalism has also been reflected to a degree among Catholic writers like Pascal, Hans Urs von Balthasar, Simon Tugwell, Hans Küng and Romano Guardini.

The biblical life- and world-view is oriented about the mighty deeds of God in a particular history—that mirrored in the Bible. It emphasizes hidden meanings in the unfolding of history rather than the birth of God in the soul (as in mysticism). The climax of the biblical revelation is the historical incarnation of God in Jesus Christ. Faith does not entertain the idea of a cosmic incarnation, which compromises the particularity of the biblical witness.

Biblical spirituality is also an evangelical spirituality because its focus is on the life-giving flow of the revelation of God in a particular person—Jesus of Nazareth. It is well to recognize that the emphasis in the New Testament, which claims to be the fullness of biblical revelation, is on the work of Christ rather than on his person as such. The incarnation is seen in the light of the atoning sacrifice of Christ on the cross. Indeed, the purpose of the incarnation is the deliverance of a lost humanity through the suffering and death of Jesus Christ. Apart from Christ the Old Testament revelation becomes easily misunderstood as the keeping of the law or subjection to moral codes, which we find in rabbinic Judaism.

Biblical personalism has an incontestably extrinsic orientation: it is centered not on the travails of the soul but on the promises of God. God, moreover, is not the core or ground of the soul but the Wholly Other who infinitely transcends the human creation. Evangelical spirituality celebrates the alien righteousness of Christ rather than an immanent, inherent righteousness, which is insufficient to guarantee salvation because of the taint of original sin. Our hope rests not on the searchings of humanity but on the revelations of a mighty and glorious Savior from above.

This extrinsic focus of biblical revelation was especially noticeable in the mainstream Protestant Reformers: Luther and Calvin. God is not the interior silence but "the outer outerness" (Luther). Luther's recommendation was, "Go out of yourself, away from yourself to Christ."[11] He admonished his hearers not to remain in their experiences of God but to rise above their experiences in an act of faith and obedience.[12] And in the words of Calvin, "Our righteousness is not in us but in Christ. . . . We possess it only because we are partakers in Christ."[13] Karl Barth, who incontrovertibly stands in the Reformation tradition, also insisted on the extrinsic character of the faith of Christians:

> Grace points them away from self, frightens them out of themselves, deprives them of any root or soil or country in themselves, summons them to hold to the promise, to trust in Him, to boast in Him, to take guidance and counsel of Him and Him alone.[14]

Evangelical spirituality appeals to a norm outside conscience and experience: God's self-revelation in Jesus Christ. This norm is attested in Scripture and witnessed to in church tradition. The final criterion in this kind of spirituality is the paradoxical unity of Word and Spirit. A place is made for silence, but not as an attempt to get beyond the Word to an ineffable reality—the undifferentiated unity. Instead, the function of silence in an evangelical or biblical context is to prepare us to hear the Word. Luther held that sustained solitude is detrimental to the soul.

A spirituality that rests on the Bible and the evangel is both theocentric and Christocentric. The glory of God is given priority over personal happiness, even over salvation (cf. Ps 115:1; Jn 7:18). The early Calvinist ordinands in New England were asked by the church elders, "Would you be willing to be damned for the glory of God?" This kind of question underscores the radical theocentricity of Calvinism, though it cannot claim full biblical sanction, since Scripture plainly tells us that what most glorifies God is the salvation of his people, indeed of the entire world. In the biblical story the glory of God takes precedence over the fulfillment of the self, though it does not negate the longings of the self for a restored relationship with God. While the mystical ethos concentrates on the cultivation and nurture of the soul, biblical faith gives much more attention to the advance of the kingdom of God in history.

In both mysticism and biblical religion love is seen as the highest of the virtues, but in the former this love is generally defined as eros—the possessive, acquisitive love that seeks the security and salvation of the self above all other things. In New Testament religion love is depicted as agape, the love that does not seek its own (cf. 1 Cor 13:5 NKJV). Agape love is unconditional, spontaneous and sacrificial.[15]

Otherworldly asceticism is frowned upon by those who subscribe to prophetic piety, but such piety does not rule out the salutary role of spiritual disciplines in the religious life. Evangelical spirituality upholds what Max Weber calls an inner-worldly asceticism, which devotes itself to the realization of the believer's vocation in the world.[16] Ascetic disciplines can be helpful in equipping the saints for ministry, but they can become spiritual snares once they are treated as meritorious. They do not play a role in procuring our salvation, but they do enable us to remain true to our faith commitment as we live it out in society. Ascetic practices in the context of evangelical piety do not depreciate the world, but they relativize the things of this world. They do not cancel out worldly pleasures, but they relegate these pleasures to second place.

Prayer in biblical piety is not the contemplation of the essence of an impassible God but the pouring out of the soul to God, pleading with God for help and strength in the midst of adversity. The Bible makes a prominent place for importunate prayer.[17] This note is also discernible in the apocryphal book of Sirach:

> The prayer of the humble pierces the clouds, and he will not be consoled until it reaches the Lord; he will not desist until the Most High visits him, and does justice for the righteous, and executes judgment. (Sirach 35:17 RSV).

Biblical personalism is a world-transforming spirituality. It does not draw us out of the world but challenges us to bring the world into submission to the Lord Jesus Christ. Military metaphors abound in this kind of spirituality. Life is portrayed as a combat against the forces of darkness that have gained partial control of the world through the emergence of sin and death in the human creation. We are summoned to battle with the devil, not to secure our salvation but to manifest and demonstrate a salvation already achieved.

In the biblical understanding faith is radically personal because it has its basis in an I-Thou encounter. We are made able and willing to believe because we have been addressed by the holy God who calls us to obedience. The subject-object relationship is not overcome (as in mysticism) but is transfigured. Through faith we now have fellowship with God, but we are never absorbed into God (as in Neoplatonism). Evangelical theology speaks of the sanctification of believers, not of their divinization or deification.[18]

In contrast to those who embrace mystical spirituality, biblical Christians are given a commission to witness, not an invitation to embark on a spiritual quest. We do not need to find the truth, for the truth has already found us—in Jesus Christ. Our task is to bear witness to what God has done for us in Christ—in our words and in our lives.

Faith in biblical perspective is not a mystical feeling of absolute dependence (as in Schleiermacher) but an acknowledgment of God's incomparable sacrifice of himself in the person of his Son. Faith is not "the darkness of unknowing"[19] prized by the mystics but "a firm and certain knowledge of God's benevolence toward us, founded upon the truth of the freely given promise in Christ, both revealed to our minds and sealed upon our hearts through the Holy Spirit" (Calvin).[20]

Evangelical Protestantism teaches the imputation of the grace of God to the believing sinner on the basis of the obedient life, vicarious suffering and death, and resurrection of Jesus Christ, the one representative of humankind who is perfectly righteous in the sight of God. While the Reformers did affirm the new life in Christ through the Holy Spirit, they envisaged this not so much as an effusion of grace into the self (as in the mystical view) but as the birth of a new self who is discontinuous with the old. Our hope rests not on the discovery of a divine spark within the soul, but on the invasion of the Spirit of God into the human soul, creating a vision of reality that overthrows as well as fulfills natural hopes and expectations. In the born-again experience we do not sink into the All but rise into creative fellowship with the God who rescues us from sin.

A New Spiritual Vision

A new spiritual vision has captured the imagination of a growing number of people, a vision that patently contradicts both biblical, evangelical spirituality and classical mysticism. This new spiritual orientation can be called a naturalistic or secular mysticism. It can also be described as a new naturalism or a practical idealism. It is closer to vitalism than to mysticism in the traditional sense. It is biocentric—centered in life—and holocentric, that is, focusing on the whole of reality. The cleavage between idealism and naturalism is overcome in this latest spiritual quest. All of nature is viewed as being alive or animated. In philosophical terms, this point of view is denominated panpsychism or hylozoism.

The focus in the new spirituality is neither on the vision of God nor on union with God but on the discovery of the identity of self and God. The new mystic seeks unity not with an unchanging Absolute but with the universal stream of consciousness or the creative pulsating ground of existence. The goal is not simply the liberation of the self but the liberation of God through self-affirmation and world-affirmation (Kazantzakis).

The new spirituality is anchored in the Renaissance, the Enlightenment and Romanticism. It was already anticipated in Stoicism and Gnosticism. There are even points of contact with Plato and Aristotle, though the pre-Socratics are probably more influential, particularly thinkers like Heraclitus, who envisioned ultimate reality as becoming rather than being.

In the spirit of the Renaissance the new spirituality celebrates the infinite possibilities of humanity over both the uncreated light within humanity (as in classical mysticism) and the depravity and helplessness of humanity (as in evangelical Christianity). Ralph Waldo Emerson voices the new mood: "Man is weak to the extent that he looks outside himself for help. It is only as he throws himself unhesitatingly upon the God within himself that he learns his own power and works miracles."[21]

The key words in this new worldview are *evolution* and *progress*. This emphasis has shaped not only modern thought but also postmodern thought, which clings to the hope of a new heaven on earth. The old mysticism fixed its attention on emanation and return. Biblical faith is much more concerned with creation and redemption. The new spirituality calls its devotees to world-immersion and world-affirmation. The body is the seed of the soul, not the tomb of the soul (as in the mystical heritage of the church).

What we see in these new spiritual movements is a dynamic-process panentheism, which is to be contrasted with both biblical theism on the one hand and mystical pantheism on the other. In classical theism God stands over the world as its creator and sustainer. In pantheism God and the world are identical. In panentheism God and the world are viewed as inseparable: God is *in* the world and the world is *in* God.

Modern and postmodern spirituality has given rise to new symbols for deity such as the Life-Force, the Creative Surge, Creative Emergence, Primal Energy, the Creative Event, the Power of Creative Transformation, the Womb of Being, the Creative Process, the Great Ecstatic, the Cosmic Whirlpool, the Eros of the Universe, the Slumbering Deep Within You, the Over-Soul, the Pool of Unlimited Power and the Midwife of Change. The foundational symbol that fuels the modern and postmodern quest for truth is the volcanic eruption, God emerging out of the depths. How radically different is Luther's depiction of God as "a traveling Cloud Burst," or the older mystical vision of a beatitude that lies beyond history.

What gives the new spirituality its distinctive configuration is its emphasis on the striving and struggle of God rather than on the impassibility of God or the eternity of God. In contradistinction to the old spirituality, the new movement postulates risk in God—the vulnerability of God to sorrow, tragedy and pain.

In this new world outlook faith becomes a venture in creative living or a commitment to a future with promise. This is a far cry from the Reformation depiction of faith as trust in the mercy of a holy and all-powerful God. Faith is reconceived by secular religionists as a means to human fulfillment and inward liberation. In its crasser forms, faith becomes the key to worldly success, health and prosperity. Prayer in the new orientation is action designed to alleviate human distress or free the human spirit for its advance into novelty.

The goal in life is mastery over nature or harmony with nature as opposed to escape from nature into the realm of pure spirit. Carnal enjoyment (libido) is celebrated over a purely spiritual love (the higher kind of eros). Two strands can be discerned in this new consciousness. One takes its cue from psychology, the other from sociology and politics. The first emphasis has given birth to the ideal of the therapeutic society. The second applies its energies to the creation of a just world order. Salvation is either mentalized or politicized. What commands our attention is consciousness raising rather than justification or sanctification. The burning need of humanity is for therapy, not pardon for sin. The aim is interior peace in the sense of absence of tension and conflict. In stark contrast to this attitude stand Luther's words of wisdom: "When God makes alive, He kills; when He justifies, He imposes guilt; when He leads us to heaven, He thrusts us down into hell."[22] In this view peace is realized in and through tribulation.

The new spirituality teaches not the fear of God nor the inaccessibility of God but the availability of God. God is a power we can tap into rather than a holy Lord we must submit to. God is "the fellow-sufferer who understands" (Whitehead) rather than the sovereign overseer of history.

Not only is this secular spirituality world-affirming and self-affirming, it also proves to be world-conforming. This is true even for the liberation theologies in their fusing of the Christian ideal of the kingdom of God and the modern ideal of the classless society. In the new theology the highest values of the culture are equated with the values of the kingdom of God. It is not God's act of self-sacrifice that is celebrated but the passions of life experienced by all mortals. The cure for the human malaise is found in zest for living rather than in acts of penance and reparation. This world is neither a vale of tears nor the theater of God's glory but the field of human experimentation and evolution. The vision that spurs us on is that of an open future, an open universe. Infinity lies in the future rather than in a timeless eternity.

Among the theological movements that feed into the new spirituality are process theology, liberation theology, feminist theology, neomystical theology, story theology and the openness of God theology. In all of these movements God is seen as the creative force that galvanizes the human quest for peace and justice on earth. Philosophical representatives of the new worldview include F. W. J. Schelling, J. G. Fichte, Friedrich Nietzsche, G. W. F. Hegel, Henri Bergson, Alfred North Whitehead, Martin Heidegger, Pierre Teilhard de Chardin, Nikos Kazantzakis, D. H. Lawrence, Charles Peirce, William James, Samuel Alexander, Ralph Waldo Emerson, Henry David Thoreau, Walt Whitman, Carl Jung, Rudolf Steiner,

Miguel de Unamuno, Alan Watts and Wilhelm Reich. Key theological figures in this movement are Friedrich Schleiermacher, Ernst Troeltsch, Paul
Tillich, Bernard E. Meland, Henry Nelson Wieman, Jay McDaniel, Rosemary Radford Ruether, Mary Daly, Morton Kelsey, Naomi Goldenberg,
Matthew Fox, John Cobb, James B. Nelson and Jürgen Moltmann. Some
of these persons are more intent on maintaining continuity with Christian
tradition than others. All of them herald a God beyond the God of theism,
a God who is closer to the Earth Mother than to the Sky Father.

Ideal Types

It is important to understand that these three types of spirituality are ideal
types. This is to say, they exemplify overarching patterns of thought that
are only approximated in actual writers and movements. They are ideal
constructs rather than concrete historical embodiments. For Max Weber
and Ernst Troeltsch the purpose of a typology is to promote understanding, not to demonstrate the superiority of one type over the other. These
men were very clear that a typology is mainly descriptive, not normative.
By contrast I shall be giving a Christian evaluation as well as a historical
and theological analysis of these types.[23] Phenomenology in this study
will be in the service of theology.

   Because we are dealing with ideal types, no one theologian or spiritual
writer can be completely identified with any one of them. In classical or
traditional mysticism some thinkers stand much closer to biblical faith
than others. Augustine and Bernard, for example, display a marked evangelical thrust, though the heritage of Platonism and Neoplatonism is still
determinative in how these men articulate their theologies. Augustine reveals his discomfiture with Platonism when he argues that "it is not the
bad body which causes the good soul to sin but the bad soul which
causes the good body to sin."[24] Interestingly, the Reformers appealed to
both Augustine and Bernard as well as various other church fathers in
their articulation of a biblical, evangelical theology.

   In some Christian mystics Neoplatonism is so pronounced that the biblical worldview is partially eclipsed. Among those especially indebted to
Platonic and Neoplatonic philosophy are Evagrius Ponticus, John Cassian, John Scotus Erigena, Nicholas of Cusa, Catherine of Genoa and

Meister Eckhart. In evangelical tradition one can discern the reappearance of mystical motifs in Pietism and radical Pietism.[25] Yet it is well to note that such leading evangelicals as John Wesley, Count Zinzendorf and Kierkegaard all warned against mysticism.[26]

One temptation we should guard against is to treat the typology of mystical, biblical and secular as correlative with Catholicism, Protestantism and liberalism. This kind of thinking represents an unwarranted reductionism that fails to do justice to the complexity of the issue. Some exponents of Catholic and Orthodox spirituality are closer to evangelical or biblical piety than first appears. Among those in whom a pronounced biblical thrust is evident are Augustine, Bernard of Clairvaux, Pascal, Greek Orthodox Patriarch Cyril of Lucaris (seventeenth century), Russian Orthodox saint Tikhon of Zadonsk (eighteenth century)[27] and Catholic Carmelite nun Thérèse of Lisieux (nineteenth century).[28] Some Protestant spiritual writers have more affinity with mysticism than with Reformation faith. Among these are Jacob Boehme, George Fox, Gerhard Tersteegen, William Law, Robert Barclay, Albert Day, Rufus Jones and Douglas Steere.

Again it should be noted that some contemporary evangelicals are very much at home in the philosophical milieu of rationalism. Here one can place Benjamin Warfield, Charles Hodge, Gordon Clark, Carl Henry, R. C. Sproul, Ronald Nash, Norman Geisler and Clark Pinnock, though several of these transcend the rationalist legacy in favor of a view that is more personal and spiritual.[29]

Not everyone in the new spirituality can be legitimately classified as a mystic or even a neomystic. Many of these thinkers have an emphasis on empirical validation rather than on mystical insight or intuition. It is naturalism, activism and vitalism more than mysticism that characterize the new world vision. Yet this new movement has an incontrovertible mystical element as well, for its goal continues to be the unity of the One in the All.

While there are marked convergences between the three types, there are even more conspicuous divergences. The old mystical spirituality encourages an ascent to a holiness beyond this world. Evangelical spirituality signifies a response to a holiness won for us by a divine incursion into the world. The new spirituality finds holiness in involvement in the ongoing struggle for a new world order. In all these forms of spirituality the doctrine of God is pivotal. Yet here we see more than in any other place the lines that separate these competing visions. The God of classical spirituality is the transcendental ideal that moves all things toward itself by the magnetism of its beauty. The God of modern spirituality is the infinite abyss, the bottomless depths out of which all things emerge. The God of biblical spirituality is the almighty Lord who creates and rules over all things.

4

CLASSICAL MYSTICISM

The only way to pray is to approach alone the One who is Alone.

PLOTINUS

Do not wander far and wide but return into yourself.
Deep within man there dwells the truth.

AUGUSTINE

What is love but to desire and to long to have and to possess and to enjoy?

HUGH OF ST. VICTOR

Nothing better helps a religious to remain silent
than flight from the company of others and the pursuit of a life of solitude.

BONAVENTURE

Love wishes to be free and apart from every worldly affection,
lest its inner vision be hindered.

THOMAS À KEMPIS

Mysticism makes a place for the experiential dimension in Christian faith, but in its radical form it subverts the paradoxical unity of Word and Spirit, subordinating the former to the latter. Rationalism also fosters a break in the dialectic of Word and Spirit, and it ends with a purely logos Christology. Evangelical catholicity strives to unite Word and Spirit by viewing them as inseparable and indissoluble.

The biblical view does not abrogate mysticism, but it challenges the salient motifs of mysticism. In mysticism meaning is swallowed up in mystery. In rationalism meaning is reduced to logic. In biblical faith meaning shines through mystery. In biblical Christianity the real is the historically incarnational as opposed to the rationally inescapable (as in rationalism) or the mystically ineffable (as in mysticism).

Because classical mysticism in this context is virtually synonymous with Christian mysticism, it is not surprising to find conflicting motifs in the Western mystical heritage.[1] Those mystics who are more Christian than mystical tend to contradict themselves in their efforts to remain true to the affirmations of New Testament faith. It is an open question whether the great Christian mystics succeeded in holding together the sovereignty of divine grace and the necessity of good works in the Christian life. It is incontestable that the mystics often subordinated Scripture and tradition to the inner light and that the latter was in fact their ruling norm.

The Mystical Experience

The tie that unites Christian and non-Christian mysticism is the mystical experience, a direct awareness of God that bypasses the senses. Mysticism strives for a knowledge beyond rational discourse and a vision beyond images. According to Abbé Bremond, mysticism is based on "a real knowledge, a direct intuition, which, without the intermediation of images and concepts" establishes "between the real, whatever it may be, and ourselves a kind of immediate contact, amounting to complete adherence or possession."[2] Radical or thoroughgoing mysticism leaves sacraments behind, but in a Christian context sacraments are preparatory for the mystical experience. Mystical religion portrays the mystical rapture as a "meeting of the one with the one" (Dionysius). In this meeting the subject-object relationship is dissolved and the human soul loses its individuality as it merges with the world soul.

Mystics generally agree that the mystical experience lies beyond verbalization and is thus incommunicable. It furnishes not a rational content that can be preached but a joy that can be shared. In the words of Angela of Foligno (c. 1248-1309), "I beheld the ineffable fullness of God, but I can relate nothing of it, save that I have *seen* the fullness of Divine Wisdom, wherein is all goodness."[3]

The God of the mystics is shrouded in mystery. We can make experiential contact with this God, but we cannot adequately describe his being or his workings. The experience of this God is ineffable, but it is not unintelligible. We can have negative knowledge of God, but not positive knowledge or univocal knowledge.[4] We can say what God is not, but we cannot comprehend his majesty. God is beyond reason, but he is not irrational. We can have an immediate awareness of God but not a rational grasp of his being and his attributes. The names we give to God are but metaphors rooted in religious experience. The mystical God is suprapersonal and suprarational. We cannot rise to God's level, but we can experience God's presence. The hope of the mystic is to be transfigured in God's image, though a full understanding of God's being and working will always elude us. God is both the Wholly Other (Rudolf Otto) and Wholly the Same, since the core of the soul *is* God or the place where we meet God.

The God Above God

The God upheld in the classical mystical tradition is a God above God—the ground of being beyond all particular beings. Showing the influence of Neoplatonism, mystics posit a God beyond all thought, beyond growth, decay and death. Plato could even describe God as "beyond all existence." And in the words of Plotinus, "The One is an Absolute transcending all thought and is even beyond Being."[5] This is the immutable, impassible God of Greek philosophy, and this God was identified by both Christian mystics and scholastics with the living God of Christian faith. This is a God beyond the personal, the infinite ground and depth of all being (Tillich). Meister Eckhart enjoined, "Love him as he is . . . apersonal, formless. Love him as he is the One, pure, sheer and limpid, in whom there is no duality."[6] According to Paul Elmer More, Eckhart's theology "brings into the open the universal drift of mysticism towards an anti-theistic, or supra-theistic transcendentalism."[7]

The Trinitarian legacy of Christian faith resisted the mystical reduction of God to a primordial One beyond all diversity and duality. A number of the great mystics of the church seeking to be faithful to their commitment to the catholic and apostolic faith strongly adhered to the Trinity and sought to bring this doctrine into accord with Greek tradition. The German mystics of the fourteenth and fifteenth centuries distinguished between the Godhead and God, the former connoting the infinite abyss beyond all trinitarian distinctions. The God of mysticism is an undifferentiated unity beyond the Trinity. Dionysius the Pseudo-Areopagite described God as the "super-essential Essence," the "super-essential Darkness" and the "unspeakable darkness."[8] All of these appellations reflect a God beyond the personal and therefore one that contradicts the original vision of Christian faith.

Even while positing the transcendence of God on the epistemological level, the mystics held to the radical immanence of God on the ontological level. God is above human thought, but at the same time he is the ground of human thought and the core of human selfhood. In the words of Plotinus, "God is not external to anyone, but is present with all things, though they are ignorant that He is so."[9] Mysticism posits a divine spark within the human creature, an uncreated light within the soul. The anonymous author of the *Theologica Germanica* voices the sentiments of the mainstream of Western mysticism: "This eternal Good does not have to come into the soul, for It is already there, albeit unrecognized."[10]

Whereas biblical Christianity emphasizes the outer word, the cross and resurrection of Jesus Christ, mysticism focuses on the inner word, the eternal light resident within the human soul. In the mystical ethos we meet God in the innermost part of the soul, sometimes called the cave of the heart. We find God by journeying to the center of the soul, which comprises the point of contact between the divine and the human. We discover God by looking upward, above history to the eternal, but this upward dimension is at the same time an inward dimension, for the eternal is the ground of the temporal. The God of mystical devotion is the center of the world and the center of the self.[11]

The Eternal and the Temporal

The polarity of the eternal and the temporal is pervasive in mysticism, though sometimes the mystics find aspects of both in God. While on the one hand God is the Unmoved Mover, absolutely immutable and transcendent, on the other hand he is sometimes described as being in movement. The One goes out of itself and returns to itself as light diffuses itself into darkness; then the lights in the darkness return to their source—the eternal light. Meister Eckhart described this movement in terms of *Fluss* and *Wiederfluss,* a stream and a counterstream. It moves away from itself and then returns back into itself.[12] This means that the mystics perceived a dynamic dimension in God, though their philosophical speculation remained fairly close to Greek philosophy, which could not countenance any real change in God. The mystic John Ruysbroeck (d. 1381) declared, "This flowing forth of God always demands a flowing back."[13] This same sentiment is echoed in Paul Tillich: "Everything temporal comes from the eternal and returns to the eternal."[14] We find it also in the Anabaptist mystic Hans Denck (c. 1500-1527): "God, the all-highest, is in the deepest abyss within us and is waiting for us to return to Him."[15] The Quietist Madame Guyon held a similar position: "Then it is that this spirit which went forth from God, returns back unto God; this being its sole end."[16] The contradiction with the biblical view of God appears when the mystics describe the outgoing or outflowing of God as an inner necessity rooted in God's eternal fecundity. In the biblical view God's going out to the world is an act of divine grace and is rooted in God's freedom, not in his nature.

When the world is seen as an emanation of God rather than a creation out of nothing *(creatio ex nihilo),* the reality of a world distinctly other than God is called into question. Paul Elmer More maintains that mysticism is characterized by "the conviction of supernatural realities accompanied with a sense of the illusory nature of the phenomenal world."[17] To find God we must turn away from the world—which is basically appearance—and proceed to a spiritual reality that is obscured by a fascination with the corporeal or the material.

In classical Christian mysticism the plight of humanity is found in separation from Being-itself, and salvation is found in reunion with the ground and center of all things. Sin thereby becomes privation and separation from being. It is not so much a deliberate rebellion of the self against its maker as a deficiency of being or a lack of goodness. Mystics often posit an ontological fall in addition to a historical fall. The ontological fall is synonymous with creation. It is separation from the ground of being, a turning toward nonbeing. In this *Weltanschauung* sin becomes practically indistinguishable from finitude.

In the mystical understanding love is a longing for unity with the eternal from which we have come. Love is the desire for the highest value. This is eros love, which is acquisitive and self-regarding. It stands in palpable contrast to the love described in the New Testament—going out to the lowliest in order to help the lowliest.[18]

The goal of the mystical quest is the vision of God, the perception of the Good, the Beautiful and the True (Plato). Salvation is both the possession of God and the deification of humanity. Catherine of Genoa (1447-1510) put it this way: "God became man in order to make me God; therefore I want to be changed completely into pure God."[19] Mysticism focuses on the journey of the soul to an Absolute outside of time and history. Prophetic religion concentrates on the battle of the soul to reclaim the world as the domain of God. It is the difference between a radical individualism that turns our attention to transcendental realities and a social Christianity in which the world is the arena of the glory of God (Calvin).

Ascent to Divinity

One of the fundamental motifs that runs through almost every kind of mysticism is the ascent to divinity. The hope of the restless spirit to become joined to divinity was already evident in Platonism and Neoplatonism. For Plato the aim of a person's action should be to gain freedom from the bonds of the flesh and to strive with virtue and wisdom "to become like God, even in this life."[20] For Dionysius the Pseudo-Areopagite, the goal of the Christian life is "coming nearer and nearer to God and finally uniting with him."[21]

The mystics also teach that the way to unity with God is not to get out of ourselves but to go deeper into ourselves. According to Isaac of Nineveh (d. c. 700),

> The ladder leading into the kingdom of heaven is hidden within you, in your heart. And so purify yourself from sin and enter your heart; there you will find the rungs of the ladder by which you can climb to the heights.[22]

A similar sentiment is expressed by Albertus Magnus (c. 1200-1280): "To mount to God means to enter into oneself. Whoever enters within and penetrates his own depths, goes beyond himself and in truth mounts to God."[23]

The ascent to God presupposes a descent from spiritual to earthly reality. Mystics who speak out of the Christian ethos generally see this descent as one of grace and therefore as undeserved. At the same time many of these same persons can describe the descent as the fall of the soul into multiplicity and temporality (the Neoplatonic emphasis).

As we have seen above in Isaac of Nineveh, mystics frequently portray the return of the soul to God as climbing the mystical ladder to heaven, though we need divine grace to complete the ascent. A closely related metaphor is the stairway of perfection (the *scala perfectionis*) leading from earth to heaven. Another prominent image is the mountain of purgation, which often includes a cloud of unknowing that hides the summit of the mountain from view.[24]

The climax of the spiritual quest is the vision of God—when we see God face to face. But this goal is a possibility only for those who purify themselves from sin and mount up the ladder of salvation. The downward way is God's way to humanity. The upward way is the pilgrim's way to divinity. Athanasius expressed it thus: "God became man so that man might become God."[25]

The developing mystical spirituality began to articulate stages in the ascent to God. Many mystics, showing their indebtedness to Proclus and Dionysius, posited four stages in the road to perfection: purgation, illumination, union and ecstasy. Union with God in the state of ecstasy was regarded by Christian mystics as a gift of sheer grace. Yet we would not experience this blessing unless we strived for "the holiness without which no one will see the Lord" (Heb 12:14). For some mystics like Richard of St. Victor (d. 1173), in the fourth stage of spiritual life the soul descends from the lofty heights of contemplation to practice charity in the world.[26] This biblical note was also discernible in Meister Eckhart, who counseled his hearers to break off their contemplation if they came across a person in real need.

Again, the followers of mysticism postulated stages in the life of prayer. We begin with petition and then go on to meditation, finally ending in contemplation. The highest prayer is one beyond words in which we simply gaze upon the glory and majesty of the holy God. The elevation of mental over vocal prayer is conspicuous in this remark of Isaac of Nineveh: "Vocal prayer acts as a stimulus to contemplation, in such a way that the words disappear little by little from the lips and the soul enters into ecstasy, becoming unconscious of the world."[27] For Augustine petitionary prayer is for beginners, but when we make progress in the spiritual life we go on to meditation and contemplation. Teresa of Ávila was convinced that unless we let go of verbal prayer and enter the silence of contemplation we have not yet arrived at spiritual maturity.

At the same time, the mystics sometimes warned against the perils of reaching too high and leaving the cares of this world behind. Teresa of Ávila observed, "It seems to be a kind of pride when we seek to ascend higher, seeing that God descends so low, when he allows us, being what we are, to draw near unto him."[28]

In the Eastern church the repetition of the Jesus prayer—a call upon Jesus for mercy—was viewed as a helpful preparation for higher prayer, but it was never the goal of the prayer journey. The goal in Eastern Orthodox mysticism is immersion in God, transfiguration by the Spirit of God.[29] John Climacus (c. 570 - c. 649) spoke for many when he described the highest form of prayer as "the remembrance of Jesus," "the wordless prayer of the spirit," the stillness of adoration.[30]

The idea of an ascent to God through the cultivation of the spiritual life was sharply challenged by the Protestant Reformers. Luther warned against a relapse into mysticism: "God will not have thee thus ascend, but He comes to thee and has made a ladder, a way and a bridge to thee."[31] It is not "man's search for God" but "God's search for man" that is the biblical theme (Barth). The mystics of the church have nevertheless kept alive the truth that salvation involves not only the forgiveness of sins but also the transfiguration of the believing soul into glory (2 Cor 3:18). By virtue of our inclusion in the resurrection and exaltation of Christ through faith, we are given a foretaste of the glory that is yet to come (Rom 6:3-11; Col 2:11-13).

Call to the Desert

Classical mysticism is noted for its call to the desert, a call to extricate ourselves from worldly entanglements and confront the invisible God apart from visible signs and aids. In the mystical worldview, the "desert is a place of stripping and purifying, a place where there are no luxuries." The desert "witnesses to the confrontation with God in terrible simplicity, it is the 'primal scriptural symbol of the absence of all human aid and comfort.'"[32] The desert connotes a place of solitude, a place for overcoming illusions and purifying desire. The call to the desert is a call to withdrawal from worldly society, from the outer, external world. It is a call "of the Alone to the Alone" (Plotinus). It is an invitation to embrace solitude as a necessary step to the knowledge of God. As Bonaventure put it, "Nothing better helps a religious to remain silent than flight from the company of others and the pursuit of a life of solitude."[33] A similar sentiment is expressed by Teresa of Ávila: "We need no wings to go in search of Him but have only to find a place where we can be alone and look upon Him present within us."[34]

Life in the desert does not necessarily imply the breaking of all contact with fellow humans. Instead it means detaching ourselves from the aimless activities that ensnare ordinary mortals in order to relate to others at a deeper level. Thomas Merton advised: "Go into the desert not to escape other men but in order to find them in God."[35]

Christian mystics often appeal to Scripture in order to justify their world-denying stance. Some of them cite Hosea 2:14: "Now I shall woo her, lead her into the wilderness, and speak words of encouragement to her" (REB). Psalm 55 also seems to offer possible support for the monastic vocation: "Oh, that I had the wings of a dove! . . . I would flee far away and stay in the desert" (Ps 55:6-7 NIV). Jesus' withdrawal into the wilderness for forty days is often pointed to as illustrating the dialectic between action and contemplation (Mt 4:1-11; Mk 1:12-13; Lk 4:1-13).[36] Just as Jesus in his wilderness journey was confronted by the devil, so the mystics too go into the desert with the expectation of battling the devil and triumphing over him. In the mythology of the time, the desert was the place where the demons dwelt. To withdraw into the desert was to go to the front lines in the war between light and darkness. To separate from the world is at the same time to make oneself available to God for the sake of the redemption of the world.

Mysticism in its classical sense is united with an otherworldly asceticism that depreciates the joys of earthly life in order to prepare us for the higher joys of the contemplative life. According to Augustine the good things of the world are to be used, not enjoyed.[37] In the words of Thomas à Kempis, "All worldly pleasures are either vain or unseemly: spiritual joys alone are pleasant and honorable."[38] Indeed, "If you wish to possess the blessed Life, despise this present life."[39]

The elevation of virginity and celibacy over marriage is also indicative of the world-denying spirituality fostered by mysticism. Origen was convinced that "love, which is God, and takes its existence in Him, affectionately loves nothing earthly, nothing material, nothing corruptible."[40] In the words of John Climacus: "If you long for God, you drive out your love for family. Anyone telling you he can combine these yearnings is deceiving himself."[41] A similar stance is found in Jerome: "That battering-ram of affection, by which faith is shaken, must be beaten back by the wall of the Gospel."[42] Angela of Foligno regarded the members of her own family as obstacles to her spiritual growth and saw in their deaths a hidden blessing.[43]

The mystics were firm in their contention that the eternal world is alone the object of joy, that the present world is there to be endured. According to Jerome, "we must not laugh, for this is the world and this is the time for tears; the future world is the world of joy."[44] Thomas à Kempis advised that we renounce the pursuit of worldly happiness and focus our attention on the delights of the spirit.[45]

As Catholic theology developed, a distinction came to be drawn between three types of discipleship: the active life, the contemplative life and the mixed life. One could be a true Christian in any of these vocational choices, but generally the monastic life was valued over the secular life, contemplative existence over worldly activity. A few mystics like Thomas Aquinas saw the need for the mixed life—combining contemplation and action. But in general even a missionary vocation was held to be less conducive to the spiritual life than a purely contemplative vocation. As Thomas Merton put it, "The monastic life is a search for God and not a mission to accomplish this or that work for souls."[46]

Mystical devotion viewed the two sisters of Bethany, Mary and Martha (Lk 10:38-42), as types of the contemplative and active lives, respectively. Not surprisingly Mary is lauded for embracing the one thing needful—sitting at the feet of Jesus and reflecting on his words. Martha's task in preparing the food was necessary but not nearly as praiseworthy as Mary's. It is interesting to note, however, that both Meister Eckhart and Teresa of Ávila spoke highly of Martha, even elevating her to the same plane as Mary. According to Eckhart, Martha had already achieved the contemplative state and was now sharing the fruits of her contemplation.[47]

The Church Within

One of the hallmarks of mystical spirituality is to uphold the invisible church over the visible church. The true church is the company of the committed who reside in all denominations and sometimes outside of any particular religious fellowship. According to Gerald Heard, the true church is comprised of holy souls in all religions.[48] The real people of God are those who are making progress toward sainthood. They are those who have put to death the animal nature within them and have become fully or purely spiritual.

Christian mystics, in contrast to generic mystics, continue to affirm the role of sacraments and rituals in the life of faith; yet they consider these things expendable or at least not absolutely essential. Meister Eckhart regarded the sacraments and even the "human shape of our Lord Jesus Christ" as obstacles to spiritual growth.[49] The important thing is to get beyond visible signs to invisible reality. According to Geert Grote, founder of the mystical Brethren of the Common Life, the valiant soul will leave "the Scriptures and external signs behind" as he or she makes progress in the Christian life toward the perfection of faith.[50]

As a type of religious association, the mystical society is a fellowship of kindred souls, not a mission station to convert the world. The mystical society will often take the form of a parachurch fellowship that is generally supportive of the church as a social institution. Yet mysticism in its celebration of religious experience unwittingly loosens the tie to the institutional church.

Mystics see their task as sharing the fruits of their contemplation with the world. This means showing others the road to God that they too must follow. In evangelical perspective sharing the fruits of our faith entails making known to others God's way to us in Jesus Christ. For mystics the ministry of evangelism is not proclaiming a definite message but sharing a personal experience that is designed to edify searching souls. According to Plotinus, whose influence on mystical spirituality is incalculable, "If we here speak and write, it is but as guides to those that long to see: we send them to the Place Itself, bidding them from words to the Vision."[51]

While recognizing the value of fellowship for seekers after truth, mysticism is fundamentally an individualistic type of religion. What is all-important is the individual's discovery of truth within the self rather than a special revelation in human history. Augustine here mirrors the individualism rampant in mysticism: "All I desire to know is God and the soul, the soul and its God."[52]

As I have noted earlier, institutional Catholicism has always mistrusted mysticism, though it has sought to use the mystical witness to consolidate its hold over the faithful. Christian mysticism at its best calls us to rise above parochial loyalties to a genuinely catholic vision of the truth. At its worst it encourages people to place their trust in their own experiences of God rather than in the witness of Holy Scripture or the wisdom of sacred tradition; the journey of the soul to God is more important than the fellowship of those gathered together to hear the Word of God.

The Biblical-Classical Synthesis

Mysticism becomes understandable when seen in the light of the biblical-classical synthesis—the attempt by Christian thinkers to unite biblical and classical themes.[53] The question is whether the living God of biblical faith can ever be reconciled with the God of Greek philosophy, the impassible Absolute. We find both Gods in Christian mysticism, but the Hellenistic vision is dominant. The God of the mystics is basically a God impervious to suffering and change. Angelus Silesius (1624-1677) puts it this way: "We pray: Thy Will be done. . . . But look: he has no will—he is eternal silence."[54] The metaphysical vision of Hellenism is also expressed by Gregory of Nyssa: "As the Divine Nature is altogether impassible, a man who is always entangled in passions is debarred from union with God."[55] Nevertheless in their personal devotions and in the liturgy of the church the mystics demonstrated that they too believed in a God who answers prayer and who intercedes for the redemption of humanity.

The indebtedness of the mystics to Platonism and Neoplatonism is evident in the way they seek to relate history and eternity. In mysticism we gain our fulfillment outside history, not within. Many of the mystics (such as Meister Eckhart) seem to value the birth of God in the soul more highly than the incarnation of God in history. The eternal Christ has far greater significance than the historical Jesus. Emil Brunner observes:

> Mysticism in the strict sense exists only where one soars above the sphere of history, and where in place of the Mediator and the historical event are put the inner word of God, the inner motions of the soul, in order to reach immediacy between soul and God, and in the end, the identity of both.[56]

Whereas historic Christian faith upholds the creation of the world by the fiat of God, mystics who stand in the tradition of Platonism and Neoplatonism prefer to speak of the emanation of the world out of the being of God. Instead of God being over and other than the world, they portray God as standing in basic continuity with the world. In Neoplatonism the world is explained in terms of the necessary derivation of essences. In Gnosticism, which is also a source for mysticism, creation is viewed as something lamentable rather than wondrous and praiseworthy. According to Simone Weil, creation is "good broken up into pieces and scattered throughout evil."[57] The goal of spirituality is to rise above the created order in order to make contact with the unchangeable Good.[58]

The Platonic imprint upon Christian thought is evident not only among the mystics but also among Pietists and evangelicals. Jonathan Edwards is an example of a respected biblical theologian who nevertheless drew upon classical thought in order to make the case for Christianity more credible. One critic remarks: "In genuine Neo-Platonic fashion," Edwards "regards being itself as a good, and he goes on to draw the conclusion that excellence is proportioned to the degree of existence. The more of existence any being has, other things being equal, the more excellent it is. The infinite Being God is immeasurably more excellent than all crea-

tures, for He possesses an infinitely greater amount of existence than
they, and is infinitely farther from nonentity."[59] Edwards also favored
speaking of creation in terms of emanation, another Neoplatonic emphasis. Edwards was partly a mystical and partly an evangelical theologian.
In contrast to Barth, who posited an antithesis between biblical Christianity and classical humanism and mysticism, Edwards sought a synthesis of
these disparate worldviews.[60] Yet biblical motifs definitely have priority
in his thought.

Another polarity that theologians of synthesis try to overcome is that
between revelation and recollection. In Platonic theory we find truth by
bringing into the open transcendental ideas or ideals implanted in the human soul. We recall to mind our preexistent unity with being or the
ground of being. In biblical prophetic religion, on the other hand, we
come to truth only when we are grasped by the truth in the event of
preaching and hearing. We find truth not by looking to the uncreated
light within us but by going to Scripture and reflecting on its witness to
the mighty deeds of God. Søren Kierkegaard put his finger on the incom-
patibility of the two approaches in his seminal book *Philosophical Fragments*.[61] For Kierkegaard the key to biblical hermeneutics is not an underlying congruity between the divine and the human but an antithesis
that cannot be surmounted by human reason. Humanity is separated from
God not only by its finiteness but also by its sin. The breach between God
and humanity is only healed by the incarnation—God becoming man in
Jesus Christ. And this is an event in history, not an eternal idea that can
be uncovered through unceasing introspection (as in mysticism).

A further polarity that constitutes a challenge to synthetic theology is
that between agape and eros, the self-denying love of New Testament
faith and devotion and the self-regarding love that typifies the Platonic
ascent of the soul to the heavenly realm.[62] Plato defined love as "desire
for the perpetual possession of the good [or the beautiful]."[63] The apostle
Paul by contrast envisaged a love that does not seek its own fulfillment
or happiness, that loses itself in sacrificial service to others. Agape is the
paradoxical love of the cross—making oneself vulnerable for the sake of
another without expectation of personal gain. Eros is the aspiring, acquisitive love that seeks possession of the divine. Anders Nygren brilliantly

shows in his groundbreaking *Agape and Eros* that the assimilation of classical thought to Christian faith led to a focus on *caritas,* which combined insights from both biblical and classical traditions but ended in subordinating agape to eros.[64]

The Christian mystics sought to do justice to the altruistic or other-regarding character of Christian love, but the goal in Christian life remained for the most part egocentric. We love God and our neighbor in order to find our own fulfillment in God, that is, in unity with God. The highest love, according to Bernard of Clairvaux, is the love of self for the sake of God.[65] Love is not the descent of the highest to the lowest (as in evangelical spirituality) but the ascent of the lowest to the highest (as in Platonism and mysticism). In the view of the anonymous author of *The Cloud of Unknowing,* love is the "longing" and "desire" "to achieve perfection."[66]

While generally articulating their conception of love in Neoplatonic terms, the Christian mystics nevertheless often broke through philosophical verbiage in demonstrating a real, caring concern for others. Teresa of Ávila could even say that the surest sign for knowing whether we are in a state of grace is the love of our neighbor.[67] Yet Paul Elmer More utters this word of caution in attributing a biblical basis to the mystical vision of love:

> The fact cannot be overlooked that the mystic's violent repudiation of the world very frequently narrowed and desiccated his religion to a caricature of the Gospel. Nor can we forget that what may appear as an affectionate care of men may be no true love at all but an egotistical aspect of asceticism which commands us to revel in self-sacrifice.[68]

Augustine made contact with the New Testament idea of love as agape in his theology of grace. Yet grace is given that we might ascend to God by virtue of our love for God. We are called to love what is worthy of love, but such a precondition seems to undercut the command to love our neighbor. Augustine does speak of love for neighbor, but he appears to understand it as really a love for the image of God in our neighbor. And when God loves us he is actually loving the reflection of himself in us.

Just as the key word in biblical personalist religion is self-sacrifice, so the key word in mysticism is self-fulfillment. As Evelyn Underhill beauti-

d it, "Attraction, desire and union as the fulfillment of desire; this is the way Life works, in the highest as in the lowest things."[69]

Yet the mystics as people of Christian faith and commitment did not reject the idea of self-sacrifice. On the contrary they made clear that we are called to sacrifice ourselves in order to fulfill ourselves. As has already been noted, Richard of St. Victor referred to a fourth stage in the spiritual life—after purgation, illumination and union. This is when the soul descends from the heights of contemplative glory to bear the cross in the midst of the world's anguish.[70] The agape element is unmistakably present in much mystical devotion, but it is fused with the eros element and is thereby relegated to second place.

The effort to reconcile the biblical with the Hellenistic vision of truth and reality appears in the emphasis accorded by the church fathers to divinization or deification rather than to justification, the leitmotif of Pauline theology. For the church fathers, being elevated into godlikeness played a more determinative role in the shaping of theology and spiritual life than being pardoned by God on the basis of the substitutionary atoning sacrifice of Jesus Christ. The forgiveness of sins was still integral to patristic and medieval theology, but it was clearly subordinated to the goal of being transformed into the likeness of God through the struggle of faith and obedience. According to Athanasius, God became human so that humans might become like God.[71] Divinization is possible only because of the incarnation. The ascent of the human person to divinity has its basis in the descent of God to humanity.

It is well to note that the biblical story says little of divinization but very much of justification and sanctification. At the same time, the idea of being "partakers of the divine nature" is not absent from New Testament thinking (2 Pet 1:4; cf. 1 Pet 4:13; 5:1). One should recognize, however, that the Neoplatonic goal of being merged into God through spiritual exercises is completely foreign to New Testament faith. The New Testament focus is on fellowship with God, not absorption into God. It is a fellowship, moreover, based not on whether we have purified ourselves of sin but on God's unconditional love that goes out to sinners. Holy living is the outcome of fellowship with God, not its foundation.

Whereas biblical faith puts the accent on reconciliation, mysticism un-

derlines the theme of reunion with God. In the former the important thing
is for the sinner to be reconciled with a God of majesty and holiness. We
can be reconciled because God has taken upon himself in the person of
his Son our sin, guilt and shame. Our responsibility is to accept this gra-
tuitous gift of God and live accordingly. In the mystical vision the human
dilemma lies first in being separated from God through creation and then
being entangled in the web of sin. In Neoplatonism the soul goes out
from the world soul and then returns to it by climbing the ladder to perfection. In Paul Tillich's theology, "Prayer is a spiritual sighing and longing of a finite being to return to its origin."[72] Reinhold Niebuhr scores Tillich for introducing a Platonic notion into the biblical schema of
salvation.[73] For the Christian mystics, justification is the first stage in the
heavenly return. Reconciliation becomes the basis for reunion with God.
None of the biblical aspects of salvation are overlooked, but the tie that
unites them is the upward ascent of humanity to divinity.

The history of Christian spirituality also includes an underlying cleavage between blessedness and happiness. The latter has its basis in *eudae-
monia*—the fulfillment or development of human potentiality. Blessedness is rooted in the Greek word *makarios*—being full of God or being
at peace with God. Happiness connotes the fulfillment of desire; blessedness signifies conformity to God's will. The Christian mystics and church
fathers sought to bring the two notions together by positing a higher happiness—the satisfaction of our yearning for God on the basis of God's
grace. Self-fulfillment is still important, but now we find our fulfillment in
God rather than in the perfection of virtues as such.

Augustine is significant for turning the Christian vision to the anthropocentric goal of satisfaction and fulfillment of the human desire for
union with God. In this perspective unhappiness is a state of being in
need. Happiness is a state where our deepest needs are satisfied.[74] The
theocentric notion of giving glory to God is not eclipsed in the Augustin-
ian vision but is linked to the human striving for eternal happiness. What
gives glory to God is the reunion of the soul with God. The love for God
becomes a love of the self that is fulfilled in union with God. He could
even say, "The more we love God the more we love ourselves."[75]

It is true that certain biblical passages endorse the idea of satisfying the universal human desire for communion with God (cf. Ps 37:4). Jesus himself said, "Blessed are those who hunger and thirst for righteousness, for they shall be satisfied" (Mt 5:6). The important point to consider, however, is that satisfaction of personal need and desire is contingent on God's blessing and not vice versa.[76] We are called to celebrate the undeserved blessing of God that does speak to our innermost needs but relegates them to a secondary status—after the impartation of divine grace.

No polarity reveals the gulf between Hellenistic and biblical worldviews more strikingly than that of grace and merit. In Greek philosophy and religion virtuous action was deemed meritorious—deserving of divine approval and reward. Cicero considered the noblest person to be one "who has raised himself by his own merit to a higher station."[77] According to Aristotle the attainment of virtue lies in the practice of virtue. Later Catholic theology endorsed the four cardinal virtues of Hellenism: prudence, justice, fortitude, temperance. Yet it subordinated these to the theological virtues: faith, hope and love. Moreover, one can attain these higher virtues only with the assistance of divine grace. The natural virtues are within human capacity, but to be retained they must be exercised. This latter note also applies to the theological or supernatural virtues.

The battle over the role of the human will in salvation was highlighted in the debate between Augustine and Pelagius. The former insisted that not only is salvation a free gift of God, but the act of receiving is itself produced by grace. It is not natural free will but a liberated will that brings people into the kingdom of God. Pelagius taught that we can do good on our own apart from grace, though grace makes the task easier. Semi-Pelagians held that we by ourselves can take the first step in the process of salvation, but grace is necessary for us to complete this process. According to Thomas Aquinas, we can merit an increase of grace, but not the first grace. For the mystical theologian Bonaventure, as soon as the soul has mastered the steps on the mystical way, "it becomes holy, and its merits increase in the measure of its completion of them."[78]

In the mystical ethos the goal of our seeking is to be made worthy of God's justification and salvation. We are made worthy with the aid of grace, but we ourselves can do much to facilitate this salvific process. The idea of being made worthy can possibly be found in 2 Thessalonians

1:11: "We always pray for you, that our God may make you worthy of his call" or "will make you worthy of his call" (NJB). Yet as one biblical scholar observes:

> In no other passage known is the meaning "to make worthy," but always "to deem worthy." Paul prays that God may deem them worthy because of that purpose and faith which he sees in them.[79]

Indeed, the King James Version of this text together with the NKJV, NEB, REB, NIV and NASB reads "count you worthy." In the overall biblical perspective we are not made worthy either by grace or by works, but we are counted or deemed worthy on the basis of Christ's righteousness that is imputed to us by faith. We are presented as holy before the Lord because of our faith in Christ's meritorious death (Col 1:22-23). We are accepted by God not because God finds righteousness within us but because his righteousness covers our sinfulness. We are accounted righteous by virtue of Christ's sacrifice, but a process of inward cleansing begins with repentance and faith and continues throughout life.

Finally we must consider the marked divergence between these two types of religion regarding immortality. Mysticism draws on the legacy of Greek and Roman philosophy, which depicts the soul as inherently immortal. In evangelical theology, which leans on Hebraic sources, death claims both body and soul, but we are given the promise of the resurrection of the whole person, body and soul, on the last day when Christ comes again. Mystics who stand in the mainstream Christian tradition have sought to synthesize these two understandings by contending that in the eschatological consummation our souls will be reunited with our bodies.

Augustine, who blended Hellenic and Hebraic themes in his theology, taught that the soul is eternal in its essence and also immortal in that it persists through the travail of death. The mystical writer Angelus Silesius opined: "If you, my soul, return to what has been your source, you'll be what you have been, that which you honor and love." Indeed, "The body out of earth, again to earth must come. The soul, derived from God, will it not God become?"[80] Biblical faith, by contrast, forthrightly denies the supposition that the soul is impervious to death by virtue of being at one

with God. Instead, it looks forward to the immortality of a personal relationship with God, which death cannot sever (Rom 8:35-39). One of the
most insightful studies on this subject is that of the Lutheran theologian
Oscar Cullmann, who presents a credible case on the intractable differences between Greek and Hebraic conceptions.[81]

Epilogue

Despite the explicit Christian commitment of so many of the great mystics, it cannot be denied that there is a fundamental incongruity between
mysticism and biblical Christianity. In stark contrast to the biblical ethos,
mysticism is uncompromisingly introspective. Its focus lies on the exploration of the depths of the soul, not the preaching of Christ to the masses.
The gospel does not come from outside the self but is implicit within the
self. According to Meister Eckhart, "What is truthful cannot come from
outside in; it must come from inside out and pass through an inner
form."[82] A similar sentiment is expressed by Catherine of Siena: "If thou
wouldst arrive at a perfect knowledge of Me the Eternal truth, never go
outside thyself."[83] Jesus mingled with the people, whereas mystics elevate
solitude over fellowship. This inward proclivity comes not from the Bible
but from Platonism and Neoplatonism. According to Plotinus, "The only
way truly to pray is to approach alone the One who is Alone. To contem-
plate that One, we must withdraw into the inner soul, as into a temple,
and be still."[84]

At its core, mysticism is a world-denying spirituality. The pleasures of
the world are to be viewed at most as stepping stones to a higher world,
which is spiritual, not material. We are allowed to use the things of the
world for the sake of human survival, but we are commanded to enjoy
only the things of the spirit.

Mysticism makes a place for both the vision of God on the boundary
of eternity and the service of God in the squalor of the world. But the
latter is clearly subordinated to the former when we speak of ultimate
concerns. The mystical priority is articulated in a prayer based on a pas-
sage from Plato's *Symposium:* "Open my eyes, O God, to behold true
beauty, divine beauty, pure and unalloyed, not clogged with the pollu-
tions of mortality."[85] Sight much more than hearing is the pathway to

knowledge of God. In the philosophy of Philo, a Hellenized Jew, "hearing holds second rank to seeing." "It is possible to hear the false and take it for true, for hearing is deceptive, but sight, by which existing things are truly apprehended, does not lie."[86] Visible signs of the eternal are acknowledged as aids in the spiritual journey, but when we make progress toward the perfection of faith we leave such things behind.[87]

In addition, mysticism is incorrigibly synergistic. While the Christian mystics generally upheld salvation by grace alone *(sola gratia),* they nevertheless placed the accent on human responsibility for cooperation with grace. We ourselves are summoned to climb the ladder to perfection, though admittedly with the help of grace. As John of the Cross phrased it, "If we would find God it is not enough to pray with the heart and the tongue, or to have recourse to the help of others; we must work ourselves, according to our power."[88] In the mystical perspective, good works are not simply the aftereffects of salvation but the means to the fulfillment of salvation.

Despite the emphasis on cultivating intimacy with God, the mystical God is actually quite distant from the human scene of personal interaction. This is because God, who is the summit of perfection, the Impassible Absolute, is radically removed from the cares and concerns of humanity. A God who is incapable of change cannot enter into a personal relationship with the human creature, who is subject to growth, decay and death. The mystical God is enwrapped in himself, "thought thinking thought" (Aristotle). In the words of John Ruysbroeck, "The Godhead is, a simple essence, without activity; Eternal Rest, Unconditioned Dark, the Nameless Being, the Superessence of all created things."[89] He is a God beyond all anthropomorphism, separateness and multiplicity. The human subject cannot add glory to God because God is already the fullness of perfection. Our efforts therefore can only go toward improving and elevating the human soul.

Finally we should note that mysticism is incurably elitist. Its secrets are too deep to be grasped by mere mortals. Its message is intended for those who would be spiritual adepts, not for the common person. Only a few reach the heights of perfection. As Gregory of Nyssa phrased it, "The knowledge of God is a mountain steep indeed and difficult to climb—the majority of people scarcely reach its base."[90] Aldous Huxley contrasts "the mass of ordinary human beings" who "think and act anthropocentrically" with the "enlightened" ones who pray not that their carnal desires be satisfied but that God might be worshipped so that "the latent and potential seed of reality" within the human soul "may become fully actualized."[91] The truth that mysticism discovers can be appreciated only by the spiritually attuned. In the Christian context these are the saints who are reaching toward the pinnacle of perfection with the aid of divine grace.

CHRISTIAN MYSTICISM AND GNOSTICISM

One of the principal challenges to apostolic faith in the early church period was Gnosticism, which drew upon a variety of sources, including the Greek mystery religions.[1] Gnosticism was an eclectic movement characterized by a cosmic dualism. It emphasized not the incarnation of God in human flesh but escape from materiality. Those Gnostics who considered themselves Christian still made a place for Jesus Christ, but their focus was on the cosmic Christ rather than on the historical Jesus. Among the leading Gnostics in the first centuries A.D. were Valentinus, Basilides, Marcion, Manes and Saturninus.

Hallmarks of Gnosticism

Gnosticism is often confounded with mysticism, but actually it represents a force inimical to the mystical tradition, even to Neoplatonism.[2] It could be deemed an aberrant form of mysticism. Gnosticism is irremediably dualistic, for it posits a basic cleavage between God and the world, the spiritual and the temporal. Mysticism on the contrary is inclined to be monistic, emphasizing the all-comprehensiveness of God.

In gnostic mythology humanity is in a state of alienation from God, but a divine spark within the human self constitutes a point of contact with divinity. The goal of the seeker after truth is to acquire knowledge of one's essential identity with divinity. By this knowledge we can gain liberation from the alien world that surrounds us.

Christ is a cosmic power who descends to earth in order to give us knowledge of our essential self. Christ did not really become human, nor did he really die on the cross.[3] Jesus shows us how to tap into the spiritual resources within us in order to extricate ourselves from the bonds of the flesh.

Gnosticism exemplifies a radical cosmic dualism. On the one hand, there is the intrinsically evil nature of the world that we must strive to overcome. On the other hand, there is the enduring spiritual nature within every human being that is waiting to be discovered.

Marcion (d. c. 160) set out to purge Christian faith of its Judaic accretions in order to make way for a religion of pure grace. He rejected the Old Testament and most of the New except for a heavily edited version of the Pauline epistles and a portion of the Gospel of Luke. According to Marcion there are two different gods: the creator God of the Old Testament and the redeemer God of Pauline Christianity. Salvation is liberation from the domain of the law and entrance into the kingdom of "grace, redemption and hope." One critic observes:

> One consequence of Marcion's system was the literal elimination of time, of history. Marcion's church is severed from Abraham's descendents and becomes a community of spiritualized souls freed from the ongoing course and curse of world history. If there is no historical continuity, no connection between the God who makes us and the God who saves us, then in Marcion's gospel the church becomes a free agent. There is no past to which we are beholden.[4]

Gnosticism did not discount the reality of a supreme being, but this being is unknown and ineffable. Nothing can be predicated of him. The true God is alien to the world, but at the same time he is at one with the human spirit *(pneuma)*.

The god who created the world is an inferior deity. He is the demiurge of the Old Testament. He is a god of justice and wrath, not of love and mercy. To know the merciful God we must ascend from the realm of the material into that of the spiritual. This higher realm is the Pleroma—the fullness of being.

Gnosticism posited a pre-mundane fall to account for humanity's present state. We can return to our spiritual origin through probing the innermost depths of the self. The Christian mystics also looked forward to a return to undivided unity with God, but this was conceived in terms of the practice of love.

The gnostic vision sees a spark of heavenly light imprisoned in a natural body. The body is an obstacle to God's redeeming work, not a vehicle (as with Christian mystics). According to the Gnostics, the saving gnosis awakens seekers after truth to their essential value and to their eternal origin.

The Gnostics spoke of both emanation and devolution to account for the mystery of the world and of God. In Basilides the nameless original ground is called the not-yet-existing god. The deity unfolds itself from the darkness of its primeval essence. We also find this theme in Valentinus, who envisioned an unfolding of the dark and mysterious primitive Depth *(Bythos)* to self-revelation.

Differences from Christian Mysticism

In contrast to the Gnostics, the Christian mystics affirm a real incarnation and a real death of Christ on the cross. The mystics acknowledge the goodness of creation but see it as a ladder to a still higher realm. They posit an upward ascent—from the realm of created light to the realm of glory. The Gnostics by contrast view creation as a foil for redemption. Meister Eckhart here typifies the positive value accorded to creation by Christian mystics: "This, then, is salvation, when we marvel at the beauty of created things and praise the beautiful providence of their Creator."[5] Yet Eckhart also asserts that the soul does not ascend into God until it falls into a forgetfulness of all temporal things.[6]

For Christian mystics we find God through love, not through esoteric knowledge. Our union with God is one of aspiring love, not absorption into the Pleroma. The goal is the remaking of the self, not its extrication from matter. What is given in faith is not simply self-understanding but the forgiveness of sins. We are challenged to embark on a life of discipleship, not a life of unceasing introspection. The focus in Christian mysticism is love to God; in Gnosticism, knowledge of hidden mysteries. An anti-Judaic strand is also discernible among many Gnostics. And this is true for some of the Christian mystics as well, including Simone Weil.

In the Christian mystical vision nature is perfected rather than annulled by grace. The mystics of classical tradition spoke of creation and emanation, not of evolution. Evil in Christian mysticism has a privative character. It is never a positive principle (as in Gnosticism). There is no ultimate metaphysical dualism. The mystics of the classical heritage veered toward monism rather than dualism. Everything that really exists is in a state of continuity with God as its infinite ground and source. The mystics championed a spiritual idealism that transfigures the world, not a cosmic dualism that depreciates the world. It is well to note that Plotinus also objected to Gnosticism partly because of its world-denying propensity.[7]

The mystics loved the Psalms, which testify that the glory of God is revealed to the whole creation. For Simone Weil, a modern mystic, we approach God through the beauty of the world, which leads to God. We are called to go into the world in order to break through the world to the God who lies beyond the world. Yet for her, true Christianity consists of only "drops of purity" in the general ugliness of human history.[8] "God has created a world which is not the best possible, but at every stage of good and evil. We are situated at the point where it is as bad as possible."[9] Simone Weil taught not the denigration of the material world but its depreciation.

Both Neoplatonic and gnostic motifs are conspicuous in Nicolas Berdyaev: "History is a horrible tragedy. Everything is distorted in it, all great ideas are disfigured. And revelation has been perverted in it."[10] The call is to rise above history into the eternal rather than to redeem history through works of justice and mercy.

According to a respected authority on gnostic spirituality, Carl Raschke, the true mystic delights in union with the Infinite. The gnostic by contrast agonizes over the gulf between our present situation and our transcendent goal.[11]

There are nonetheless points of convergence between Christian mysticism and gnosticism. Both movements posit a ladder of perfection and a return to an original unity with God. Both depict the body as the prison house of the soul. Both affirm the need for spiritual purification through the knowledge of God.

Gerald Heard (d. 1971) represents a synthesis of Christian mysticism, Neoplatonism and gnosticism.[12] There is also an element of Oriental mysticism in his philosophy. While he was open to the insights of the Christian mystical tradition, it is indisputable that Gnostic and Neo-Platonic motifs are dominant in his system.

Both gnosticism and Christian mysticism are introspective: both encourage the seeker after truth to gaze within. Augustine, who sought to build bridges between Christian faith and classical philosophy, declared, "Do not wander far and wide but return into yourself. Deep within man there dwells the truth."[13] For gnostics truth dwells in the divine Pleroma that summons us to break free from the earthly self. We probe within, but through enlightenment we do not remain within the confines of our earthly habitation.

In contradistinction to Christian mystics, gnostics seek knowledge of the real or inner self and then of God. The second is sometimes viewed as unnecessary, for fulfillment lies in the first. In gnosticism the quest for salvation is more important than the quest for God.[14] Yet at times these are practically identical. The Christian mystic seeks escape from the turmoils of life by union of the soul with God or with Christ. The gnostic strives to escape into the self. Salvation for the gnostic is not from sin but from ignorance. The significance of the gospel is that it brings illumination of the human condition.

Gnosticism connotes a knowledge from below. We begin with the self—entangled in the web of history and materiality—and end with the self, now liberated and reunited with its divine source. Evangelical Christianity espouses a knowledge from above. We begin with divine revelation and end in a divine-human fellowship that takes us out of ourselves into the service of God and neighbor. Gnostics stress the utter inaccessibility and unknowability of God. Christian mystics by contrast emphasize the nearness and immediacy of God.

Platonism and Neoplatonism, which supplied the philosophical underpinnings of Christian mysticism, sought to reinterpret the world rather than denigrate the world. Their aim was to penetrate through the world of appearance to the spiritual basis of the world. The Gnostics tried to transcend the material world completely. Their intention was to leave the world behind in fulfilling a purely spiritual task.

The Gnostics envisaged a cosmogonic fall—the devolution of spirit into matter. The Christian mystics, in contrast, saw matter created by spirit but lacking the plenitude of being that is in spirit. The Neoplatonists filled the void between God and the world with intermediate spiritual beings to underscore the continuity between God and the world. The Gnostics, however, inserted spiritual beings into this void in order to highlight the distance between God and the world. Plato's distinction between illusion and reality becomes for the Gnostics an alienation between the material world and the spiritual world.

Hans Jonas, one of the foremost scholars of Gnosticism, provides a cogent analysis of gnostic dualism:

> The dualism is between man and the world, and concurrently between the world and God. It is a duality not of supplementary but of contrary terms; and it is one: for that between man and world mirrors on the plane of experience that between world and God. . . . In its theological aspect this doctrine states that the Divine is alien to the world and has neither part nor concern in the physical universe; that the true God, strictly transmundane, is not revealed or even indicated by the world, and is therefore the Unknown, the totally Other, unknowable in terms of any worldly analogies. Correspondingly, in its cosmological aspect it states that the world is the creation not of God but of some inferior principle whose law it executes; and, in its anthropological aspect, that man's inner self . . . is not part of the world, of nature's creation and domain, but is, within that world, as totally transcendent and as unknown by all worldly categories as is its transmundane counterpart, the unknown God without.[15]

Gnosticism is paradoxically a form of agnosticism, for the mysteries of God and the self defy rational comprehension. God is the totally other even after one makes contact with this god within the deepest recesses of the self. Paul Tillich sees a gnostic thrust in Protestant neo-orthodoxy by its emphasis on the extreme transcendence of God.[16] It should be noted, however, that Karl Barth's position is that we can really know God because God has made himself known in his incarnation in Jesus of Nazareth. Even though God remains the hidden God in his revelation, he is not totally hidden, for his Spirit grants us a luminous perception of the significance of God's work of redemption in Christ. This is the opposite of Gnosticism, which takes us out of history and out of materiality into a purely spiritual realm. Mainstream Christian faith speaks not of the entrapment of the soul in the body but of the resurrection of the body into fellowship with Christ and our neighbor.

BIBLICAL PERSONALISM

God has created mankind for fellowship, not for solitariness.

MARTIN LUTHER

The gospel snatches us away from ourselves and places us outside ourselves.

MARTIN LUTHER

The body is not a tomb but a wondrous masterpiece of God,
constituting the essence of man as fully as the soul.

HERMAN BAVINCK

We are not saved by the love we exercise, but by the Love we trust.

P. T. FORSYTH

I can know Him only by His self-communication.
Before He speaks, He is absolute mystery.

EMIL BRUNNER

A second form of the old spirituality is what I have chosen to call biblical personalism. This stream of spiritual life has its source not in ancient philosophy but in the prophets and apostles of biblical faith. Other names for this pattern of spiritual consciousness are prophetic religion, evangelical piety, revelational religion and Puritan spirituality.

Biblical personalism is not to be confused with philosophical personalism. The first focuses upon the self-revealing God who calls people to fellowship with himself. The second appeals to a universal principle and then defines God in terms of this principle. Emil Brunner reminds us that the God of biblical revelation is not the god of theism: "The thought-of person—say, the idea of God in theistic metaphysics—is not truly personal, because it does not assert itself over against me but is immanent in my thoughts." "Christian faith maintains . . . that God Himself asserts Himself as a subject, that He interrupts the monologue of our thought of God, or our mystical feeling of God, and that He addresses me as 'Thou.'"[1]

Between the God of biblical faith and the god of the philosophers stretches an insurmountable chasm, as Abraham Heschel makes incisively clear:

> The God of the philosophers is all indifference, too sublime to possess a heart or to cast a glance at our world. His wisdom consists in being conscious of Himself and oblivious to the world. In contrast, the God of the prophets is all concern, too merciful to remain aloof to His creation. He not only rules the world in the majesty of His might; He is personally concerned and even stirred by the conduct and fate of man.[2]

The great mystics of the church sought to combine the God of biblical revelation and the god of theistic metaphysical speculation, but too often the biblical vision of God was irremediably compromised. The mystics for the most part conceived of God as impassible, distant and totally other, as practically divorced from human experience. Prophetic religion also speaks of God as transcendent and as other than humanity, but it insists that the God of the heights descends into the world of pain and death and battles with us and for us.

The Sovereign, Creator God

The God of biblical faith is the sovereign Lord of the universe. He is the One who brings the worlds into being. He is the One who sustains the world and guides it to completion. He directs its course through history. He is not the creator of evil in the sense of being the direct cause of evil, but he has power over evil. He brings good out of evil. In the words of second Isaiah: "I form light and create darkness, I make weal and create woe, I am the LORD, who do all these things" (Is 45:7; cf. Amos 3:6).

This God is ever active and ever working. He is not a passionless observer of the human scene but is deeply involved in the human drama, overcoming evil with good. He is not the impassible Absolute of classical theism but being in action. He is not simply the Architect of the universe but its Sustainer and Renewer. He is unchanging in the integrity of his purposes, but he is not removed from the sufferings of a fallen humanity. According to Kierkegaard, God's changelessness is not a "chilling indifference" nor a "devastating loftiness" but a perpetual concern.[3]

The God of biblical revelation does not lift humanity above sorrow and tribulation but guides humanity in the midst of tribulation. The goals of the self are realized through being countered and overcome. Wilhelm Herrmann articulates a theme that was prominent in Luther's evangelical understanding:

> God takes away our self-confidence, and yet creates within us an invincible courage; He destroys our joy in life, and yet makes us blessed; He slays us, and yet makes us alive; He lets us find rest, and yet fills us with unrest. . . . God gives us a new existence that is whole and complete; yet what we find therein is always turning into a longing for true life, and into desire to become new.[4]

Biblical spirituality focuses not on the human quest for God but on God's search for humanity. The Bible teaches that the natural person does not even seek for God because sin has irrevocably bent the human will. The person who is corrupted by sin is not in search of God but in flight from God (Rom 3:9-18). We need to be completely turned around if we are to know God and see God. Conversion is a crisis more than a process, though it may nevertheless involve stages in which the old nature is supplanted by a new nature. In the perspective of biblical and Reformation faith the knowledge of God is not a possibility within humanity but a gift of free grace. We do not know God until God addresses us in the awakening to faith. Luther put it this way: "God will not have thee thus ascend, but He comes to thee and has made a ladder, a way and a bridge to thee."[5] Here the ladder imagery of mysticism is reversed and becomes a means of divine descent rather than of human ascent.

The God of the Bible is not troubled by a need for completion or fulfillment, but he actively seeks to answer human need. He is the summit of all perfection, but he wishes his people to share in this perfection. In the words of C. S. Lewis, "In God there is no hunger that needs to be filled, only plenteousness that desires to give."[6] God is with us and for us and makes himself partly dependent on how we respond to his gracious initiatives. He works his purposes out in history in cooperation with his subjects, sometimes overruling their decisions and commitments. God wants what is best for us. In acting to fulfill human need he gives glory to himself. His glory is other-regarding, for its ground lies in the selflessness of his love.[7] He seeks his own glory not in order to magnify himself over humanity but in order to redeem humanity. He is not content for us to be simply his servants: he wants us as sons and daughters—active participants in a fellowship of love. Prophetic piety does teach submission to the will of God but only for the purpose of becoming covenant partners with God in the unfolding of his kingdom in sacred history.

The Divine-Human Encounter

The leitmotif of biblical spirituality is not a descent into the depths of the self where we make contact with the all-pervasive World Spirit but a confrontation with the living Christ, who answers the longings of the human heart. What occurs is not a divine-human fusion but a divine-human encounter, which we see first in Jesus himself and then in the members of his mystical body. The subject-object antithesis is not overcome, as in mysticism, but is transfigured. God is no longer an object but now a living Subject who relates to us by his Spirit, empowering us from within.

The meaning of prayer is drastically altered in the context of biblical faith. No longer an attempt to control God and bend God to our purposes (as in primitive religion), prayer is now submission to the will of God but only after sharing with God our deepest needs and concerns. Prayer is not the silencing of petition (as in mysticism) but the deepening of petition, the subordination of personal need to the glory of God and the advancement of his kingdom.

In rationalistic philosophy prayer is reduced to reflection on the infinite ground of all being or resignation to a divinely appointed destiny. In the Aristotelian view the ultimate universal datum is an Absolute Mind with whom we make contact by the abstraction of thought. In the biblical view it is an Absolute Subject who meets us in a personal encounter. In

Platonism and Neoplatonism the final goal of the spiritual life is the vision of God—when we are lost in the contemplation of primordial being or of the eternal ideas. In biblical Christianity the vision of God takes the form of fellowship with God. It also includes fellowship with all the saints through the medium of God's Spirit. It is not a solitary meeting of the one with the One (as in Plotinus) but creative interaction with the Creator and Redeemer of humanity.

For Jonathan Edwards we are called not simply to the vision of God but to conversation with God. "God and we will indeed *sing* to one another, beatitude will be the perfected eternal chanting of 'God's word and prayer.'"[8] Edwards reconstrued the beatific vision, "apprehending it not on the paradigm of seen beauty but on that of heard beauty."[9]

The ineradicable gulf between biblical and mystical spirituality is also apparent in Søren Kierkegaard, who like Edwards nevertheless remained in contact with the mystical tradition. In his *Philosophical Fragments* Kierkegaard recognized that God could reveal his truth to us by raising us to his level by way of ascent, thereby transforming us. Yet this would so overwhelm us that we would be incapable of understanding the very thing God desired to teach us. So God chose to descend to our level, taking on a lowly form.[10] We are energized not by retreating into the self but by being seized by a will and purpose outside the self. We enter into personal communion with God when we are addressed by God, not by meditating on his being but by hearing his Word.

Kierkegaard poignantly challenged the philosophical tradition epitomized by Socrates that truth is resident within the individual and needs only to be brought into the open by a process of introspection. In Kierkegaard's view there is no identity between thought and being but instead "an infinite qualitative difference." Truth is found not by fostering self-awareness or even God-awareness but by looking to that moment in history when God descended to earth in the form of man. We are edified by the knowledge not that we are one with God but that our sins are forgiven by God's gracious act of mercy.[11]

In biblical perspective prayer is not being transported into glory but entering into a dialogue with God. When we speak God answers; when God speaks we answer. In the mystical outlook of Evagrius pure prayer is immediacy, without images and ideas.[12] By contrast biblical prayer involves an exchange of ideas for the purpose of doing the will of God.

The divine-human encounter happened in past history—when God became man in Jesus Christ. But it happens ever again when mortals are confronted by the Spirit of Christ in the moment of decision. This is not simply an external meeting but an internal one as well. God not only speaks to us from the outside, but he also comes to dwell within us. By his Spirit he enters into us, though he never becomes part of us. We are elevated to fellowship with God, but we never become part of God. Christian faith rests on a personal confrontation, yet one that has a mystical dimension.

In classical mysticism we are not confronted by the Wholly Other, but we are given an awareness of our essential identity with the One. The Wholly Other turns out to be the Wholly Same. The transcendent God proves to be the immanent Eternal Spirit.

The picture is radically different in biblical personalism. We do not have a direct or immediate knowledge of God as he exists in himself, but we do have an indirect knowledge. We experience God not in his naked majesty but in the Jesus Christ of history. The biblical view might be described as a mediated immediacy. As Luther put it, "David does not talk with the absolute God but with God clothed and mantled in the Word."[13] In biblical Christianity we need a mediator between God and humanity—not only for the purpose of redemption but also for the purpose of adequate knowledge of God. To know is to be known by God (1 Cor 8:3; Gal 4:9). It is not we who discover God but God who finds us, as the Shepherd finds the lost sheep (Mt 12:11; Lk 15:3-10). We find God not by the negation of the self nor by an expansion of the self but by being found by God, who gives us a new will, a new nature, a new existence. The old self must die; a new self must be born. The creative dialogue between God and the human creature begins only when God takes the initiative and calls us to decision and repentance. Our answer, which is made possible by the empowering of the Spirit, sets the dialogue in motion. The life of prayer is not basking in the glory of God but engaging in meaningful conversation with God. The object-subject relationship is not annulled but placed on a new foundation.

The Scandal of Particularity

The divergence between biblical personalism and mysticism is particularly striking in the doctrine of revelation. Whereas the mystical-idealist tradition sees revelation as an inward process of enlightenment, biblical faith posits a revelation in a particular history—that mirrored in Holy Scripture. God is not discovered within the depths of the soul through unceasing introspection, but God makes himself known in a particular person and in particular events in history. In the classical worldview we are saved by coming to an awareness of truth that lies within us.[14] In the biblical worldview truth must seize us from without and challenge us to a decision.

Persons who stand outside the biblical framework of meaning regard the Christian claim to truth breaking into the history of a particular people (the Jews) as arrogant and offensive. The arrogance is compounded, they believe, when this revelation is considered definitive and final. Yet Scripture clearly affirms that God has revealed himself "once for all" times in Jesus Christ (Heb 10:10; 1 Pet 3:18). In sharp contrast to Gnosticism, as represented by Marcion and in more recent times by the "German Christians," the Gospel of John affirms that "salvation is from the Jews" (Jn 4:22).

In Christian perspective history itself is not the source of our knowledge of God, nor does it unveil the content of faith. The infallible criterion for faith is eternity breaking into history. History itself is not the theme of revelation; this theme is the mighty deeds of God attested in a particular history—that recorded in the Bible.

In a spirituality anchored in scriptural revelation there can be no bona fide natural theology, even though all of creation reflects the presence of the living God (Ps 19:1-4). A natural theology assumes that the knowledge we gain from nature and universal history is sufficient to yield dependable information regarding God and his plan of salvation. We do have knowledge of God by finite reason alone, but it is grossly inadequate for a full or true understanding of God. It is sufficient to render us inexcusable but not sufficient to enable us to construct a system of thought rooted in the living God himself. Only in the light of the one great revelation in Jesus Christ can we discern the lights that illumine the mystery of God in creation (Ps 36:9). This is no longer natural theology but now a theology of creation.[15]

The pagan opponents of Christian faith in the early church period were especially disturbed by the Christian doctrine of the incarnation—that the Word of God became flesh in Jesus Christ. In Greek idealistic philosophy the Word of God is an eternal idea or ideal; it is nonhistorical, outside of history and temporality. Rational philosophy can affirm a cosmic incarnation, a God reflecting his light everywhere in nature and in history, but reason is confounded by the audacious claim that God who is pure Spirit entered into time and became subject to the vicissitudes of history. This allegation goes directly counter to the classical idea of a god who is immutable, impassible and immobile.

Christian faith steadfastly asserts that there are no other sources of revelation that supplement or go beyond Holy Scripture. There is the ongoing illumination of the Spirit in the life of the church, but this inner work of renewal constitutes a revelation that is wholly dependent on God's self-revelation in Jesus Christ as attested in Scripture. In evangelical understanding the source of revelation is in the past, in biblical history; yet signs of revelation can appear again and again in the history of the church, even in universal history, which transcends the parameters of the church. Only those whose inward eyes have been opened by the Spirit of God can discern these signs, which are of no use to those whose eyes are blinded by sin, whose wills are bound to the power of evil in the world.

The scandal of particularity is simply one form of the scandal of the cross. The idea of substitutionary atonement—that Christ was made sin so that we might be accounted righteous (2 Cor 5:21; Gal 3:13-14; 1 Pet 2:24)—is especially offensive to the natural person, who trusts in moral effort to guarantee a place in the kingdom of heaven. Yet Paul claims that the scandal of the cross is the very heart of the gospel (1 Cor 1:18-25; 2:1-5). It is a stumbling block to Jews and folly to Greeks but constitutes the pathway to salvation. The cross of Christ is to be valued not so much because it is a model of perfected human life but because it is a declaration that the Son of God suffered and died in the place of sinners so that all who believe might be saved. Most Christian mystics are ready to affirm the reality of the crucifixion of Christ, but they generally have difficulty with the Pauline doctrine of imputed righteousness—the view that what saves us is the alien righteousness of Jesus Christ laid hold of only by faith. Mystics are inclined to embrace the position that we are justified by faith *and* works, that our progress in justification rests partly on our works. By contrast in biblical, evangelical faith we are justified while we are still sinners (Rom 5:6-8). The ground of our justification lies completely outside ourselves—in the unmerited grace and mercy of the living God.

Word and Spirit

Evangelical spirituality upholds the complementarity of Word and Spirit. The Word is not a dimension of human nature but a personal address directed to the one who believes. Emil Brunner has discerned the personal character of the Word more than most theologians:

> Revelation . . . means that God no longer speaks *out of* us, but *to* us; we do not know him as being *in* the world, and therefore we do not know him *through* the world, but we know him as the One who comes *into* the world. For he himself is an other than the world, an other than the content of the soul. He is the *Other One,* the mysterious and unknowable One, who has his own proper name and whom we do not know because he is *person.*[16]

Mysticism has tended to elevate silence over the Word. The aim is to get beyond the logos to the ineffable One who defies rational articulation. Simone Weil here reflects the ethos of mysticism: "The speech of created beings is with sound. The Word of God is silence."[17] By contrast Francis Schaeffer reveals his affinity to the prophetic tradition of Christian faith when he argues that God is there and is not silent.[18]

In biblical faith the knowledge of God has its roots in the paradoxical unity of Word and Spirit. Against rationalism we do not appeal to the Bible in and of itself but to the Bible illumined by the Spirit. Against mysticism and spiritualism we insist that the Spirit acts in conjunction with the revealed Word of God. The Spirit does not speak directly to the human soul, that is, apart from historical mediation. Instead, the Spirit deigns to act through the outward means of Word and sacraments, the visible signs of invisible grace.[19]

The Reformers were adamant that the Holy Spirit acts and speaks freely but ordinarily binds himself to the Word. As Luther expressed it, the Spirit of God "works in the hearts of whom he will, and how he will, but never without the Word."[20] In Reformation thought the Bible is the final criterion, but the Spirit brings the Bible to life. Whereas both mysticism and rationalism contend that the truth lies within us, biblical religion insists that the truth lies in the God outside of us. In the words of Brunner, "Faith . . . declares: truth is in God's own Word alone; and what is in me is not truth."[21]

Biblical spirituality seeks to avoid both the objectivism of ritualistic and rationalistic religion on the one hand and the subjectivism of mysticism on the other. Revelation is not an external datum but an internal experience that is nonetheless grounded in historical fact. It contains both an ecstatic and a rational dimension. Revelation is not a body of information that lies before one in a book but the act of being personally addressed by a God who is hidden from direct observation—yet who has made himself known in Jesus Christ and in the biblical testimony to Christ. Revelation is not simply the imparting of propositional truth but the dawning realization that we have been grasped and turned around by the truth. Revelation is the welling up of an irreversible conviction that what the Bible says about God's act of deliverance in Jesus Christ is universally true.

In the mystical tradition of the faith, revelation is generally conceived of as an experience of oneness with God. In the biblical strand of Christianity revelation is an encounter with the Wholly Other. What comes to the fore is not our essential unity with God but God's judgment on our desire to be autonomous and independent of God.

As an alternative to both rationalism and mysticism I propose a theology of Word and Spirit in which the rational and mystical elements of the faith are united.[22] We have real knowledge of God but only through the power of the Spirit. We are truly directed by the Spirit of God but only insofar as our thoughts are in accord with the written Word of God. We need to move beyond the polarity of a dead orthodoxy focused on logical symmetry and an amorphous mysticism focused on feeling and experience. Only then will we be in contact with the living Word of God—Jesus Christ—who speaks to us by his Spirit and who points us to his witnesses, especially the prophets and apostles of biblical history.

Salvation by Grace

The leitmotif that runs through biblical and evangelical spirituality is salvation by grace alone *(sola gratia)*. It was not only a cardinal theme of the Reformation but belongs to the wider catholic tradition.[23] To be sure, the Council of Trent insisted that our final justification is dependent on human cooperation with grace, but it also held that the salvific process is begun by the undeserved infusion of grace from a holy and beneficent God. Catholic theology nevertheless has difficulty in maintaining the *sola* in the salvation equation because of the critical role it assigns to the human will in the fulfillment of salvation. Reformation theology gives a more consistent witness to the doctrine of free salvation by contending that what truly saves is the righteousness of Christ imputed to us by faith rather than an interior righteousness that presupposes human acceptance and obedience for its salvific efficacy.

Biblical Christianity advocates a spirituality of substitution as opposed to a spirituality of imitation. Our task as Christians is not to duplicate the righteousness of Christ but to believe in this righteousness, which in God's plan takes the place of human sinfulness. The principle of imitation is not annulled in the evangelical perspective but is subordinated to a higher principle—justification by the alien righteousness of Christ. We are commissioned to take up our cross and follow Christ—not in order to gain or secure our salvation but to demonstrate a salvation already accomplished for us through the cross and resurrection of Jesus Christ.

Sola gratia is correlative with total depravity. It is only because our wills are bound to the power of sin that salvation becomes contingent solely on what God can do for us and in us. Total depravity does not mean that there is no remnant of goodness within us; it is rather the admission that in our sin we no longer have the capacity to believe and obey the gospel message. Not only faith but the very condition of faith must be given by the Spirit of God if we are to break with the old way of living and thinking and embrace the salvation offered by Christ without any merit on our part. In the fifth century Augustine staunchly affirmed *sola gratia* in opposition to Pelagius, who insisted that grace is the reward for human effort.[24] The semi-Pelagians held that grace must accompany our spiritual journey if it is to culminate in final salvation, but we of ourselves can take the first steps toward grace. The Second Council of Orange (529) condemned semi-Pelagianism as a heretical intrusion into Christian thinking. In the sixteenth century Martin Luther, in a strident debate with Erasmus, argued that the will of the natural person is bound to sin and can be liberated only by God's undeserved grace, which alone enables us to believe and to understand.[25] In the twentieth century the controversy between Karl Barth and Emil Brunner revolved around this same issue: Can we of ourselves do something to gain or actualize the salvation assured to us by Christ? Barth's position was that the very capacity for revelation has to be given by the Spirit of God. The natural person cannot contribute in any way to the procuring of either revelation or salvation; yet one can bear witness to these inestimable gifts that come from the hand of a gracious God.

While totally opposed to any idea that the human will can cooperate with divine grace in realizing salvation, biblical spirituality insists that the delivered person is under a tremendous obligation to manifest this salvation in good deeds and in life. We are justified by grace alone and faith alone, but as P. T. Forsyth trenchantly reminds us, we are justified *for* holiness alone.[26] Our duty is not to win salvation for ourselves through works of reparation and penance but to proclaim God's salvation to others through preaching the gospel and living the Christian life. We do good works not to call attention to our holiness but to publicize God's unfathomable generosity in taking upon himself our sin and guilt so that we might be accounted righteous in faith. As Luther put it, "Our righteousness is not by the Law and good works but by the death and resurrection of Christ."[27]

In biblical, evangelical perspective Christianity begins and ends in the forgiveness of sins. It begins with forgiveness because it was God's will to forgive when he poured out his love for us in Jesus Christ. It ends in forgiveness because even the best of human works cannot alter the fact that we will appear before the judgment seat of God with works inadequate to redeem because they are mixed with impure motives. Our works as well as our inner being need to be sanctified and purified through undeserved grace. In the last analysis we are only sinners saved by grace, though we can nevertheless make progress toward holiness by battling against sin and cleaving to the righteousness of Christ. Yet even while we are sinners saved by grace, we are also sons and daughters of the most high God who are summoned to leave sin behind and strive for the holiness apart from which no one will see the Lord (Heb 12:14). But contrary to perfectionists, both Catholic and Protestant, I contend that in this life no one will ever arrive at the point where sinful inclination is completely eradicated. "Nothing in my hand I bring, simply to Thy cross I cling" (Toplady).[28] The ubiquity and tenacity of sin can be countered by faith working through love, but on the day of judgment even those who are holy need to hear again the word of God that announces pardon for sin.

Our vocation is to be rich in good works (Eph 2:10), but we celebrate not our works, which always fall short of the moral ideal, but his great work—the work of redemption and reconciliation that alone restores repentant sinners to God's favor. In Christ we can do works that are pleasing to God, but we should never place our trust and hope in these things because they are imperfect and inadequate as they stand by themselves. Grace alone brings us into the kingdom of God, and grace alone spurs us to a life of self-giving and self-sacrifice. A holy life does not guarantee us a place in the kingdom of heaven, but it is a sign that a place has already been set apart for us by virtue of God's gracious election revealed and fulfilled in Jesus—in his life, death and resurrection.

The Paradoxical Love of the Cross

Nowhere is the contrast between biblical and mystical religion so glaring as in the way they conceive of love. When read in the light of the gospel, the Bible teaches a love that contradicts eros or natural love.[29] In the New Testament this higher form of love is called agape. Whereas eros is a self-regarding love, a love that seeks its own perfection in union with the Absolute, agape is a self-effacing love that seeks the good of one's neighbor, even above one's own good. Emil Brunner astutely observed: "God's love is not a covetous love, not a passion, not an *eros,* which in some way desires the other for his worth, but devotion, self-devotion, sacrifice."[30] Anders Nygren viewed agape as spontaneous and unmotivated—not conditional on the worth of the one loved.[31] Christian love as Luther understood it is a *quellende Liebe,* a love that rises up from the heart apart from external considerations. It is also a *verlorene Liebe* ("lost love"), one that continues even when it is betrayed. Love itself creates worth and beauty; it does not necessarily gravitate toward those who are endowed with such qualities.[32] We should love our neighbor not because he or she is lovable but because Christ commands us to do so. Luther put it this way: "Sinners are beautiful because they are loved; they are not loved because they are beautiful."[33]

Agape is the descending, outgoing, self-giving love of the cross. But it also has an upward movement. We present our work on behalf of our neighbor to God as a sacrifice of praise and thanksgiving. Precisely by going down to the needs and travails of our neighbor, we grow nearer to God who meets us in our neighbor. Agape is a paradoxical love. It gains by showing that it is willing to lose. It creates value; it is not based on value. The Christian overcomes not through the coercion of law but through the power of the powerlessness of love. We are summoned to love our enemies and thereby shame them into repentance (Rom 12:20-21). This is a love that goes beyond mutual love. We see it displayed most strikingly in the death of Jesus Christ on the cross. He died not to make himself secure with the Father nor to realize a higher perfection but out of compassion for a lost human race. His deity was manifested in his solidarity with a sinful and despairing humanity.

The Christian mystics also encouraged love for one's neighbor. Yet our neighbor is to be loved not as a sinner but as one who still reflects the image of God. It seems that we love not our neighbor as such but the presence of God in our neighbor.[34] Eros love is attracted to that which has the greatest value. Agape love goes out to the powerless, the forsaken, the despised. The mystics seek their salvation and fulfillment in union with God. The biblical prophets were willing to let go of their concern for their own salvation in service to God and neighbor.[35] Moses was willing to be cursed for the salvation of Israel (Ex 32:32). Similarly Paul declared his willingness to let go of his eternal security for the salvation of the Jews (Rom 9:3). Calvin insisted that the goal of the Christian is to "ascend higher than merely to seek and secure the salvation of his own soul."[36] We should be concerned for our own salvation precisely because such concern gives glory to God. But God is even more pleased when we focus on the good of others, even to the detriment of our own good.

Biblical faith does not rule out the right love of self, but love for God and neighbor must take precedence. Christian love takes us out of ourselves into zeal for the glory of God and the welfare of our neighbor. In Luther's words, "Self-love is always sinful as long as it stays in itself; it is not good unless it is out of itself in God, that is, unless my inclination to have my own way and my love for myself are dead and I seek nothing but to have the will of God alone done in me."[37] Indeed, "To be blessed means to seek in everything God's will and his glory, and to want nothing for oneself neither here nor in the life to come."[38]

The mystics condemned self-love in the sense of *cupiditas* but allowed for self-love in the sense of *caritas*.[39] What should be avoided is love that seeks the satisfaction of the pleasures of the flesh. What is permissible and indeed salutary is a purely spiritual love that strives to satisfy the desires of the heart for the higher happiness—union with God.

In evangelical perspective our love for God is based on thankfulness and joy for what God has done for us in Jesus Christ. We love not in order to possess God as a lover seeks to possess the beloved, but we love in order to please God by serving our neighbor for whom Christ died. We seek not the rapture of the soul in union with God but the well-being of our neighbor for the sake of the glory of God.

The God of the Bible is not pure agape but the unity of agape and *nomos* (Brunner). Love fulfills *nomos* (law) rather than cancels it. Jesus Christ not only demonstrated the generosity of God's grace and love but also satisfied the demands of God's holiness. In our love for our neighbor we endeavor not only to meet that person's spiritual and material needs but also to direct that person to the law of God as the regulating principle of the moral life. Obedience to the law is what brings life to the righteous, but this obedience must be done in the spirit of love, a spirit that often goes beyond the letter of the law. We sometimes need to reprimand others in order to help them bring their lives into conformity with God's law, but we may also be asked to sacrifice ourselves for the sake of others out of an overflowing love that exceeds all legal obligations and decorum.

Holy Worldliness

The commandment that we hear in Scripture is not that the people of God withdraw from the world into a hermitage or monastery but that they permeate the world with a message of healing and redemption (Jn 17:15-18). As Bonhoeffer phrased it, "The really *lived* love of God in Jesus Christ . . . does not withdraw from reality into noble souls secluded from the world. It experiences and suffers the reality of the world in all its hardness."[40]

The goal of the Christian is to bring the world into subjection to Jesus Christ, not in a legal or political sense but in a moral or spiritual sense. The gospel should not be made into a law imposed on society, but the members of society should be so transformed by the gospel that they will spontaneously make themselves ready to heal and to serve.

A quite different picture is found in the post-Christian mystic Gerald Heard, who saw the hope of the world resting on an elite of neo-Brahmins, mystics trained in the spiritual life. The challenge is to overcome the animal nature within ourselves and allow our spiritual nature to develop and flower.[41] What society needs is a mystical infusion, one that we can prepare for and precipitate. By contrast the Christian hope rests on the outpouring of the Holy Spirit through preaching the gospel, pondering Scripture, and the fervent practice of intercessory prayer.

French Reformed lay theologian Jacques Ellul was convinced that the criterion for Christian social action cannot be derived from culture, which is dominated by ideological interests. At the same time, our standard for faith and practice cannot remain in the heavenly realm, entirely removed from the burning issues that engulf society. "The point is not to break off the dialog or to retire to the desert, but the word of God can be proclaimed only by someone who places himself outside 'the world,' while staying at the very heart of the questioning that goes on within it."[42] Ellul, like Bonhoeffer, championed a holy worldliness, a vocation lived out in the world but separated from the idolatries that prop up the world. Ellul himself was active in civic affairs and politics. He served for a time as mayor of Bordeaux, and before that he was a member of the resistance movement—hiding Jews from their Nazi persecutors. He was intimately involved in the political process, but he was adamant that politics in and of itself cannot change the human person and that social justice must never be confounded with the kingdom of God, which grants people a new identity and a new social and spiritual vision.[43]

To borrow a phrase from H. Richard Niebuhr, the social strategy of the Christian should be "Christ transforming culture" as opposed to "Christ against culture" and "Christ above culture."[44] We are not to *flee* from the culture but to *fight* for mastery over the culture. This is a spiritual battle, for it concerns ultimate loyalties and priorities. We cannot bring in the kingdom by political schemes, but we can set up signs and parables of the kingdom. We cannot build the kingdom on earth, but we can bear witness to the reality of the kingdom, which is already in our midst.[45]

Biblical Christianity embraces an inner-worldly asceticism, one that involves self-mastery for the sake of service to God and our neighbor. Luther broke with the monastery because he believed that it had become penetrated by worldliness and thus rendered ineffectual as an instrument for social and spiritual change. He went back into the world in order to battle against the principalities and powers that wreak havoc in society. Both as a monk and as an active religious leader in society he was a disciplined person, living according to a schedule dictated by the events of the time. He reformed the church and changed the face of the continent as a prophet who urged people to embrace a higher righteousness, which both purifies the soul and keeps intact the fabric that holds society together.

Whereas mystics generally favor the celibate life over the married life, biblical Christians have always held the married life in high esteem. Its purpose, however, is no longer to insure progeny but to serve as a model of the fellowship of the saints. For the Puritans married love is a form of heroic chastity and as such belongs to the kingdom of God. The Reformers did not rule out the celibate vocation, but their intention was to show that married and family life too can serve the cause of the kingdom of God. Calvin even acknowledged that the single life has a practical, though not a moral, advantage because it enables one to devote all of one's time and energy to the dissemination of the faith.[46]

The evangelical revival movement has given birth to new forms of Christian discipleship: Bible colleges, conventicles, evangelistic crusades and missionary training centers. The monastic vocation is not excluded by evangelical piety but is given a new rationale and direction. A monastery is now a training center for Christian mission rather than a school for developing the spiritual life. Its purpose is to send forth people to the field of spiritual battle rather than to aid people in their quest for a higher sanctity.[47]

The Struggle of Prayer

In the framework of biblical faith prayer is essentially a struggle—making known our needs and concerns to a holy and all-merciful God.[48] Biblical prayer culminates in submission to God's will, but this follows a struggle to make known to God the depth of our predicament and need. God, of course, already knows our needs even better than we do ourselves; yet it pleases him when we share our innermost thoughts and desires with him. Prayer in the biblical sense often takes the form of importunity—a passionate pleading with God. Sometimes we seek to change what appears to be God's will so that his greater will might be fulfilled. Prayer may involve wrestling with God and with the powers of darkness so that God's triumph over the powers might be more fully sensed in our lives (cf. Gen 32:24-30). Paul gives voice to this element in the life of prayer: "For this purpose also I labor, striving according to His power, which mightily works within me" (Col 1:29 NASB).

The heart of biblical spirituality is petition, the pouring out of the soul before a loving, heavenly Father. Petition is not the only form of prayer, but is present in all prayer, including adoration, thanksgiving and confession. We ask God to accept our sacrifices of praise and thanksgiving. In mysticism petition is a lower form of prayer. The highest kind of prayer is beyond words. Prayer reaches its climax in silent adoration and contemplation. For Luther by contrast contemplation is simply the life of faith, not a higher stage within this life. Biblical prayer is characterized not by the stillness of passionless resignation but by the confident expectation that God is in control. The struggle of prayer ends in a "comforted despair" (Luther), not in the cessation of desire (as in Quietism).

In our own day Richard Foster gives a ringing endorsement of the prayer of petition, which far from being "a lower form of prayer" is "our staple diet," for it connotes our continual dependence on God. Interestingly Foster speaks as a dedicated Quaker who is open to and supportive of evangelicalism.[49]

When we compare the two types of prayer (biblical and mystical) we cannot avoid the conclusion that these are strikingly different—both in their ground and goal. According to Calvin, "Prayer is a communication between God and us whereby we expound to him our desires, our joys, our sighs, in a word, all the thoughts of our hearts."[50] In diametrical opposition the mystic Gerald Heard defines prayer as "not asking for things—not even for the best of things—it is going where they are."[51] Nevertheless when one reads the lives of the great saints and mystics of the church, one is clearly reminded that naive or petitionary prayer remained part of their legacy. Even in the state of contemplation the saints offer petitions to their God. Teresa of Ávila advised, "Talk to Him as to your Father: ask for what you want as from a father: tell Him your sorrows and beg Him for relief."[52]

Prayer in the biblical context has an indisputably paradoxical dimension. It is rooted in both the experience of Godforsakenness and the sense of the presence of God. It is inspired by both a felt need of God and gratitude for his work of reconciliation and redemption. It involves both pleading with God and trusting surrender to God in the confidence that God will act in his own time and way. It consists both in striving with God in the darkness and resting in the stillness. There is a time to argue and a time to submit. Prayer involves both joy and agony.

Biblical prayer, unlike ritual prayer, is spontaneous. Heiler describes it as a spontaneous outburst of emotion. Prayer may well take structured forms, but these forms prepare the way for what is truly momentous and significant: the I-Thou encounter. Prayer is not a technique that bends the will of God through repetitive utterances. Prayer beads and prayer chains belong to ritualistic and primitive religions. Biblical faith sees these things as snares that direct our attention away from the infinite to the finite, to what we can possess and control. Biblical prayer on occasion seeks to alter the ways in which God realizes his will for our lives, but it is deeply aware that what is most important is the altering of our wills so that we might more fully comprehend the greater will of God as it takes effect in our lives.

The Great Commission

All spirituality that claims to be evangelical gives prominence to the commission of our Lord to his disciples to go into the world and preach the gospel to the whole creation (cf. Mt 28:19-20; Mk 16:15; Lk 24:47; Acts 1:8). The objective of Christian faith is to redeem lost sinners by bringing them into a right relationship with the living Christ. This task includes preaching, teaching, prayer and nurturing. We are enjoined not only to invite people to place their trust in the Lord Jesus Christ but also to train them to be disciples engaged in service to Christ and their neighbor.

This spiritual mandate of the church is not its only mandate. We are also called to be a leaven in society, to guide society toward a higher degree of justice and to do all things to enhance peace in the world.[53] The cultural mandate of the church, however, does not give the church its uniqueness and significance. The church preeminently is called to speak to the problem of human sin and to announce the coming of the kingdom of righteousness. Its involvement in the political issues of the time is clearly subordinate to its spiritual mission—to be the vanguard of a new social order ruled by the law of love. The cultural mandate is there to serve the spiritual mandate, but these mandates must never be confused, for otherwise we will end by politicizing the mission of the church. Evangelism is both the goal of faith and the heartbeat of faith (Nels Ferré). A church not involved in evangelism is destined to wither away and die.

Whereas the Greek mystery religions were oriented about the manifestation of the sacred, appealing to the visual sense, biblical religion rests on the proclamation of the faith and has an iconoclastic dimension. In Catholic and Orthodox theologies art can serve the proclamation of faith; in Puritan theology art often undermines the proclamation by directing attention to the visible rather than to the invisible, to the finite rather than to the infinite.[54]

Those who embrace a mystical spirituality are generally not interested in proclaiming the faith to the masses. Their concern is to share insights with fellow travelers on the infinite way.[55] In Roman Catholic religious orders we see a combination of the biblical and the mystical, though with the latter often predominating. In radical mysticism contemplation becomes an end in itself and is severed from the apostolic mandate of preaching the gospel. According to the Quaker-Vedantist theologian Gerald Heard, mystics have a single desire which takes up their whole life and heart: "seeing God."[56]

H. Richard Niebuhr makes a helpful distinction between the vision of God and the service of God.[57] The former typifies the mystical stance and the latter the Protestant or evangelical. We find both elements in Scripture, but there the vision of God signifies an encounter with God, a meeting with God, not the perception of the divine essence. To "seek the face of God" in the Hebraic ethos is "to seek to know God, to live in his presence . . . to serve him faithfully."[58]

In evangelical perspective the highest service is sharing the good news of what God has done for us in Christ. It is winning souls for the kingdom, conferring the blessings of peace and salvation through the power of the Holy Spirit. Count Zinzendorf confessed that his greatest joy was "to win souls for the Lamb."[59] William Booth, founder of the Salvation Army, enjoined his officers, "Go for souls and go for the worst."[60] A maxim reflecting the spirituality of Mother Teresa identifies what is most important in the Christian mission: "The soul of the care of the poor is the care of the poor soul."[61] Here we see a convergence between a certain kind of practical mysticism and biblical evangelicalism.

Evangelism in the biblical worldview is not primarily sharing with others our personal journey of faith but telling others what God has done for us and the whole world in Jesus Christ. According to D. T. Niles, evangelism is "one beggar telling another beggar where to get food."[62] Contrast this sentiment with that of Gerald Heard: "As each individual becomes aware of his real nature in God, his enlightenment gives him the power to kindle the same illumination in others."[63]

Our calling is not to a new self-awareness or to a higher state of consciousness but to the decision of faith. We are invited to celebrate not the divinity of our origin nor our infinite possibilities but God's saving act in Jesus Christ. In the biblical worldview we are not thrown back on our own experiences but raised to a universal priesthood in which we intercede for others and point them to the One who alone pardons and redeems.

Epilogue

Biblical Christianity is a historical religion based on actual events in the history of a particular people—the Jews. In contrast to Greco-Roman philosophy it is founded not on eternal ideas or universal principles but on a divine incursion into history—the incarnation of the Son of God in Jesus Christ. Historical investigation can uncover the historical context of God's self-revelation in Jesus Christ, but it cannot certify the truth of this revelation. The truth of the gospel of God must be given by God himself in a personal encounter that involves but also transcends rational communication.

Biblical faith is theocentric and Christocentric, not anthropocentric. Luther put it succinctly: "The Gospel commands us to look, not at our own good deeds or perfection but at God Himself as He promises, and at Christ Himself, the Mediator."[64] This God-centered way of speaking and thinking was also underscored by the maverick Pietist theologian Christoph Blumhardt:

> It is God's honor which we must now exalt in our own persons, both physically and spiritually. Not our own well-being must be in the foreground, but the one desire that God may come into His well-being, into His right on earth. His Kingdom must gain ground in us and in our lives before we can enjoy all the goodness through the miracle-working hand of our Savior Jesus Christ.[65]

At the same time we must be careful not to reduce the self to nothingness. We should steer clear of a theocentric objectivism that severs the glory of God from any human happiness and well-being. We should neither elevate the self unduly nor demean it unnecessarily but see it in its proper perspective. Brunner is right when he terms the Christian position "theanthropocentric": it is centered in the glory of God, which does not cancel but fulfills the human search for inner peace and beatitude. This kind of theology can also be found in the church father Irenaeus (c. 130-c. 200): "The glory of God is humanity fully alive."

Søren Kierkegaard exemplifies the biblical outlook when he posits an infinite qualitative difference between God and humanity. Faith does not surmount this difference but acknowledges it and even rejoices in it.

Kierkegaard's position stands in striking contrast to that of mysticism, which posits a basic continuity between God and humanity. Yet Kierkegaard goes too far in his attack on human culture and philosophy. He claims that Christianity wants "to burn up the *human zest* for life" so that our aim in life becomes purely spiritual.[66] In my opinion Karl Barth is closer to the truth when he recognizes that the Christian faith includes an affirmation of life in its fullness, though never an affirmation of sin.

Rudolf Bultmann veered toward another kind of imbalance in which faith is reduced to ethics. In his view, "Jesus calls us to *decision,* not to the *inner life.* He promises neither ecstasy nor spiritual peace."[67] Yet Bultmann overlooks the fact that we must draw near to God if we are to receive power to draw near to our neighbor. He also forgets that Christ does promise interior peace to those who seek it, though this peace is qualitatively different from the peace the world gives (Jn 14:27; Phil 4:7). Bultmann could be corrected by some of the mystics of the church who partially succeeded, sometimes against their own philosophical presuppositions, in holding the spiritual and ethical dimensions of the faith together in a higher unity.

While biblical personalism is associated much more with evangelical Protestantism than with Catholicism, it is well to keep in mind that Catholic authors too have tried to retain the personal and dialogical dimensions of the faith and have to some extent resisted the lure of mysticism and Neoplatonism. Although the Platonic element in his thought is very pronounced, Hans Urs von Balthasar seeks to construct a theology rooted in the Bible, not in cultural philosophy.

> The whole order of reason is theologically embedded in the order of faith, just as the order of creation lies embedded in the order of grace. . . . To enter into a relationship of knowledge and will with the God of *this* creation means to be placed before the God of Jesus Christ and before no other.[68]

In his view anything that "smacks of technique" is "opposed to the gospel's grace of childlikeness."[69] He appears to call into question the mystical quest when he observes, "the natural man wishes to climb or at least to stand. But Jesus, who descended from heaven, chooses to fall."[70] In Balthasar's theology the human ascent to God is clearly subordinated

to God's descent to humanity in Jesus Christ. We must not be too hasty
in dismissing the contributions of Catholic theologians; at the same time
it is important to recognize that Catholic spirituality, especially on the
popular level, conflicts with the biblical witness on many levels. If honest
all partners in the ecumenical dialogue will acknowledge that many problems remain unresolved; yet in our common focus not on ourselves but
on Christ, we can overcome some of these difficulties.

6

THE NEW SPIRITUALITY

Body am I entirely, and nothing else;
and soul is only a word for something about the body.
FRIEDRICH NIETZSCHE

The word must be rediscovered in the flesh.
Religion must turn to dance. Perhaps Zorba is the saint for our time.
SAM KEEN

Blessed be you mighty matter, irresistible march of evolution,
reality ever new-born.
TEILHARD DE CHARDIN

A new God is being formed in our hearts to teach us to level the heavens and
exalt the earth and create a new world without masters and slaves, rulers and subjects.
ROSEMARY RADFORD RUETHER

Out of our different religions, a "religion of the earth" will emerge
that will teach us the spirituality of the earth in order that we may
recognize ourselves as "children of the earth."
JÜRGEN MOLTMANN

It is incontrovertible that we are witnessing the dawning of a new spirituality that stands in dramatic contrast to both classical mysticism and biblical personalism. This spirituality affirms life rather than negates life, upholds not the renunciation of power but the will to power. It is a spirituality that augurs the recrudescence of paganism. It is both pre-Christian and post-Christian. It is this-worldly more than other-worldly. It can be legitimately described as a secular mysticism.

Sam Keen typifies the new mood when he calls for a visceral theology that places the emphasis on "touching" rather than on hearing or seeing.[1] He proposes a theology of the flesh as opposed to a theology of the head. One must start not with a meta-story but with one's own story and then seek to relate this to other stories that open up for us a new future.

Nikos Kazantzakis, the spiritual father of Sam Keen and many others in the new theology, envisioned a god who is struggling to realize its potentialities:

> I firmly believe in the nobility and power of a Spirit that passes through plants, animals, humans, and is now consciously struggling inside me, wanting to surpass me, to free itself from my unworthy nature.[2]

Postmodernity entails a profound mistrust of reason and a dependence on instinct and imagination. It calls for a radical emancipation from the taboos that bind us to an outmoded morality. Zorba the Greek, one of Kazantzakis's fictional characters, observed that a person may have everything in the world except one thing—madness. Unless we have a little madness we cannot cut the rope and be free. Life challenges us to dance with the powers of destiny.[3]

The new spirituality seeks not an amalgamation with the old spiritualities but instead their overthrow. This belligerent spirit is especially conspicuous in its attitude toward historical Christianity. Carl Jung here speaks for many: "One way to kill the soul is to worship a God outside you."[4]

Reinhold Niebuhr, a modern defender of biblical faith, describes the reigning philosophy of the modern world as "a naturalistic idealism." I prefer to call it an idealistic naturalism. The new spirituality makes a place for spirit forces within nature that can help or hinder us but not for a God who transcends and directs nature and history toward a supramundane end.

Historical Roots

One of the major sources of the new spirituality is the Renaissance of the fifteenth and sixteenth centuries, which sparked a rediscovery of the humanistic values of Greco-Roman civilization. The emphasis was no longer on the helplessness and depravity of the human race but now on its infinite possibilities. We no longer need a heavenly Savior; we can become our own saviors by tapping into the spiritual resources within us. A robust optimism began to supplant a medieval pessimism, which portrayed this world as the valley of the shadow of death. Pico della Mirandola echoed the new mood: "We can become what we will."[5]

Even more important in shaping the new spirituality was the Enlightenment of the late seventeenth and eighteenth centuries, which championed human autonomy and freedom. In the more radical circles God was relegated to the status of a grand Designer or Watchmaker. The human person was free to work out his or her own destiny according to the light that resides within the soul. The truth claims of Christian faith must be validated by reason. Revealed religion exists in harmony with natural religion, and the latter looms as more significant than the former. Among the pivotal figures of Enlightenment thought were René Descartes, John Locke, George Berkeley, G. W. Leibniz, David Hume and Immanuel Kant.[6] Some philosophers of the nineteenth century (such as Hegel and Herbert Spencer) continued to manifest the Enlightenment trust in reason.

The Romantic movement of the late eighteenth and early and middle nineteenth centuries also contributed to the building of a new spirituality. Now the emphasis was on feeling rather than on reason as the key to knowledge of the Absolute. We look not for the infinite beyond the finite but for the infinite in the finite (Schleiermacher). We are no longer stewards or masters of nature but worshipers of nature. Nature no longer exists in antithesis to the divine but is now the vehicle of the divine. According to Schelling, "It is a blasphemy of the Creator to think that nature is only there in order to be the material for our moral glory; nature has the divine glory in itself."[7] Dostoevsky gives voice to the Romantic impulse when he advises: "Love to throw yourself on the earth and kiss it. Kiss the earth and love it with an unceasing, consuming love."[8]

In more recent times Langdon Gilkey assigns a positive role to nature in communicating the glory of God. In his view nature is not a mask that hides the glory of God (as in Luther) nor a reality that detracts from his glory, but a sacrament that functions as an effectual sign of God's glory and grace. We know God not by fixing our gaze on an eternity beyond nature but by celebrating our kinship with nature.[9]

Still another source of the new spirituality is the voluntarist idealism that we see in Fichte, Schelling, Schopenhauer and Nietzsche. In this worldview God is defined in terms of will rather than of static being. The motivating force in all culture and religion is the will to live (Schopenhauer) or the will to power (Nietzsche). Our wills become effective as they are united with the primordial will that moves the universe.

Closely related is existentialism, which we find in Kierkegaard, Martin Heidegger, Unamuno, Paul Tillich, Karl Jaspers and many others. Kierkegaard brought a uniquely Christian perspective to the philosophical discussion; yet he mirrored the existentialist vision by contending that truth is attained not through abstract speculation but through existential passion and commitment. In Heidegger's philosophy eternity is reconceived "as a more primordial temporality which is infinite."[10] For Unamuno love is passion and empathy: "To believe in God is to love Him, and to love Him is to feel Him suffering, to pity Him."[11] In loving God we love ourselves, for our eternal happiness is found in God: "It is ourselves, it is our eternity that we seek in God, it is our divinization."[12]

Perhaps no movement more fully embodies the new spirituality than Transcendentalism, which we associate with Ralph Waldo Emerson, Theodore Parker, Henry David Thoreau, William Ellery Channing and Amos Bronson Alcott. Emerson gives voice to the immanentism fostered by this movement: We become strong not by positing a god outside ourselves but by drawing upon the creative power within ourselves; then we are enabled to work miracles and shape history.[13]

Pragmatism—assessing truth by its ability to strengthen the individual and remold society—is a kindred movement that has left an indelible imprint on the American religious scene. Its leading lights include William James, Charles Peirce, John Dewey and Richard Rorty.[14] It was James who said: "Be not afraid of life. Believe that life *is* worth living, and your belief will help create the fact."[15]

Postmodernism, which reinterprets truth from a pluralistic perspective, is still another hallmark of the new spirituality. The prophet of postmodernism was Friedrich Nietzsche, who taught that truth is a matter of changing perspectives on reality. His hostility to traditional Christianity is evident in his call for a transvaluation of values in which Christian precepts are repudiated as encouraging human weakness and insularism. D. H. Lawrence reflects a similar outlook: "Human desire is the criterion of all truth and all good. Truth does not lie beyond humanity, but is one of the products of the human mind and feeling." True worshippers are called to be "proud and strong," not submissive and pliant.[16]

Like the old spiritualities, the new draws upon classical philosophy, including the pre-Socratics. Heraclitus, with his emphasis on becoming over being, and Epicurus, who celebrated chance over necessity, have also been important influences. Other thinkers who have played a modest role in forging the new spirituality are Plato, Plotinus, the Stoics and the Gnostics.

The German mystics of the late medieval period also constitute a spiritual resource for secular spirituality, especially Meister Eckhart, whom Matthew Fox considers his foremost spiritual mentor.[17] For Eckhart, "spirituality is a constant expansion of the divine potential in us all."[18] Mechthild of Magdeburg is appreciated for introducing the anguish of desire in God himself.[19]

The New Metaphysics

The new spirituality rests upon the new metaphysics, which subordinates being to becoming. The whole world, including God, is in a process of creative change and evolution. The ultimate universal datum is neither mind nor matter but creative will and energy. Henri Bergson describes God as "unceasing life, action, freedom."[20] According to Fichte, God is "not a being but a *pure activity.*"[21]

In contradistinction to the old metaphysics, the new world outlook conceives of God as life rather than as idea, as temporal rather than eternal. The Absolute unfolds itself in history (Hegel) rather than blithely towering above history. God does not stand still but is creatively advancing in history (Whitehead). The infinite is known only in the finite (Schleiermacher), the absolute only in the relative.

Instead of a God of the heights, as in historical Christianity, we are presented with a God of the depths. This is not a God who descends into history from eternity but one who emerges out of history into an open future. This is not a God who stands outside of nature but one who is the creative principle within nature. This is a religion that celebrates the beauty of the earth rather than the transcendent beauty of eternal ideas (as in Plato). Dostoevsky's Father Zosima enjoins his hearers:

> Love all God's creation. . . . Love every leaf, every ray of God's light. . . .
> If you love everything, you will perceive the divine mystery in things.[22]

God and the world are inseparable in this strand of philosophy. As Matthew Fox explains, "The cosmos can and needs to be imaged as a cosmic womb, a cosmic soup, in which all creatures swim. The cosmos is God's womb, the divine womb."[23] Classical theism has been supplanted by a this-worldly pantheism. Or better we should designate this new metaphysical stance as panentheism—God in the world and the world in God.

Another aspect of the new spirituality is its futuristic bent. Even God has a future that he looks forward to and strives to bring into actuality. In the words of André Gide, "God lies ahead. I convince myself and constantly repeat to myself that: He depends on us. It is through us that God is achieved."[24] Lewis Mumford's stance is similar: "God is the faint glimmer of a design still fully to emerge, a rationality still to be achieved, a justice still to be established, a love still to be fulfilled."[25] According to M. Scott Peck: "We are growing toward godhood. God is the goal of evolution."[26] Bultmann could even define God as "the Openness of the Future."

In stark contrast to both Christian mysticism and biblical personalism, the new god is finite rather than infinite. This god represents not supernaturalism but neo-naturalism. In this perspective God is in process, luring the world onward toward eternal ideals that have yet to be fully realized. In place of classical theism we have a process panentheism. Instead of a closed universe in which everything has been preordained, we have an open universe where new possibilities are being realized through evolution. William James could describe the universe as "an unfinished skyscraper" brought into being by God and humanity working together.[27]

The new metaphysics transcends the dichotomy between idealism and materialism. Its commitment is to panpsychism, in which all of nature is infused with intelligence. It also embraces hylozoism, the view that all matter has life. In addition it breaks through the antithesis between pluralism and monism. There is one creative energy, but it exists in an infinite variety of forms.

The new metaphysics encompasses an ecstatic naturalism—one that is self-transcending (Tillich). The spiritual and physical worlds totally interpenetrate each other. The spiritual is the depth dimension of the physical. According to Matthew Fox, our goal is to "sink" into existence rather than rise above existence.[28] Larry Rasmussen expresses the new mood when he declares, "Don't look up for God, look around. The finite is all there is."[29]

God is not so much the creator of the world as its vitalizing agent. Ralph Waldo Emerson described God as "the flowing river of Nature."[30] For Theodore Parker, God is "the immanent and ever active force" who brings nature to perfection.[31] "The whole world will be a temple, every spot holy ground, every bush burning with the Infinite, all time the Lord's day, and every moral act worship and a sacrament."[32] In this view "the material universe and God, in every point of space and time, are continually at one."[33]

Our fidelity is not to a God beyond the world but to the earth, which is pulsating with divine energy. Nietzsche put it well: "I conjure you, my brethren, *remain true to the earth,* and believe not those who speak unto you of superearthly hopes!"[34] We are commissioned to alter the face of the earth on the basis of power that comes to us from the earth. In this sense we are creating a new god or enabling this new god to create itself as it opens to us a new future. This new god is not the universe as such, but the "Roar of the Universe" or the animating fire of the universe.

Key Concepts

One of the salient hallmarks of the new spirituality is the quest for heroic freedom. The hero brings a boon to humanity by his prodigious feats of daring and courage, not by serving the downtrodden (as in historical Christianity). Joseph Campbell observes: "The hero strives to conquer the world, not to help others."[35]

In contrast to the traditional Christian worldview, this new worldview envisages the human person as a free moral agent. We are bound neither to fate nor to sin but are free to plot our own destiny. Like Hercules at the crossroads we are summoned to make decisions in which the future is entirely in our own hands. While historical Christian faith holds that humanity is created with free will, it insists that this is a freedom impaired by sin and therefore incapable of insuring a safe conduct through the wilderness of earthly life. What we need for our redemption is a will liberated by grace, and this becomes an actuality only through faith.

Another key concept of the new spirituality is growth. According to John Dewey, "Growth itself is the only moral 'end.'"[36] Growth entails human planning, but it has its basis in evolution. In the view of Schleiermacher, the human person is itself a product of the evolutionary advance: "The living spirit of the earth, rending itself from itself as it were, links himself as a finite thing to one definite moment in the series of organic evolutions and a new man arises."[37]

It is not only humanity but God himself who is believed to be caught up in the drama of evolution. Even God experiences struggle and growth. For the later Schelling, God is "Life"—subject to suffering and growth. God is not an Unmoved Mover (as in Aristotle) but a free moral agent giving direction to the universe. In the words of Schleiermacher, "Freedom, you are for me the soul and principle of all things."[38] In those theologies that identify God with mother Earth, the same theme is apparent. Rosemary Haughton alleges, "The earth herself struggles to bring to birth a new humanity."[39]

The modern view looks not to an eternal decree that determines the course of world history but to unceasing change that spurs the world on to a higher vision—best described as an advance into novelty (Whitehead). In the words of Ivan Illich, "The specific task of the church in the modern world is the Christian celebration of the experience of change."[40] For Langdon Gilkey, "Change is the basic reality of history; it is in some way the character of whatever being there is."[41]

The emphasis on change is conspicuous in the judicial systems of Western nations, including the United States. In this postmodern milieu the courts tend to deny "permanent truths" on which their dictums rest and are ready to celebrate "the inevitability of change." Our highly controversial Supreme Court has tried to justify its judicial activism on the ba-

sis of commitment to a constantly evolving "living" Constitution as opposed to a "dead" Constitution.[42]

No less important in the modern worldview is chance. Whereas the
Greek tragedians and the Stoics bowed before the mystery of fate,
moderns and postmoderns celebrate chance. Contingency characterizes
not only the world but God himself. William James regarded chance as
the basis of hope. Charles Darwin referred to "omnipotent Chance." For
Nietzsche the truly blessed have learned "to dance on the feet of
chance."[43] Alan Jones confesses: "I believe in the God of Chance! Chance
in the universe means that the story isn't over. The drama hasn't yet
played itself out."[44] According to Jacques Monod, "Pure chance, absolutely free but blind, [is] at the very root of the stupendous edifice of evolution."[45] Charles Peirce sought to develop an ontology of chance, which
he called tychism after the Greek goddess Tyche.[46] Openness of God
theologian Gregory Boyd calls chance "a beautiful mystery."[47]

The emphasis on chance is especially prominent in postmodern philosophy, which itself is a product of modernism. Whereas the modern
(Enlightenment) worldview regarded human choice as the determiner of
world history, the postmoderns celebrate chance. The biblical or Christian worldview by contrast attributes the unfolding of world history to divine Providence.

In this new world vision even God becomes subject to risk, since the
future is entirely open.[48] This means that the future is unknown even to
God. It seems that God does not know an event until he experiences
it.[49] Both process theology and the openness of God theology (open-
view theism) hold to a god that cooperates with humans in building a
new world.

Creativity is also a salient concept in the new worldview. The inner life
of God is conceived by Schelling as "a dynamic process of self-creation."[50]
Tillich spoke of "God's directing creativity" that "drives" or "lures" a seeking humanity toward fulfillment.[51] Whitehead regarded creativity as "the
universal of universals."[52] For Henry Nelson Wieman and John Cobb, God
is "the power of creative transformation." Gordon Kaufman rejects the
classical theistic view of God for "serendipitous creativity," which makes
the world go around.[53]

Equally significant is the idea of the world as a living organism. The sharp demarcation between the material and the spiritual is overcome in this latest brand of spirituality. All of matter is pulsating with life and desire. All things are linked together, forming part of an organic whole. In the new mysticism the human being is linked to the world just as much as he or she is linked to God. We enter into mystical communion with the World Spirit, a communion already actualized at birth.

The new world vision is also marked by inclusivity, pluralism and diversity. The only true church is the invisible church of the Universal Spirit that binds humans together in a quest for happiness and purposefulness. There are many roads that lead to God because the World Spirit is ever-present, directing all people on spiritual pathways to the goal of world transformation.

The new spirituality has both a communitarian and a libertarian thrust. We come together to share our experiences of depth encounters, but all people must make their own choices in realizing their divinely given possibilities for wholeness and meaning in life. Authority is finally centered in the self rather than the group, but the self is a microcosm of the universal world self, which lures us to new heights in life's adventure.

Love in the new spirituality takes the form of *amor fati*—living on the edge, in the heights, being open and vulnerable, following one's bliss. *Amor fati* is the joyous embrace of the destiny allotted to one by history. Teilhard de Chardin put it this way: "Love is an adventure and a conquest. It survives and develops like the universe itself only by perpetual discovery."[54] According to Paul Tillich, love is the vitalizing principle that ignites the human quest for wonder and beauty. Love is not directed to a god beyond the world but to the world itself in its yearning for fullness and wholeness. In his theology, "Love is the urge for the reunion of the separated. It is a universal love for everything that exists."[55]

Such exuberance is fueled by the myth of progress, which animates both modernity and postmodernity. The "fall of man" is a fall upwards (Hegel, Matthew Fox). The fall makes possible growth toward maturity. Only when we throw off our dependence on taboos and stifling traditions can we meet the challenges that life has to offer. Spiritual progress is intimately linked with moral evolution, but it is an evolution not imposed on the human creation but one directed by the human creation in collaboration with the World Spirit.

In the new spirituality the tragic flaw is neither fate nor hubris but inflexibility and rigidity. The challenge facing the spiritual wayfarer is to break out of insularism into a global perspective in which we assimilate insights from all peoples. We are summoned to give shape to a new religion inspired by the universal human quest for a worldview that meets human needs on all levels of existence—material, moral and spiritual.[56] We need a mysticism that does not take us beyond the world but unites us with its deepest impulses, one that is inclusive of all who seek for a greater truth whatever their cultural background and ethos.

Secular Mysticism

The new spirituality signifies a new mysticism—one focused on life on earth rather than life beyond death. It beckons us to live life to the fullest rather than to impose restrictions that curb a zest for life. It bids us go directly to God apart from all external mediation, and here it shows its affinity to the old mysticism. In the words of Emerson, "To reflect is to receive truth immediately from God without any medium. . . . It is by yourself without ambassador that God speaks to you. You are as one who has a private door that leads to the King's chamber."[57] Also echoing themes from the past, Simone Weil declares, "If we go down into ourselves we find that we possess exactly what we desire."[58] For Jürgen Moltmann the journey of mystical experience is a journey "not of the world beyond but of this one, the experience not of a spiritual life but of vital life in the midst of the world in which we live."[59]

Whereas the old mysticism affirmed the immortality of the soul, the new champions an immortality on earth. Schleiermacher spoke of an immortality in time, not in eternity.[60] In Whitehead's philosophy the values that we have produced live on in the consciousness of God. In process circles this is called objective immortality. According to Charles Fillmore, founder of the Unity School of Christianity, through meditation, proper exercise and diet we can overcome the fact of death.[61]

Prayer in the new spirituality is reaching out to unknown possibilities. It is not bowing before an all-powerful God but releasing the god power within us. The life of prayer is not one of withdrawal but one of engagement. According to Kazantzakis, "Solitude is no longer the road for the man who strives, and true prayer, prayer which steers a course straight for the Lord's house and enters, is noble action. This, today, is how the true warrior prays."[62]

Worship is transposed from a ritual of adoration to a technique of human empowerment. In the words of Whitehead: "The worship of God . . . is an adventure of the spirit, a flight after the unattainable."[63] For Gerald Heard the life of the Spirit is a "voyage of discovery."[64] It is opening doors to a glorious future rather than celebrating what God has done in past history.

In a spirituality shaped by the technological society, the locus of the sacred is utility, productivity and efficiency. An action is worthy if it is useful in expanding human potential. A spiritual program can be adopted if it furthers human enrichment. Technology furnishes us the means to become superhuman.

The new paradigm of transcendence is the future and also paradoxically the depths. Our hope rests not on the intervention of a transcendent God into history but on the coming of a new god as history unfolds. God is calling us to meet him in the future as well as in the depths of our own being. God is within, and god is also at the end of the cosmological process.

The new spirituality promotes a new asceticism, one that involves building up the body rather than suppressing bodily appetites. It entails mastering the flesh for the sake of the flesh rather than for a purely spiritual life. Spiritual disciplines are still in order, but their purpose is to enhance human creativity, not to extinguish human desire.

In congruity with classical Christian mysticism, the new mysticism celebrates the heroic. Yet heroism lies not in self-sacrifice for the good of others but in the display of power over the self and over others. The hero of the technological society is the one who makes an impact on society through the mastery of technique. The hero wins praise from the culture by virtue of being a culture creator, not one who flees from the culture into a monastic enclave.

The new mysticism places the accent not on identification but on unification (Teilhard). It is not identity with being but the unifying of all things in God that constitutes the culmination of world history. The goal is not mystical communion with a God outside of us but vitalization by a God who surrounds us and indwells us.

Matthew Fox, one of the luminaries of the new mysticism, advocates a spirituality symbolized not by climbing Jacob's ladder (as in the old mysticism) but dancing in Sarah's circle. We ascend to God by living out a destiny that leads to unity with God. In the Christian view we are already united with God through faith in his Son; the goal is not to gain power over the world but to be servants of God in the world.

In contrast to the old mysticism which draws on Neoplatonism, the new draws on pragmatism and modern naturalism. The key word in the old is emanation; the key word in the new is evolution. Whereas the old is inspired by the mountain of purgation, the new fixes its gaze on the mountain of evolution. While the old is otherworldly, the new is this-worldly. The new is not a mysticism of being but a mysticism of the earth. The key to knowing God is not inner purification but creative emergence.

Rebirth of the Gods

The new spirituality signifies the rebirth of the gods of ancient Greco-Roman civilization. These are gods who represent the cycles of nature and therefore can be harnessed in the service of an immanentist worldview.

One of the old gods reappearing in the culture and in the religious world is Gaia, the Earth Mother. The impact of this goddess can be seen in the Marian cult of Roman Catholicism, though official Catholic theology vigorously opposes any trend toward deifying the Virgin Mary. Gaia is even more prominent in the New Age movement, which seeks to retrieve the folklore of Native American religion and other tribalistic expressions of animism and primitivism. Gaia is also celebrated by the radical feminist movement, in its campaign to dethrone the monarchial god of patriarchalism.

A deity who is increasingly being appreciated in the modern world is Dionysus, the god of vitalistic intoxication. D. H. Lawrence expresses a religious devotion to the passions of the flesh, thereby giving them divine status: "The great eternity of creation does not lie in the spirit, in the ideal. It lies in the everlasting and incalculable throb of passion and desire. . . .

Without the deep sensual soul man is even inconceivable."[65] In the words of Starhawk, a New Age guru, "Sex is the manifestation of the driving life force energy of the universe. Sexuality is an expression of the moving force that underlies everything and gives it life."[66] "In a world where the endlessly transforming, erotic dance of God and Goddess weaves radiant through all things, we who step to their rhythm are enraptured with the wonder and mystery of being."[67]

Mars, the god of war, is also arousing new interest. In the devotion to this god violence becomes the crucible by which we encounter divinity. Conflict is regarded as the gateway to freedom. Here the new spirituality becomes a source for the resurgence of militarism in the modern world. Militarism here signifies an attitude—one that finds the security of a nation in its armaments and alliances rather than in its commitment to peaceable relations among nations and its recognition that a nation's destiny lies in its submission to a higher power—the living God.

Time (Chronos) is not so much a rebirth of an ancient god as the birth of an entirely new god.[68] In the ancient worldview time is something to be overcome. In the new metaphysics time itself is divinized. For Gerald Heard, time and history simply indicate the ebb and flow of eternity.

Earlier I mentioned Tyche (Greek) and Fortuna (Latin), signifying the elevation of chance as the determiner of human destiny. In this excursus in metaphysics, contingency is attributed not only to the world but also to God. Becoming triumphs over being, process over crisis.

The cult of youth is still another manifestation of the old religiosity now reappearing in a new form. Adonis, the object of devotion for many of the ancient Greeks, symbolizes the ideal of youth, which increasingly pervades modern culture. Schleiermacher gave voice to the resurgence of this confident mood: "I will not see the dread infirmities of old age; I vow a mighty scorn of all adversity that does not touch the aim of my existence, and I pledge myself to an eternal youth."[69]

Hermes, the god of commerce and invention, fits in well with the technological society that celebrates productivity as a spiritual goal. This may be the area where ancient Greek and Roman religion makes its greatest impact on the modern scene—where ideology becomes the servant of technology.

We must also consider the titans or divinized mortals, who likewise are making their presence felt in a postmodern and post-Christian society. Hercules has become known as a slayer of dragons. Prometheus, who stole fire from heaven, is noted for his defiance of the gods and his challenge to fate. The titans or demi-gods were driven by a passion to be superhuman. This emphasis stands in striking contrast to the saints in Christian tradition who are content to be human and who acknowledge themselves as fallible. The model of the saint or holy person is John the Baptist, who declared, "He must increase, but I must decrease" (Jn 3:30). The Christian doctrine of the saints rightly understood contradicts the Greek idea of heroism, though the Greek ideal certainly penetrated the doctrine of the saints as this developed in Catholic and Orthodox traditions.[70]

The modern age connotes a movement from monotheism to pluralism, from trinitarianism to panentheism, from deism to paganism. In the new spirituality the Holy Spirit becomes "the Stream of Life" or "the Wellspring of Life." Jesus Christ becomes the model of a superhumanity rather than a paradigm of vicarious suffering love. The passion that dominates postmodernity is the will to power and the will to life rather than the desire to serve without expecting anything in return. Friedrich Nietzsche rightly perceived that we are talking about two different worldviews, which finally cannot be reconciled. The new spirituality heralds a transvaluation of values in which the powerful are celebrated over the weak. This is the challenge facing a church that is obliged to utter a prophetic warning to a culture that is unashamedly engaged in the worship of new gods, which in reality are the old gods in new forms.

Priding itself on its openness and sensitivity to the winds of the age, this new brand of spirituality translates into an inflexible insistence on "diversity" that tolerates no deviation from its dictates. This totalitarian spirit has come to permeate virtually every area of Euro-American society to the detriment of genuinely creative inquiry and moral sensibility, not to mention the traditional faith and values that constitute the glue that has held society together. By relativizing the standards of faith, the spiritual forces now regnant in the culture are preparing the way for a new civilization that aspires to be all-controlling as well as all-embracing—provided, of course, that people conform to what the elites deem acceptable in a new world order.

THE NEW AGE MOVEMENT

W hat I call the new spirituality is wider and deeper than the New Age movement, but the latter represents a concrete manifestation of the former. The New Age constitutes a curious blend of naturalism and occultism, shamanism and gnosticism. Its focus is on the spiritual evolution of the race, often called "transformational evolution." In this new worldview the evolutionary process can be accelerated. Evolution directs us toward a super-Intelligence that has been anticipated in various periods of history by sages and holy persons including Jesus and Buddha.[1]

In contrast to the old mysticism, the outlook toward the earth is strikingly positive. The New Age is biocentric, centered in life. Its goddess is Gaia, the Earth Mother of ancient mythology. The New Age is occultic, for it encourages the exploration of a realm hidden from the senses. It is also gnostic in its supposition that knowledge of reality lies in unlocking the secrets of the self. It celebrates immediate experience over faith. Carl Jung declared, "I don't believe, I *know*." Similarly Joseph Campbell says, "I don't need faith. I have experience."[2]

Like ancient shamanism and primitive religion in general, the New Age holds to a belief in spirit guides and ascended masters—superbeings who place humans in contact with the cosmic or universal Mind. As in panentheistic and panentheistic religion, the New Age reconceives God as the pulsating ground of nature, the Life-Force.

Manifesting a marked affinity to the religions of the East, the New Age generally holds to reincarnation, though this is not the Hindu doctrine of the transmigration of souls in which one may descend into lower forms of life. In New Age ideology reincarnation is united with the idea of progress, especially of the moral and spiritual kind. The doctrine of karma is accepted but reinterpreted. One's final destiny lies not in the karma one inherits but in the free decisions one makes, which alter the

karmatic effects of reincarnated lives. Our lives are not inexorably determined by the law of sowing and reaping, but they are shaped by decisions that belong to the sphere of human freedom. Ralph Waldo Emerson, one of the gurus of the New Age movement, summarized the new
Weltanschauung in his injunction: "Build . . . your own world."[3]

The New Age spawns a this-worldly mysticism, which in an earlier section I called a secular mysticism. The stages in the spiritual life are not
purgation, illumination and union (as in the old mysticism) but now
struggle, growth and freedom. It is neither God's search for humanity nor
humanity's quest for God, but God's *birth* in humanity that describes the
New Age venture. God is resymbolized as Primal Energy, the Creative
Surge, the Immanent Mother, the Womb of Being, the Universal Cosmic
Consciousness, the Pool of Unlimited Power, the Slumbering Deep
Within and the Spring of Life.

A dark side of the New Age movement is a racist proclivity that casts
doubt upon the viability of democratic political experiments. For Ralph
Waldo Emerson the hope of the world lies in "the instinctive and heroic
races," especially in the "imperial Saxon race." He declared, "Before the
energy of the Caucasian race all the other races have quailed and done
obeisance."[4] In occultic circles a division is often made between spiritual
races, the highest of which is "the Aquarian and Aryan man." Vera Alder
sees a golden age ahead of us when planet earth will be ruled by a race
of man-gods.[5] According to Alice Bailey, "We are laying the foundation
for the emergence of a new species of human being—a more highly
evolved unit within the human family." She referred to a New Age vanguard, a superior race centered in Shamballa in Tibet, marked by "group
. . . consciousness and idealistic vision."[6] Helena Blavatsky, founder of
Theosophy, envisioned human evolution in seven stages; we are on the
eve of the final stage—a deified humanity.[7]

Trademarks of the New Age

The New Age is a diversified movement without any centralizing base.
Yet it is tied together by common concerns and similar perceptions of nature and of history. One of these is wholism, also known as holistic health
and interconnectedness. We are united not only with all of humanity but

with all living things and indeed all things, since everything is animated by a Cosmic Consciousness. New Agers strive for the integration of body and spirit rather than for the release of spirit from body.

Global awareness is high on the agenda of the New Age. National loyalties must be superseded by a commitment to the ideal of the global village, which ties humanity together as in a family. The goal of spiritual endeavor is planetization, the "unifying of the world into a corporate brotherhood."[8] This entails the celebration of ethnic diversity, often called multiculturalism. It also involves the liberation of human potential, which often takes the form of consciousness raising. Much is made of the distinction between left-brain (the cerebral) and right-brain (the intuitive); the latter is given precedence over the former. Many New Agers look forward to a one-world government ruled by a coterie of social scientists and other adepts intent on creating a new humanity.[9]

Other trademarks of this movement are tapping into occult powers, the centering of the self, UFO contacts, astrology, channeling and spiritism. New Agers often teach submission to a guru or spiritual master, who represents a higher stage in spiritual evolution. Mantras are important in promoting the spiritual life. Prayer takes the form of incantation and meditation instead of petition to a holy God. Biofeedback is another important emphasis, for it connotes the power of mind over matter.

With William James and other pragmatists, the New Age champions an open universe—one that allows for human participation in the unfolding drama of history. We may well be burdened by a past in which we have accumulated karmic debt, but we can create a new future for both ourselves and others with the aid of spirit guides and avatars—incarnations of the gods in human form. Our focus should be not on our finite limitations but on our infinite possibilities.

The New Age is more supportive of oligarchy than democracy, since its trust is in the elite who have mastered spiritual laws. It upholds an egalitarian society albeit based not on equal distribution of goods but on spiritual equality—the equal opportunity to tap into human potential. Its commitment is really to meritocracy over egalitarian democracy. Its goal is a society of achievers.

Even while it looks to an academic elite for guidance in fashioning a new society, it paradoxically champions political decentralization. Changes must finally be initiated from below. This accounts for its support of grass-roots democracy—yet not with the view of promoting a diversity of opinion but in order to serve the civilizing of humanity. It celebrates not community control but community empowerment.

The key to a new society is personal transformation or the alteration of consciousness. Its hope lies in a human-scale technology that permits people to become masters of their own destinies, captains of their souls. The New Age is markedly open to feminist and environmental values. All of nature is divine; nature indeed is described as "the body of God."[10] New Agers unhesitatingly throw their support to androgyny—overcoming distinctions between male and female.[11]

Precursors and Proponents

Among the pivotal sources and shapers of New Age thinking are American Transcendentalism, associated with Ralph Waldo Emerson, Henry David Thoreau, Theodore Parker and Walt Whitman, as well as various other luminaries; and neo-Transcendentalism, comprising the New Thought movement, Divine Science, Unity School of Christianity, Christian Science and Religious Science. New Agers also draw upon occultic groups like Anthroposophy, Rosicrucianism, Theosophy and the I AM movement. In addition they manifest a deep appreciation for Eastern religions, especially Hinduism, Buddhism and Taoism. Other notable sources of New Age thinking are process philosophy, reflected in the writings of Teilhard de Chardin in particular; the pragmatism of William James and John Dewey; and the voluntaristic idealism of Schopenhauer, Schelling, Hegel and Nietzsche. The gnostic hue of the New Age is evident in Schopenhauer's thesis that we are justified neither by faith nor by works but by knowledge.

New Age organizations include the White Eagle Lodge; the Chinook Learning Community; Silva Mind Control; State of the World Forum; the Findhorn Community; est; Planetary Citizens; the Lucis Trust; Eckankar; Esalen Institute; Scientology; Transcendental Meditation; the Saint Germain Foundation; Association of Research and Enlightenment (devoted to the writings of Edgar Cayce); the Church Universal and Triumphant; Association for Humanistic Psychology; the Nirvana Foundation; the Windstar Foundation; the Movement of Spiritual Awareness; and the Collegians International Church. The New Age outreach extends to conferences, seminars, meditation groups and bookstores (estimated at 2,500).

Modern proponents of the New Age include Marilyn Ferguson, Theodore Roszak, Fritjof Capra, Joseph Campbell, Matthew Fox, Morton Kelsey, Shirley MacLaine, John Naisbett, David Spangler, Elizabeth Clare Prophet, Buckminster Fuller, John Denver, M. Scott Peck, Jean K. Foster, Charlene Spretnak, Miriam Starhawk, Deepak Chopra and Neal Donald Walsch. Key books that have shaped the New Age ethos are Marilyn Ferguson's *The Aquarian Conspiracy;* Joseph Campbell's *The Masks of God, Creative Mythology* and *The Hero with a Thousand Faces;* Fritjof Capra's *Green Politics* and *The Tao of Physics;* Shirley MacLaine's *Out on a Limb* and *Dancing in the Light;* Rudolf Steiner's *Mysticism: At the Dawn of the Modern Age;* David Spangler's *Revelation—Birth of a New Age;* John Naisbett's *Megatrends;* Alvin Toffler's *Future Shock;* Charles Reich's *The Greening of America;* Deepak Chopra's *How to Know God* and Karen Armstrong's *The Spiral Staircase.*[12] Philosophical guides include Carl Jung, Ralph Waldo Emerson, Nikos Kazantzakis, Rudolf Steiner, Annie Besant, Helena Blavatsky, Abraham Maslow, Aldous Huxley, Gerald Heard, Sri Aurobindo, Jacob Needleman and William James. Writers who seek to build bridges between the New Age and classical Christianity include Geddes MacGregor, George A. Maloney, Harmon Bro and Morton Kelsey.[13]

It should be noted that just because great thinkers of the past are coopted by New Age devotees does not imply that those thinkers are themselves New Agers or even endorse the principles of this movement. The nationalism that runs through such modern thinkers as Fichte, Hegel and Troeltsch is alien to the New Age mindset, which extols internationalism and cosmopolitanism.[14] Nietzsche belongs to the new spirituality, but his ideal of the superman *(Übermensch),* who separates himself from the common herd, does not comport with the New Age ideal of the corporate manager and freelance inventor who strive not to undermine others but to empower others. Yet this is not to deny that Nietzsche has left an indelible imprint on modern and postmodern spirituality and that one side of the New Age movement is indebted to him.

Salient Symbols

A movement is known by the symbols it embraces, and this is certainly true of the New Age movement. Among these is the rainbow. In ancient Tibetan teaching the rainbow symbolizes humanity's ultimate state of divinity—the fusion of good and evil, shadow and light. Some colors are brighter than others, indicative that some peoples or races are higher than others.

The crystal is another poignant symbol that identifies New Age belief. Crystals are understood as conduits of divine energy. They are "windows of light" to a higher realm. To cultivate "crystal consciousness" is to tap into power sources available to all seekers after truth. The crystal becomes in this movement a kind of fetish, an icon that mediates divine energy. Both crystals and people are said to be surrounded by electromagnetic fields, determined by their vibratory rates. We are invited to tune in to the vibrations that emanate from crystals.

The pyramid is also a significant emblem of the New Age movement. New Agers frequently extol pyramid power, trusting that it can provide one with the spiritual resources to overcome and prevail in the midst of difficulties. New Agers surmise that "the pyramid form emits magnetic energy that can be harnessed to control events."[15] Interestingly the pyramids of Egypt have furnished inspiration to various modern cult movements in their endeavor to master the secrets of history.

One New Age devotee, Jane Roberts, applies the pyramid metaphor to God:

> He is not one individual, but an energy gestalt . . . a psychic pyramid of interrelated, ever-expanding consciousness that creates, simultaneously and instantaneously, universes and individuals that are given—through the gift of personal perspective—duration, psychic comprehension, intelligence, and eternal validity. . . . This absolute, ever-expanding, instantaneous psychic gestalt, which you may call God if you prefer, is so secure in its existence that it can constantly break itself down and rebuild itself.[16]

For the post-Christian mystic Gerald Heard the mountain of evolution provides a fitting guiding symbol for the modern seeker after truth as opposed to the traditional mountain of purgation. The former symbol does not widely pervade the New Age movement, but it is certainly in keeping with its ethos.

The New Age guru David Spangler, founder of the Findhorn Community, suggests tents at a fair as a poignant symbol for the New Age. He contrasts this with the traditional Christian symbol of the cathedral, which points upward to heaven. In the tent metaphor the emphasis lies on choosing the implements that one needs to build a world for oneself. People will embrace many different paths in contrast to the older spirituality, which upholds only one path to salvation.[17]

A Royal Theology?

A credible case can be made that the New Age movement exemplifies a royal theology, one designed for the elite of superachievers rather than for the masses. It is a religion of the "haves" as opposed to the "have nots." It is a faith attuned to the new class (Peter Berger), those who are upwardly mobile. These are people who seek government aid but not government control. They include both political liberals and conservatives. The New Age reflects a shift from an industrial society to an electronic-computer society. It is a religion of the New Establishment. It reveals the alliance between corporate executives and the professional educational elite. The New Age upholds a humanized capitalism.

The goal of the New Age is not only eternal security—the state of being secure through submersion in God-consciousness—but also material security, being shored up by the things of this world. A virtuous life is the condition for a successful life in a consumerist culture. The New Age mentality is illustrated in the New Thought maxim that as your virtue increases, so does your abundance. In this ethos true religion does not negate the quest for health, wealth and prosperity, but rather enables one to fulfill this quest.

The New Age can indeed be faulted for refusing to see the hand of God in suffering and poverty (as in the old mysticism). In Shirley MacLaine's theology, one critic claims, "If you're poor or unemployed you have only yourself to blame. You have victimized yourself by not living up to your potential."[18] In her view, "To be a spiritual person, you should have abundance."[19] Financial profit signifies the fulfillment of human potential, the byproduct of spiritual harmony.

The New Age champions a mysticism that aggrandizes rather than denies the self. Deepak Chopra laments: "It is a great misfortune that the spiritual life has earned a reputation for being poor, reclusive, and ascetic."[20] We should not try to curtail the creative forces that abound within us but release these forces for our own good—and for the wider good. We should strive to be miracle workers—shapers of a new humanity.

In the New Age ethos you create your own reality. The emphasis on positive thinking and possibility thinking is more akin to the New Thought and New Age movements than to traditional Christian faith. In the New Age poverty is related to negative thinking. Those who are presently in poverty are presumably responsible for their predicament because their plight is rooted in misdeeds in previous existences. We who are affluent are reaping the reward for good deeds done in previous lives.

It is a cardinal tenet of New Age philosophy that by devoting ourselves to self-improvement we thereby contribute to the well-being of society. This is in accord with the Enlightenment self-interest doctrine of Adam Smith, the pioneer of modern capitalism. There likewise is a strong dose of utopianism in the New Age. It is alleged that we change society by changing ourselves. The key to a new social order lies in the transformation of consciousness. We should not overthrow established structures but humanize them.

Afterword

The New Age movement draws on animism, gnosticism, shamanism, Eastern mysticism, transcendentalism, evolutionary naturalism, radical feminism and technocratic liberalism. It is a mysticism attuned with the technological society. Salvation lies in techniques that realize human potential, control the environment, meet human need, bridge cultural barriers and overcome national rivalries. It is a religion that appeals to the affluent, since it promises material abundance for those who are motivated to strive upward in society. Its focus is on self-affirmation over self-denial. It upholds self-deification over the subordination of the self to the kingdom of God. The New Age is a religion of immanence. It teaches a one-story universe with many rooms or dimensions. The new frontier is both outer space and the inner life. The New Age urges the exploration of the unconscious as a means to tap into ultimate reality.

Like the wider movement, the new spirituality, the New Age promotes an eros over an agape spirituality. By affirming other humans and nature, we advance ourselves. Besides eros, the new spirituality is associated with *epithymia*—the drive for life in everything that is (Tillich). Even more than erotic love, the New Age champions an indiscriminate love, an embracing of all of life. It might aptly be described as biophilia—the love of life.

In a world ruled by chance God becomes subject to risk. In the words of David Spangler, "God is . . . wild, ecstatic, and utterly unpredictable."[21] Jesus is not Lord of creation but a prophet to creation. God is not sovereign over the world but the creative force within the world. He is not Lord of life but the spirit that renews life.

The New Age interprets the drama of history in terms of a progression from a geocentric to a heliocentric to an egocentric and holocentric orientation. The vision that inspires this spiritual movement is the intermeshing of all of reality. All things are seen in the light of an overarching whole. The New Age is both idealistic and naturalistic. The outer world is grasped through the forms of the mind. But the world outside is also experienced directly and immediately as we probe the interior depths of human existence. The New Age is both vitalistic and occultistic, both rationalistic and spiritualistic. It connotes one important ramification of the new spirituality, but the latter is wider and deeper, affecting not only esoteric religious and educational institutions but also the basic rhythm of the culture itself.

Worldviews in Collision

By the law of works, God says to us, "Do what I command you,"
but by the law of faith we say to God, "Give me what you command."

AUGUSTINE

We do not display greatness by going to one extreme,
but in touching both at once, and filling all the intervening space.

PASCAL

If God has really done something in Christ on which the salvation of the world depends
. . . then it is a Christian duty to be intolerant of everything which ignores,
denies or explains it away.

JAMES DENNEY

Between the man who is bound to a God in heaven,
and another who knows nothing of this bond,
there is a contrast deeper than all other contrasts which separate man from man.

KARL HEIM

In this chapter I shall recapitulate some of the themes in earlier ones in order to underscore the enduring tension between these three types of spirituality. I shall give a descriptive or phenomenological analysis of this typology without systematically elucidating my own position on these matters, which I shall do in the final chapter. Neither in this chapter nor in the others do I try to build bridges between these spiritual movements. I do, however, point to their distinctive characteristics, which are for the most part in conflict with one another. This does not imply that the persons associated with each type stand in unalterable opposition to one another, since they all incorporate in their life and vision various strands of thought and spirituality. If they are earnestly Christian, as were the older mystics for the most part, they are indeed open to fellowship with one other. But there will be marked tensions in their fellowship because of wide disparities in their understanding of both God and the world.

Authority

Authority is always a bellwether for showing exactly where a person stands on issues of fundamental gravity. In traditional or classical mysticism authority lies in the inner light or the mystical experience. It is an experience that takes precedence over all external criteria including the biblical narrative and the creeds and confessions of the church. In secular spirituality authority lies in cultural self-understanding, scientific verification or scientific rationality. In biblical faith authority lies in divine revelation through the biblical and apostolic witness to Jesus Christ. This authority includes the experience of faith; yet it is an experience that takes us outside ourselves into the promises of God that never deceive (Martin Luther). The authoritative foundation for faith is not our experience as such but the God-Man, Jesus Christ, who both descends into our experience and who draws us out of our experience into a life of faith and discipleship.

Authority in the biblical view resides in the paradoxical unity of Word and Spirit.[1] It is both logocentric—focused on the Word written and proclaimed—and pneumocentric, allowing for the work of the Spirit in giving illumination to the reader and hearer of the biblical message.

To know the truth we need to look both inward to the stirrings of conscience and Spirit and outward to the events of sacred history culminating in the life, death and resurrection of Jesus Christ. We begin, however, not with the self but with the voice of God addressed to the self, and we end not with the self but with the living Christ, who has come and who is coming again to set up the kingdom that shall have no end.

Anthropology

In biblical Christianity the human person is made in the image of God, but humanity is never confounded with divinity. God is always the Wholly Other, and we exist in relationship to God by virtue of our being elected in Jesus Christ and incorporated in Christ by the gift of the Spirit. In classical mysticism the core of the soul is practically identical with God; the goal is to extricate ourselves from the material and ascend into the purely spiritual. But this entails a descent into self, for it is there we find the God who sustains the self.

In the biblical view body and soul do not stand in antithesis but complement one another. The body is the *vessel* of the soul. In classical Christian mysticism the body is the *tomb* of the soul. In the new spirituality the body is the *seed* of the soul. Faithful disciples of both modernity and postmodernity do not denigrate the physical side of humanity (as did Origen and many others in the mystical tradition) but instead celebrate and adulate the physical.

The tragic flaw in human existence is another pivotal point of comparison. In the biblical view the tragic flaw is sin—hardness of heart and unbelief. In the Greek tragedian view the tragic flaw is fate and sometimes also hubris—rising above our limitations. In the Platonic tradition the tragic flaw is ignorance. In the new spirituality the tragic flaw is sickness; the pressing need is for therapy.

The doctrine of sin is also a critical area in anthropology. In the biblical view the human plight is the impairment of our freedom by willful assent to evil. In the mystical view the dilemma of humankind lies in being separated from God, both ontologically and morally. In the new mysticism sin is reduced to inflexibility and rigidity. The problem is "the inertia of nature" (Whitehead) rather than deliberate malice or overweening pride.

Biblical religion takes seriously human depravity and helplessness. While we are created in the image of God, sin indelibly mars this image. Sin is not something incidental to human life but perversely affects the core of human personality. Sin is not the backward pull of our animal heritage (as in modern naturalism) but the forward drive toward the enthronement of the self. By contrast the mystical emphasis is on the divine origin of humanity, the uncreated light within humanity. Sin is the obscur-

ing of this light rather than a malign effort to extinguish this light. Sin is
negation more than perverse self-affirmation. In the modern view the focus is on realizing infinite possibilities. From this perspective sin is a fail-
ure to live up to our highest potential. Sin is shrinking back from the
problems that torment the self. Virtue on the other hand is gaining mastery over the self and over the world that confronts the self.

In biblical understanding the human will is in bondage and must be
liberated by grace. The mystical view under the impact of Christian revelation makes a place for the assistance of the will by grace. The modern
view, shaped by the Renaissance and Enlightenment, celebrates the freedom of the will. Mysticism (both old and new) presupposes human cooperation with God (synergy); biblical religion holds out the promise of
deliverance by the grace of God. In the classical mystical heritage the human being is partly free. In the modern view the human being is wholly
free. In the evangelical or biblical view the human being is wholly bound.

Doctrine of God

Not surprisingly each type of spirituality has its own conception of God.
In biblical spirituality God is a personal being who graciously interacts
with his people. He discloses himself as heavenly Father, sovereign Lord,
the Friend of sinners. He is not an object of the mind but the Absolute
Subject who confronts us from without.[2] He has aptly been described as
the Wholly Other, but he does not remain so, for he accommodates himself to people in sin and converses with them on their own level. In classical mysticism God is the ground and depth of all being, the undifferentiated Unity, the object of meditation more than the partner in dialog. In
the new spirituality God is the power of innovation and rejuvenation, a
power available to us in the depths of the inner self. God is variously portrayed as the Unlimited Pool of Power, Unlimited Possibility and the Cosmic Consciousness.

Mysticism of the classical variety stresses the *eternity* of God; biblical
religion emphasizes the *sovereignty* of God; the new spirituality places
the accent on the *potential* of God, or even the *future* of God. Those who
champion open theism—the idea that God is striving to realize his own
future—fall into this third category.[3] It is fashionable in avant-garde cir-

cles to affirm that the future is hidden or partly hidden from God.

Biblical religion too can speak of the eternity of God, but not in the sense of timelessness. Eternity in the biblical panorama is not God towering above time but God entering into time, taking time into himself. Eternity is God's lordship over time. God is not the timeless Absolute (as in classical theism) but the Absolute in time. Neither is God "temporal everlastingness" (as in process thought and open theism). It is theologically more felicitous to depict God as eternal steadfastness, unceasing fidelity. God is eternity in history, but we here have in mind not the history of humanity only but God's inner history—the inner conversation of the Trinity.

Similarly in biblical, prophetic religion God is not subject to suffering. But God enters into suffering and transforms it. God is impassible in the sense that he rises above suffering; yet he also descends into suffering without compromising his unchanging vision of the world and of history.

All three strands of spirituality perceive a transcendent dimension to God, but only the biblical or evangelical strand sees God as fundamentally independent of the world. Mystics are inclined to speak of the emanation of the world from the being of God rather than *creatio ex nihilo*. Those who are consciously Christian make a place for God as the sole creator of the world, but they tend to combine this notion with that of emanation or of evolution. They are generally united in affirming the inseparability of God and nature or God and history (as in the modern version).

Jesus Christ

No doctrine is more central in relating to the essentials of the faith than the person and work of Jesus Christ. While Christ has a prominent role in all three types of spirituality, the uniqueness of his person and life is especially evident in biblical personalism. In the biblical view Jesus is the Divine Savior from sin, God incarnate in human flesh, the Absolute Paradox. In the classical mystical view Jesus is the mirror of divine love, the realized ideal of divine-human unity, the symbol of transformed human identity, a spiritual master who has realized God-consciousness to a supreme degree. In the modern view Jesus is the symbol of authentic selfhood, the supreme example of suffering love, the historical personification of liberating love, the "man for others," the flower of humanity, the maturation of the human spirit.

The meaning of the incarnation of God in Jesus Christ is especially pivotal in this discussion. In New Testament theology the incarnation denotes an event that happened once for all times (Rom 6:10; Heb 7:27; 9:12, 28). It signifies a divine incursion into history rather than an eruption from nature (as in the new spirituality). For J. A. T. Robinson the incarnation becomes "a breakthrough of cosmic consciousness" rather than the event of God becoming man in the person of Jesus.[4] Many mystics are inclined to posit an incarnation in universal history, and this is especially true of the new mystics (like Teilhard de Chardin). Karl Barth, in contrast, was adamant that the teaching of the faith concerns an incarnation at only one point and place in history.

All persons who claim to be Christian affirm the resurrection of Christ from the dead and his ascension into heaven. But in mystical circles, the emphasis has always been on the resurrection as a transformative experience, though the bodily resurrection of Christ from the grave is not denied, except among the more radical mystics or spiritualists. Regarding the ascension of Christ, the new mysticism speaks of the upsurge of divinity within nature and humanity rather than the ascent to a divinity beyond nature and humanity.

In the area of soteriology the evangelical strand of spirituality accentuates the forensic nature of justification without denying the blessing of sanctification, which involves inward renewal through faith in Jesus Christ. Barth's salvation model is reconciliation and redemption. Classical mystics are inclined to favor deification, the transfiguration of humanity by the Holy Spirit. Modern or new mystics focus upon the theme of emancipation—the freedom to build a new self and a new world.

The relation between grace and nature also forms an integral part of this discussion. In classical Christian mysticism grace perfects nature. In the new naturalism nature is the seedbed of grace. In biblical personalism grace brings a new nature. The discontinuity between the old self and the new self is emphasized in biblical and Reformation theology, whereas mystics of all stripes are inclined to stress the underlying continuity between the old and the new.

Life and Vocation

The significance of human life is a key to any spirituality. In the old mysticism life is a vale of tears to be endured. In biblical religion life is a gift of God to be enjoyed and redeemed, but not to be adored. It provides an opportunity for service and fellowship. In the new spirituality life is an adventure in creative living, an opportunity to realize one's dreams and aspirations. Life is a challenge to the human spirit to rise above itself. Life is the doorway to freedom, a ball to be celebrated.

In both biblical and mystical religion life is a pilgrimage fraught with promise and peril. For the evangelical Christian life is an experiment in holy living. For the Christian mystic life is a venture in disciplined living that must be perfected and transcended. For the gnostic life is a "horrible tragedy;" the only hope is an escape from one mode of existence into a higher mode of existence.[5] To phrase it another way, in traditional mysticism life is an exercise in self-denial and disciplined devotion. In biblical religion life is a battle to be won, a victory to be secured. Life is a triumph over adversity through faith in the living God. In the modern (and postmodern) view life is a struggle for mastery and power over the world. The world is seen as an obstacle to be overcome. It provides infinite possibilities yet to be realized.

To carry my ruminations further, I would say that for mainstream mysticism life is a quest for happiness in union with God. In biblical religion life is a witness to God's gracious election brought to fulfillment in Jesus Christ. In modern religion life is an invitation to demonstrate heroic virtue. Or life is a transmutation of matter into spirit. One might also say that in the modern perspective life is a struggle for survival and the survival of the fittest. Here we see Charles Darwin's ubiquitous influence on the shaping of modernity.

For the biblical Christian our vocation is to be a transmitter of the truth—bearing witness to unseen realities through life and words. For the mystic the goal is to be a spiritual master, a transfigured human being, a vessel of holiness. For the secular person it is to be the master of one's destiny, the captain of one's soul (William Henley).

In the perspective of biblical faith, life is a demonstration and manifestation of the holiness that the Spirit works within us. For the mystic life is the cultivation of personal holiness—an all-consuming passion to make oneself holy. For the modern person life is an exercise in human remolding or in social engineering. Realizing one's full potential is more important than helping the downtrodden (as in biblical or evangelical religion).

Faith, Hope and Love

The ethical mandates of the faith are brought to the fore in the discussion of faith, hope and love. Faith in biblical religion is trust in the undeserved mercy of God as revealed in Jesus Christ. In classical mysticism faith is a venture into the darkness of the unknown culminating in the vision of God beyond the boundary of death. In the new spirituality faith is a power force that works miracles. For the existentialist Lev Shestov faith is audacity, being willing to create one's own future in the face of adversity and death.[6] Such an undertaking entails "a mad struggle for possibility. For only possibility opens the way to salvation."[7]

In biblical, evangelical spirituality faith comes by hearing (Rom 10:17). In the mystical heritage of the church shaped by Neoplatonism, faith comes by self-emptying. In the new spirituality faith is ignited by imaging—visualizing the reality that we are trying to bring about. It is realized not in solitary contemplation but in feats of daring and sometimes madness.

Hope too is conceived differently in each type of spirituality. In the Christian or biblical view hope is a confident waiting for the revelation of the victory over evil already accomplished in Jesus Christ. In the classical mystical view hope is a gnawing desire for the highest good. In modern spirituality hope is the fervent expectation of success despite considerable difficulties.

In an earlier volume I already analyzed the conflicting views of love, but it is well to continue this discussion.[8] Agape, the love dominant in the New Testament, is not the relentless longing for the highest good (as in the mystical eros) but the surprising work of grace that creates good. It is not the desire for unity with the good but the power of good in action, restoring and transforming all it touches. Agape is not a calculated strategy to insure security for the self but the sacrifice of the self for the well-being of others.

Agape does not overthrow natural loves but places them on a new foundation. It does not curtail life so much as make abundant life possible. Dietrich Bonhoeffer rightly warns:

> There is always a danger of intense love destroying what I might call the "polyphony" of life. What I mean is that God requires that we should love him eternally with our whole hearts, yet not so as to compromise or diminish our earthly affections, but as a kind of *cantus firmus* to which the other melodies of life provide the counterpoint.[9]

Prayer and Action

Prayer is the core of spirituality, and every spirituality reveals its theological moorings by its attitude toward prayer.[10] In biblical religion prayer is humble supplication. In mystical religion prayer is contemplative adoration. In modern religion prayer is reflection on life and the world culminating in creative action. In the biblical worldview prayer bears fruit in action, but it basically is reliance upon God—crying out for help from God.

Prayer in biblical perspective is more than petition: it also takes the form of adoration, thanksgiving, confession and meditation. Yet all of these types of prayer contain the element of petition (Barth). There is no prayer without petition in prophetic religion. In mysticism by contrast the higher forms of prayer leave petition behind. The highest prayer is contemplation—when we simply gaze upon the presence of God.

Prayer presupposes a two-way conversation. It is indeed the conversation of the heart with God (Luther). Yet we cannot really enter into dialogue until we listen to what God says. As Christoph Blumhardt put it, "God can well hear the sighs of everyone, even the foolish; yet, in reality, only those can *pray* who *listen* to God."[11]

Biblical prayer consists of stillness as well as struggle. This stillness, however, is not passionless tranquility or the cessation of desire but a comforted despair, in which we sense the presence of God in the midst of our anxiety and affliction. Prayer does not remove us from the ills of the world but enables us to live in the midst of these ills in a spirit of interior calm.

Political and liberation theologies have an altruistic motif—bringing down the oppressive structures of society—but it is solidarity with the poor more than the redemption of the lost that is their chief concern.[12]

Moving in a quite different direction, the famed Mother Teresa of Calcutta was firm in her insistence that she was not a social worker but an ambassador of Jesus Christ.[13] In her theology "the soul of the care of the poor is the care of the poor soul."[14] Giving people the seed of faith energizes them to reach out and help others in the spirit of sacrificial love. Evangelicals like William and Catherine Booth, cofounders of the Salvation Army, and William Wilberforce, who spearheaded the campaign against the slave trade in late eighteenth- and early nineteenth-century England, underscored the necessity for works of justice in the Christian mission—perhaps more so than Mother Teresa. The great saints of both spiritual traditions—evangelical and Roman Catholic—have strenuously insisted that social amelioration also belongs to the Christian hope, yet always giving priority to the evangelistic mandate of the church.

Liberation theologians do not dismiss the crucial role of prayer in penetrating the bastions of oppression and deceit, but they reinterpret it so that it becomes a dramatic force for change in society. For them prayer is making oneself sensitive to the cries and needs of oppressed peoples and then acting to meet these needs through social revolution and enlightened legislation. In biblical or evangelical theology, prayer is calling upon God to deliver both lost sinners and a hurting world through the power of his Word and Spirit. Such prayer is born in the confidence that God will use human instruments as agents of personal and social change.

Ecclesiology and Eschatology

The meaning of the church is intimately connected with the new life in the Spirit. In biblical religion the church is a gathered fellowship of believers, a hospital for sick souls (Martin Luther). In the mystical worldview the church is a society of kindred souls, the company of the committed, a religious society that shares common interests. In modern religion the church is a power structure for social change or a school for creative living.

Preaching too assumes quite different roles in this spiritual typology. In evangelical religion preaching takes the form of biblical exposition and proclamation. In mysticism preaching becomes sharing one's interior journey. In the modern worldview preaching is an appeal to heroic action or a challenge to realize human possibilities.

The old spirituality of classical mysticism favors the cyclical view of history. The new mysticism embraces a spiral view of history dominated by the idea of progress. The biblical view is apocalyptic—foreseeing the catastrophic end of history. At the same time, it is not exclusively apocalyptic, for it depicts the kingdom of God as present now, moving history toward a transcendent goal and conclusion.

In the old mysticism the kingdom of God stands outside history. In the new the kingdom of God unfolds within history. In biblical religion the kingdom breaks into history from the beyond, though it is essentially beyond history. The kingdom is the new reality of the peace and reign of Christ that bursts into history and directs history to a transcendent end.

Classical mysticism is inspired by the myth of the cosmic return, the return of the soul to divinity. The new spirituality is shaped by the myth of evolution—steady progression into a higher form of humanity. Biblical Christianity is associated with the drama of divine intervention in history culminating in Jesus Christ.

In response to this dramatic manifestation of God's concern for his creation, biblical Christians see their eschatological or life goal as dedication to the glory of God, the service of the kingdom of God, the conversion of souls. For traditional mystics this goal is the possession of the supreme Good, the vision of God, divinization or union with divinity. The life-goal of moderns is earthly happiness—attaining the necessities and comforts of life, the possession of goods rather than of the supreme Good.

Life and Faith

There can be no doubt that the subject of spirituality is significantly illumined by seeing it in light of worldviews in collision. Holiness itself is envisioned in profoundly different ways. Secular spirituality finds holiness in the pursuit of peace and justice in this world. Mystical spirituality seeks a holiness that lifts us above the hopes and concerns of this world. Evangelical spirituality strives for a holiness that is other than this world but is lived out in the midst of this world.

The stages of the Christian life (or in modern parlance the integrated life) constitute the basic outline of a spiritual theology. For classical mysticism they are purgation, illumination, union and ecstasy. In biblical religion they are faith, repentance and service. As I have already indicated, for the new spirituality they are struggle, growth and freedom. Or it might be phrased this way: sensitization, involvement and liberation.

Christian spirituality is neither *climbing* nor *sinking* but *fighting* against the principalities and powers of the world. It is not mounting a heavenly stairway that leads away from this world but being raised to rulership over this world. It is not freeing the soul from the bonds of the body but raising both soul and body into a new dimension of existence that radiates the light of the glory of God.

The ruling norm for life and faith varies widely depending on one's metaphysical undergirding. In the biblical view this norm is *fidelity;* in the mystical view it is *tranquility;* in the modern view it is *utility*. In the technological society that encompasses Western civilization the value of something is appraised on the basis of its function. In authentic Christian life on the other hand the value of any person or thing is judged on the basis of its relationship to the living God.

It is who we are in the eyes of God that determines our status in the church and in the world. Our calling as Christians is not to win the praise of mortals but to give glory to God through sacrificial service to those in need. Many Christian mystics would share this authentically biblical vision, though the votaries of the new spirituality would take strong exception and uphold self-fulfillment, even self-aggrandizement, as the only goal worthy of our undivided and life-long devotion.

Appendix C

AN UNRESOLVED TENSION

The cleavage that informs this disquisition on spirituality is that between mysticism (old and new) and evangelical Christianity. I have argued that these types of spirituality represent markedly different orientations. The break with historic Christianity is especially evident in the new spirituality, which casts doubt upon the credibility of Christian and biblical truth claims. Some mystics, such as the noted Quaker devotional writer Rufus Jones, try to build bridges between these disparate types of religion. Sometimes they remind us that a "both/and" approach may be closer to the truth than an "either/or" approach, which practically denies the Christian content of the great mystics.[1] Some evangelicals, like Princeton theologian Benjamin Warfield, contend that Christianity and mysticism are mutually exclusive—that one cannot be both a Christian and a mystic.[2] I hold to the contrary that many of the great mystics have been consciously Christian, partly because of their immersion in the Bible. Mysticism as a philosophy of religion or an ideology necessarily conflicts with Christian faith, but mystical writers and teachers who appeal to Scripture in constructing their schema may be welcomed and honored as fellow believers in the gospel of reconciliation and redemption. The fact that many of them stand in diametrically opposed traditions accounts for the inconsistency and ambiguity in their arguments. As I have made abundantly clear, though, there is little viable common ground between the old or historic mysticism and the secular mysticism of the New Age. Both types exist in considerable and unmitigating tension with biblical religion.

The tension between historic Christianity and classical mysticism can be readily discerned in John Wesley, the renowned eighteenth-century revivalist, who while freely drawing upon the mystics in shaping his theology took stern issue with mysticism as a type of religion that contradicts such Christian claims as salvation through faith alone and grace alone. A book that has been helpful in this regard is Robert G. Tuttle's *Mysticism in the Wesleyan Tradition,* which acknowledges Wesley's indebtedness to many of the leading mystics of the church but makes strikingly clear that mysticism and evangelicalism are competing worldviews that challenge rather than build upon one another.[3] Tuttle convincingly shows the pervasive influence of William Law upon the younger Wesley, who began to see the widening chasm between mysticism, as represented by Law, and a vital evangelical faith. Through his evangelical conversion, which occurred in a small chapel on Aldersgate Street in London, Wesley was led to break with mysticism and embrace the doctrine of free salvation. At Aldersgate he heard Martin Luther's *Preface to the Romans* being read, and his heart was "strangely warmed." This crisis in spiritual horizon brought him to a full realization that we are justified by the righteousness of Christ alone and not by a mystical ascent to a paradise restored.

Wesley had both a profound mistrust of and a marked fascination with mysticism. He made this startling disavowal of that particular brand of piety: "I think the rock on which I had the nearest made shipwreck of the faith was the writings of the Mystics."[4] Of all the enemies of Christianity, "the Mystics are the most dangerous," for "they stab it in the vitals."[5] Wesley, however, did not throw out mysticism altogether. He persisted in seeing value in some of the mystical teachers, who encouraged seekers after truth to make experiential contact with the realities of faith. Tuttle claims that the mature Wesley anchored his theology in the righteousness of Christ to be received by faith, but retained the mystical goal—the transformation of character by perfect love. Wesley acknowledged many of the great mystics as brothers and sisters in the spirit, including in this category Thomas à Kempis, Pascal, Fénelon, Macarius, Loyola, Teresa of Ávila and John of the Cross. Wesley continued to have deep reservations regarding a speculative mysticism (as seen in the German mystics), but he was always open to a "mysticism of service," in which we mount up to God through perfect love rather than through ascetic disciplines and silence. In my opinion Wesley did not aim for a synthesis of biblical faith and mysticism, which are in some respects irreconcilable, but he assiduously sought the purification of mysticism through a faith commitment to Jesus Christ, which always remains a product of free grace.

FOR CHRIST AND HIS KINGDOM

My only hope is in your unfailing love and faithfulness.

PSALM 40:11 LB

Not all who sound religious are really godly people.
They may refer to me as "Lord," but still won't get to heaven.
For the decisive question is whether they obey my Father in heaven.

MATTHEW 7:21 LB

We are fled so far from the solitude of superstition,
that we have cast off the solitude of contemplative devotion.

RICHARD BAXTER

At our eternal best we are what redemption has made us, and not sanctification alone.
We enter heaven by a decisive change, and not merely by a progressive purification.
This is the very marrow of Protestant divinity and Evangelical faith.

P. T. FORSYTH

Christ's victory remains forever sure; the whole world will be His!

CHRISTOPH BLUMHARDT

True spirituality celebrates the coming of the kingdom of God. We are led into true worship when we are seized by the Spirit and become bearers of the love of Christ. The kingdom of God is not so much a state of transformed consciousness as the breaking in of the power of the new age. It denotes the reign of God in the hearts of his people. I uphold a triumphalism not of the church but of the kingdom. Human institutions may falter and fall, but the kingdom of God works as a leaven in the history of humanity, a leaven that cannot be permanently impeded or eradicated. Even though hidden in various movements and crises in history it continues to advance and will eventually embrace the whole of humankind.

A Churchly Spirituality

A spirituality that is biblical and evangelical will bring together an emphasis on individual salvation and community empowerment. We are saved one by one, but we live out our salvation in the fellowship of the redeemed. We receive the call of God through the Word and the sacraments; we implement this call in communion with the Spirit of God working in the fellowship of believers.

I espouse a churchly spirituality—one that stands in continuity with church tradition but also one that is judged and corrected by the Spirit of God giving illumination to Holy Scripture. Scripture remains our infallible standard for faith and practice, but its power lies in its message, not in its mode of writing. We should strive to restore not the practices of the apostolic church but its doctrine. The true apostolic succession lies in fidelity to the gospel, not in a sacramental laying on of hands that supposedly conveys a special grace of the Spirit.

The church of God will take institutional form, but it is not primarily an institution. It is fundamentally a movement of the Spirit directed to the praise of Christ. It is a catalyst that binds believers together in a fellowship of love *(koinonia)*. It contributes to the edification of the saints, but it also empowers the saints for service in the world. In this respect a gospel spirituality will be both churchly and worldly. Its goal is to advance the kingdom of God in the world.

True spirituality will be evangelical—centered in the gospel of Jesus Christ and dedicated to the conversion of a lost humanity. P. T. Forsyth correctly perceived, "Society is past saving by the philanthropists. It needs mighty evangelists."[1] The Salvation Army achieved the right balance in its slogan, "Soup, Soap and Salvation!"[2]

Moreover, true spirituality will be catholic—signifying universality and continuity. Evangelical commitment must be united with ecumenical dedication. The cause of Christian unity is just as momentous as the great commission. This does not mean that we as Christians should seek a one-world church, but it does imply that our churches should strive for altar and pulpit fellowship in order to present a united witness before a cynical and despairing world.

Again, true spirituality will be open to and supportive of the Protestant Reformation, not of its mistakes and imbalances, but of its rediscovery of the treasure of the gospel of salvation by free grace. Forsyth's words must be taken with the utmost seriousness:

> For the soul of an ethical Christianity you must go to the great Evangelical Confessions, which contain the true standard for the interpretation of the Creeds in the interest of the Gospel. And when we treat those magnificent Confessions as old lumber, when we banish from our type of Christianity the centrality of grace and live upon love, when we treat forgiveness as a decorous afterthought, when we think it dreary theology to discuss Redemption or Atonement, we are simply returning to the credal condition of Catholicism. We are falling over into a new Catholicism. We are undoing the Reformation liberty by a sentimental liberalism. For the one work of the Reformation was to restore free Grace, Atonement, and Redemption to be the centre of the Christian world, the spring of the moral world, and the authority for the free human soul.[3]

Forsyth can perhaps be faulted for his tendency to downplay the ancient ecumenical creeds and unduly exalt those that have their basis in the Reformation, whereas all of these faith affirmations should be seen as complementary and mutually supportive. The ancient creeds were an answer to misunderstandings of the person of Christ and the nature of the Godhead, and this answer must surely be reaffirmed by all churches that call themselves trinitarian. This does not imply, however, that we are not allowed to express the mysteries of the faith in new language and with new emphases so long as our contemporary versions comport with the wisdom that has gone before in sacred tradition. It is not surprising that Forsyth finds special value in the creeds and faith of the Reformation, since they pertain to the very heart of the gospel. At the same time, he has for the most part resisted the pull of insularism and has thereby proved to be an effective spokesman for the worldwide church.

The one holy catholic church will be a creedal church, though it will always subordinate its creedal expressions to the authority of Holy Scripture. It will not bow before the creeds, but it will be respectful of them. To seek a purely spiritual religion that refuses to make a public declaration of faith, that regards doctrine as ephemeral and secondary, can prove lethal to an evangelical church. Forsyth again is on target:

> A warm spirituality without the apostolic and evangelical substance may seem attractive to many—what is called undogmatic, or even unconscious, Christianity. It will specially appeal to the lay mind, in the pulpit and out. But it is death to a Church.[4]

True spirituality will be anchored in biblical revelation, but it will resist the temptation of biblicism, which narrows the scope and purpose of revelation. We appeal not simply to the Bible as a book but to the voice of the Holy Spirit as he speaks to us through the pages of the Bible and as he has guided the church through history. We do not simply repeat what the Bible says, but we interpret the Bible in light of the ongoing theological commentary on the Bible in the history of the church. We acknowledge with the Pilgrim preacher John Robinson that the Lord has yet more light to break forth from his Holy Word, but this light is not wholly new, for God never contradicts himself. Whatever church tradition upholds must be congruous with what God reveals in Holy Scripture; otherwise it must be rejected.

Just as biblicism narrows or constricts the apostolic vision of the faith, so dogmatism reduces faith to intellectual assent; both abet a false spirituality. But we must also be on guard against mysticism, which confounds the content of faith with religious experience. Against biblicism we must strive to be true to the Bible without denying its real humanity. Against dogmatism we must be forthright in our defense of the faith without reducing the gospel to a theological formula. Against mysticism and spiritualism we must recognize the experiential dimension of faith without reducing faith to a mystical experience. True spirituality is based on the paradoxical unity of Word and Spirit, and this unity is conveyed to us through earthen vessels—especially the preaching of the Word in the assembly of believers.

True spirituality will also resist the allurement of secularism, which empties biblical religion of its supernatural content. Spiritual persons in the Christian sense will not read Scripture in the light of a cultural ideology but will interpret ideologies through the lens of Scripture. We will not seek to discard the mythopoetic garb of Scripture in order to make the gospel palatable to its cultured despisers, but we will present the gospel in its poetic garb to an unbelieving world, knowing that the gospel itself contains the power of persuasion because of its inseparable union with the Holy Spirit.

The Dialogue with Mysticism

In pressing for a recovery of true spirituality we must return to the question of the role of mysticism in this enterprise. Mysticism has been treated in this book as a Christian aberration, but is there not an enduring mystical dimension in biblical spirituality? The New Testament does speak of being united with Christ in his passion, death and resurrection, but this union has already taken place in faith (Rom 6:5; Gal 2:20-21; Eph 4:3; Col 2:12; 3:10). We do not press forward into a deeper union with Christ but seek to demonstrate a union already actualized as we live out our faith in Christian service. We do not so much enter into Christ as Christ enters into us, and the gateway is the decision of faith (cf. Rev 3:20).

Where a mystical ethos seems to dominate is in the Song of Songs, which allegedly depicts God as our Lover and the object of our affections. Yet this interpretation is based on allegory, not on the natural meaning of the text. The Song of Songs is generally accepted today in scholarly circles as a wedding song, not as a depiction of heavenly love. Earthly love can, of course, be related to the paradoxical love of the cross, which is selfless and spontaneous, but in the process earthly love is purified and transformed.

The problem is the assimilation into Christian spirituality of insights drawn from Platonism and Neoplatonism, which subvert the biblical understanding of life in the Spirit. Marguerite Porete spoke for many mystics when she claimed that in the highest stage of mysticism God is "neither known, nor loved, nor praised" by the creature. God is above rational knowledge and egotistical desire. The state of beatitude is one of nonknowing and non-willing.[5] But this sentiment deviates sharply from the biblical contention that Christians have real relations with a God who loves, cares for and judges his people.

The role of silence is another area of dispute between the two spiritualities. Luther believed that sustained solitude is detrimental to both the spiritual life and creative scholarship. "The Devil likes to have the Christian alone, for then he can heap him with worries and depression."[6] Thomas Merton, by contrast, held that "physical solitude, exterior silence and real recollection are all morally necessary for anyone who wants to lead a contemplative life."[7] Merton was adamant, however, that these things "are nothing more than means to an end, and if we do not understand the end we will make a wrong use of the means."[8] The Bible is clear that the goal of the Christian life is fellowship with God and with the whole company of the saints; yet fellowship does not exclude solitude and silence but makes use of these things to deepen and expand the joy of fellowship.

Much hinges in this discussion on the definition of mysticism, and I have offered definitions earlier in this volume. In this present context Michael Ramsey's definition is helpful: "Mysticism in the proper sense is an intense realization of God within the self, and the self embraced within God in vivid nearness."[9] The biblical prophets certainly had this kind of experience, yet they did not seek it or make it the object of their labors. Their goal was the service of God in daily life, but they were animated to pursue this goal through union with the living God. Ramsey puts it well: "The effect of the experience of mystic union . . . is not to cause a person to long to have the experience again, but to long to serve God, and to do his will."[10] But there is another side to mysticism, which views the state of non-willing as higher than service in the world (as we saw in Marguerite Porete).

The mystics of the church as well as the Pietists, who drew upon mystical spirituality, remind us that we are called to delight in God as well as serve God, to adore God as well as beseech God. Yet contemplation does not take precedence over service but is the means that enables people of faith to engage in service. Against many of the mystics and pietists I contend that our relationship to God is not amorous but fiducial. Love is not a passion that drives us to God (or God to us), but a demonstration of our gratefulness to God for his glorious redemption. We do not revel in love (as a praise chorus suggests) but obey in love.

The downside of mysticism is the denigration of the world and the search for a state of consciousness that rises above earthly care and concern. Elizabeth Strakosch gives this helpful critique of the so-called German mystics:

> One must always bear in mind that preachers like Tauler, Eckhart, Suso, Ruysbroeck and others spoke primarily to enclosed nuns, and one cannot help wondering whether the German mystics of the fourteenth century sufficiently stressed the interceding aspect of a life devoted to God, instead of regarding the temporal world as something implicitly alien and evil; they searched ardently for an ever closer union with God but did they endeavour to plead for their fellowmen with the all-merciful Creator?[11]

Similarly Ida Friederike Görres, writing as a Catholic theologian, castigates what she calls the "God alone" school of mystics, namely, "those who reject and even despise and loathe Creation with as vehement a passion as they seek and love God. And there simply *is* something wrong with this attitude, extolled as it is by writers on ascesis."[12] Görres includes Catherine of Genoa among the "God-alone" mystics. Interestingly, in contrast to these mystics, she upholds nurse Florence Nightingale as a true model of holiness:

> Is her broad, glowing, generous Christianity not more truly human, more *truly* Christian than at least our present-day cloister ideal? Did she not, in fact, do more than found an order—she established a new way of life!—in the spirit of the genuine, historical founders of old?[13]

Görres concludes that "the classical way of mysticism can no longer be accounted the one and only pattern valid for us today."[14]

Mysticism should not be denigrated, but it should be deciphered. It cannot be joined to a biblical spirituality without undergoing a considerable degree of revision. We as biblical Christians can learn positively from the mystical tradition of the faith so long as we do not read into it ideas that are alien to its scope and outreach. Mysticism as a type of religion stands in contrast to biblical, evangelical faith, but a number of the great mystics of the church can be celebrated by evangelical Christians chiefly because they manifested in their piety a strong biblical thrust that exists in tension with a mystical orientation that belongs to another world of discourse and understanding.

Thomas Merton comes close to a biblical orientation when he contends that one of the imponderable paradoxes of the mystical life is this: "A man cannot enter the deepest center of himself and pass through that center into God, unless he is able to pass entirely out of himself and empty himself and give himself to other people in the purity of a selfless love."[15] Yet even here we see a cleft between mystical and biblical piety, for the latter would emphasize the gift of God to the soul in Jesus Christ rather than the labor of entering into God by passing entirely out of the self.

The Dialogue with Pentecostalism

Probably the most dynamic and provocative movement in the church today is Pentecostalism, which has its roots in mysticism and pietism.[16] Pentecostalism is basically evangelical in orientation, for its emphasis is on the substitutionary atonement of Christ, the indispensability of faith in Christ and the urgency of mission to the lost. But it also reflects mystical motifs, including inward renewal and empowering by the Holy Spirit. The danger in Pentecostalism is its tendency to elevate the Spirit over the written Word of God and thereby reduce the significance of historical revelation. Pentecostalism also reflects the new spirituality in which God is interpreted in terms of erupting power rather than redeeming mercy. Pentecostal theologian Merlin Carothers defines God as the "reservoir of power within you," which bears striking similarity to the New Age rendition of God as "the Pool of Unlimited Power."[17]

Pentecostalism must be treated as a welcome protest against certain strands in the older Calvinism, which depicted grace as reducing the sinner to nothingness. Pietist theologian Christoph Blumhardt was closer to the biblical ethos when he declared, "God's people should be exalted, full of spirit and power, and for this there has to be raising from the dead."[18] This raising from the dead occurs preeminently in the outpouring of the Holy Spirit received by faith and demonstrated in love.

One area where Pentecostalism appears to break with Reformation as well as classical Christian spirituality is its proclivity to link faith with prosperity.[19] The dubious claim is advanced that faith makes one prosperous not only in the spiritual but also in the material sense. Health, wealth and prosperity is the gospel not of the New Testament but of the New Thought movement,[20] and it again shows the affinity of Pentecostalism with the new spirituality. There are passages in Proverbs that imply that those who abide by the commandments of God will prosper in their earthly tasks, but this is a hope and expectation more than an infallible promise. Job in the Old Testament is a powerful reminder that suffering and poverty can fall even on the most godly of people. Moreover, Jesus, the model for all Christians, renounced worldly acclaim and honor in order to live a life of sacrificial service for the betterment of humanity. He also contended that it is supremely difficult if not impossible for a rich person to enter the kingdom of God (Mt 19:23-24; Mk 10:25; Lk 6:24). John Calvin did not disallow worldly prosperity for the children of God, but he was profoundly aware of the temptations that prosperity can bring in its wake: "Examples of moderation in prosperity are rare. . . . Whenever prosperity flows on uninterruptedly, its delights gradually corrupt even the best of us."[21]

Both Pentecostals and mainline Christians should ponder James Denney's asseveration that it is better to be "saved in Christ" than "lost in God."[22] Craving for an ecstatic experience of union with God beyond the gift of salvation can foster an egocentric piety in which the empowerment of the self takes precedence over helping our neighbor in need.[23] Pentecostalism at its best represents an evangelical movement of renewal that brings together people of all denominations in order to give a united witness to Jesus Christ in the power of his Spirit. At its worst it can fall into a sectarian posture in its claim to produce an immediate or direct experience of the Holy Spirit evidenced by speaking in other tongues. Pentecostalism can be appreciated by the wider Christian community for its rediscovery of the gifts of the Spirit in fulfilling the church's mission to reach the lost for Jesus Christ. But these spiritual treasures can become snares when they are used to give undue elevation to pastoral leaders who parade them for personal gain. The biblical way is to practice these gifts in the hiddenness of a personal communion with God instead of publicly presenting them as proofs of a higher spirituality.

True spirituality is not trying to make ourselves spiritual through faith, but it is living out our faith in service to God and neighbor. It is not the adornment of the soul that should command our primary attention but hearing the cries of the oppressed and deprived of the world and coming to their aid. We should address ourselves not only to the temporal needs of our hearers but also and above all to their all-encompassing spiritual need for eternal life and salvation. Our focus should be on the reconciling of a lost and sinful humanity to a righteous and holy God. In the light of God's act of reconciliation in Jesus Christ we should do all that we can to overcome the estrangement that separates peoples from one another. We should be preeminently concerned with bringing people the peace of God, but we should also be devoted to helping people live in peace with one another. Such devotion does not involve the compromise of truth but its mutual recognition. We should herald the dawning of the kingdom of God, but we should at the same time work for a just society here on earth as a sign of the perfect righteousness of the kingdom that is still coming. Many Pentecostals share the vision of a social embodiment of the faith, but we must always keep in mind that it will not be perfectly realized until the coming again of Christ in power and in glory.

Freedom for Obedience

The recovery of true spirituality entails the restoration of human freedom. Freedom is made possible not by a discovery of God in the depths of our being but by the outpouring of the Holy Spirit who creates new potentialities within us that enable us to be more than conquerors through Christ who loved us and gave himself for us (Rom 8:37). We are saved not by natural free will, which is impaired by sin, but by the Spirit of God, who grants us freedom to overcome the powers of darkness and persevere in righteousness. True spirituality signifies not a return to God (as in traditional mysticism) but obedience to God through the power of the Spirit. This obedience, which consists of works of love, is a manifestation and demonstration of a salvation already accomplished in the life, death and resurrection of Jesus Christ. It is not a means to secure or earn our salvation but a way by which we exhibit a salvation already achieved. The motivation for good works is not the hope of gaining salvation but gratitude for the salvation that is a free gift of God.

True spirituality affirms free grace over legalism and costly grace over antinomianism. It also upholds simple faith over occultism and gnosticism. Experience is certainly an integral part of true spirituality, but experience is the medium of faith, not its source or object.

True spirituality upholds the paradox of sanctity over the challenge of heroism. We are called not to feats of daring that mark us as superior beings but to faithfulness in life that confirms our election by God's grace. Our witness may very well involve acts that place us in jeopardy, but what makes our witness distinct is that the focus of attention is on Jesus Christ—his life, his obedience, his death and resurrection. We point others not to what they can do for themselves but to what Christ has done for them on the cross. Sanctity is created within us by the Spirit, but we can demonstrate and witness to our sanctity in Christ.

True spirituality affirms the God of sovereign and holy love over the impassible Absolute of mysticism and the distant god of deism. We proclaim the loving and awesome God of biblical revelation over both the vengeful god of sectarian biblicism and the sentimental god of popular religion, where love comes to mean permissiveness. We also hold to the infinite-personal God of biblical religion over the finite god of the new naturalism.

In place of frenzied activism on the one hand and quietism on the other, true spirituality encourages responsible involvement in the world. The practice of faith in the world *(orthopraxis)* flows from the right praise of God in the church *(orthodoxa)*. The ethical is rooted in the spiritual, but the spiritual finds its culmination in the ethical.

Christian faith at its best is both world affirming and world negating—joyfully accepting but relativizing the pleasures of the world. This attitude stands in marked contrast to Christian mysticism in which the pleasures of the world are tolerated but surpassed. It also contravenes gnosticism, which outrightly repudiates the pleasures of the world. In addition, biblical commitment stands in tension with the new spirituality, which unambiguously affirms and celebrates the pleasures of the world.

The paradox of faith is that we ascend to God by descending into the pain and squalor of the world. Our ascent to God, moreover, is based on his descent to us in Jesus Christ. I have difficulty with Gregory of Nyssa's observation that the "ascent to God . . . is accomplished through a sublime way of life."[24] Our hope is based not on ascetic rigorism that supposedly raises us up to God but on simple faith that brings God down to us (Luther).

In a truly Reformed spirituality law stands not in opposition to the gospel but in congruity with the gospel.[25] There is no antithesis between grace and command, for the commandment of God is itself an act of grace. With Karl Barth we can speak of "commanding grace," the gospel that includes the law. God gives what he commands, and he commands what he gives.

Instead of an exclusively agape spirituality I propose a spirituality of gospel and law, of grace and holy living. It is not only gratitude for God's gift of incomparable love but also respect for his holy law that characterize the Christian sojourn. It is not simply agape but agape in indissoluble unity with divine holiness that furnishes the foundation for Christian thought and practice.

True spirituality begins and ends with God. False spirituality begins and ends with the self. We do not find the will of God by probing into the searchings and yearnings of the self. We find hope and promise for the self by reflecting on the depth of God's love for us in Jesus Christ. We do not discover the gracious presence of God by investigating the traces of God in nature and humanity. To the contrary we find the signs of God's presence in nature and humanity by seeing all things in the light of God's self-revelation in Jesus Christ. In his light we shall see light (Ps 36:9).

Our chief concern is to seek first the kingdom of God and his righteousness, and the necessities of life will then be ours as well (Mt 6:33; Mk 10:29-30; Lk 12:29-31). We are sustained not by striving for our own security and happiness but by clinging to the promises of God as our only hope and recourse in life and in death. We are animated by the hope that we will find true happiness when we seek to give glory to God through self-sacrificing service to our neighbor.

THÉRÈSE OF LISIEUX

An Evangelical Saint?

Thérèse of Lisieux is well known in Roman Catholic circles but little known among evangelicals. Born in Normandy, France, on January 2, 1873, she received a calling to become a Carmelite nun and entered the Carmelite convent in Lisieux at the age of fifteen. She died in the convent at the age of twenty-four having contracted tuberculosis. Amazingly, considering that she led a relatively uneventful life, she was beatified by Pius XI in 1923 and declared a doctor of the church in 1997 by Pope John Paul II. This second honor implies that her writings have a normative status, which is remarkable since they patently contradict the legalism that has become imbedded in Catholic tradition. She is most noted for her autobiography, *The Story of a Soul,* which has gone into many editions and been translated into many languages.[1]

Thérèse's life was ordinary, but her doctrine appears to be extraordinary, since she contended that sanctity lies not in great experiences but in the little tasks of every day, which remain hidden from most observers. Thérèse upheld the "little way," daily surrender to God, as opposed to the "great way," justification by works. She took exception to the mystical ideal of the stairway to heaven and commended the lift or elevator of free grace, which one enters in a simple act of faith. We do not raise ourselves to a higher spiritual state, but we are lifted up by the arms of Jesus Christ, who acts out of pure mercy.

Thérèse's spirituality posed a threat to the established spirituality of the convent, and this is why she was resisted by the mother superior at the time. In the convent Thérèse "frequently encountered that crude, egoistical and arithmetical hope of reward which so constantly offends against true Catholic principle. Out of a misguided view of good works and merit the nuns zealously counted sacrifices and acts of virtue, in order to present them to God as reckonings which entitled them to their legitimate recompense."[2]

Against all legalistic spirituality Thérèse declared:

> If I had all the works of St Paul to offer, I would still feel myself to be an unprofitable servant; I would still consider that my hands were empty. But that is precisely what gives me joy, for *since I have nothing I must receive everything from God.*[3]

Thérèse did not deny that some people are more worthy than others, but she was firm in her conviction that we should not place our trust in our deeds of self-giving.

> I'm not relying on my own merits, as I have none, but I put my hope in Him who is goodness and holiness Himself. It is He alone who, satisfied with my feeble efforts, will raise me to Him, will clothe me with His infinite merits, and will make me a saint.[4]

It is my contention that in some respects Thérèse was closer to evangelical than to mystical piety, and this is why she might be a bridge to Christian unity. With the Reformers, whom she had not read, she upheld justification by grace alone, though she insisted that this grace must be appropriated in other-serving love. She lived by faith alone and continued to believe even when she felt nothing. She did not seek visions and did not receive any.[5] It was her aim to live solely by faith. Manifesting no desire to visit Lourdes, the celebrated shrine where the sick are encouraged to seek healing, she had a gnawing suspicion of the search for signs and miracles. She was critical of the Marian piety in which the glory of Mary eclipses the glory of the whole company of the saints. She conceived of prayer as crying out for help to a God who is always near though often hidden.[6] Like the Puritans, whom she did not know, she distrusted long formal prayers and viewed prayer as personal encounter with a living God. Rather than making it her goal to *see* God or the saints in glory, she wanted to live solely by faith.

She espoused a spirituality of mission. In her view the highest vocation is preaching the gospel. She also championed the apostolate of prayer in which the goal is the conversion of souls to Jesus Christ. The motivation for living the godly life is gratitude for what God has done for us in Jesus

Christ, not the hope of gaining an eternal reward. We should do good works to give joy to Jesus, not to gain for ourselves a coveted place in heaven. She espoused a love that takes the form of self-sacrifice rather than one that seeks to possess God in ecstasy. This latter note is not absent but diminished. True love "asks not the natural worth of the other, but evaluates him only by the price that has been paid for him."[7]

Thérèse's spirituality was formed by Holy Scripture, though she did not begin reading Scripture until she joined the convent. She also appealed to Thomas à Kempis's *The Imitation of Christ* and on rare occasions to John of the Cross, whom she criticized for "allowing the soul at the height of love to gaze upon its own beauty."[8] She would memorize whole sections of Scripture. She especially cherished the Gospels, and often contrasted Jesus' teachings with that of the Old Testament.

Thérèse did not wholly abandon the mystical ethos, for indeed this was the ethos that molded her from childhood. Like the mystics, she taught the renunciation of worldly pleasures and the satisfaction of our innate desire for union with God. She wrote that once the soul is raised up even in the smallest degree one can "see the bitterness in all the pleasures the world has to offer."[9] She definitely preferred solitariness over fellowship. Both the camp meetings of the evangelical revivals and the house parties of the Oxford Group movement would probably have made her uncomfortable. She perceived that loyalty to Christ takes precedence over natural affections, yet she sought to maintain family ties. She declared: "I do not understand the saints who do not love their own families."[10] With the mystics of old she regarded silence as the soil of the Word.

It would be a mistake to view the writings of Thérèse as a synthesis of biblical personalism and classical mysticism. What makes her life and thought significant is that they reflected both spiritual traditions. She fell short of the Protestant vision by underplaying the continuance of sin in the life of the Christian. According to Balthasar, she never quite comprehended the biblical and Catholic doctrine of original sin. She was willing to confess faults but not sins, though toward the end of her life she did come to see herself as a sinner. Thérèse's point was that with the help of grace one can overcome any particular sin and recover from any relapse from righteousness. There is no such thing as a hopeless case. Thérèse's message also conflicts with the high regard the Protestant Reformers held for the Old Testament. Instead of seeing the Old Testament as a covenant of works (as did Thérèse), the Reformers believed that both testaments are bound together by a covenant of grace.

Thérèse was more biblical than mystical in her view that the spiritual life consists of descending more than of climbing. We enter into the cares and travails of others in order to help them find their way in a dark and ominous world. Her goal was not the contemplation of the divine essence but the practice of Christian love. With the Pietists and the Puritans she stressed the urgency of mission and evangelism. She saw that God uses instruments to accomplish his purposes, but she was profoundly aware that God does not need instruments. God alone can sanctify our works and sanctify us without works.[11] Ida Friederike Görres aptly puts her finger on the key to the mystery of Thérèse:

> Her essential experiences of God, and her conclusions from them, were not founded upon or inspired by the special insights of the mystics, nor upon the tradition of the Carmelite Order. They derived from the homely traditions of a good family, from the simple everyday, catechism-nourished devotion of father and mother.[12]

I would add that Thérèse's encounter with Holy Scripture was even more determinative in the molding of her spirituality. This does not make her unique, since many other Catholic saints have appealed to Scripture even over church tradition, and here we could mention Blaise Pascal, whom, to my knowledge, Thérèse never cites.

Protestants can learn from Thérèse, especially from the depth of her devotion to the living Christ and her emphasis on the apostolate of prayer. Catholics can learn from the exemplars of Protestant faith that we are justified by a righteousness that is alien to our being but which is ours by faith alone.[13] Thérèse herself verges toward this Protestant conception when she declares: "In the evening of this life I shall appear before you empty-handed, for I do not ask you, Lord, to count my works. All our justices have stains in your sight. So I want to be clad in your own Justice and receive from your Love the possession of yourself. I want no other throne or other crown than you my beloved!"[14]

Evangelicals are obliged to resist the world-denying thrust of Thérèse's piety. They would never say with Thérèse, "It's impossible for one bound by human affection to have intimate union with God."[15] But they would strenuously affirm that the kingdom of God takes precedence over all human needs and obligations and that the decision of faith does involve a break with all temporal loyalties. At the same time, they would contend that once we put the kingdom of God first the goods and necessities of life are given to us as well (cf. Mt 6:33; Lk 12:29-31). Thérèse upheld the way of spiritual childhood, which means increasing dependence on God in a life of faith and surrender. Our Lord himself tells us that in order to find God we must become like a child who places unreserved trust in its father and mother. But this trust does not take us out of the world but drives us to live more fully in the world as we bring the message of salvation to lost sinners. General William Booth of the Salvation Army told the officers in his charge: "Go for souls and go for the worst!"[16] Thérèse could also say this, and we need to emphasize that the road of Christian discipleship entails many different styles of life. Both the married life and the single or celibate life give glory to God so long as Christ and his kingdom remain the goal and the center of our attention.[17]

A HYMN OF PIETISM

One of the stirring hymns of German Pietism is "One Thing Needful, Greatest Blessing" *(Eins Ist Not)*, translated into English by R. A. John.[1] This hymn can be found in a collection of hymns by Joachim Neander in 1680. The themes of Pietism are conspicuous in this beautiful hymn: contemplation as the basis for action; freedom from fear and doubt through faith; the fragile character of earthly joys; and the greater pleasure of being in communion with God. What is significant for our study is that the goal in life is still pleasure, though now not an earthly one but a heavenly one. Earthly joys are not negated, but unless they are supplemented by heavenly joys they amount to very little.

Another version of *Eins Ist Not* was given by Ewald Kockritz.[2] The hymn tune is the same, but the lyrics are strikingly different. Here the emphasis is on what God has done for us in the suffering and death of Christ. Reformation themes predominate over mystical ones. The goal is not to taste the glory of another world but to serve our fellow humankind in this world. In keeping with both the Reformation and Pietism, Christ is upheld as our example as well as our Savior. In verse 3 the law in its third use— instruction in the Christian life—follows the gospel in verse 2. A world-denying thrust is more evident in the first hymn than in the second.

Neither hymn counsels withdrawal from the world; both find our hope as lying in a kingdom that is not of this world. Both hymns, while duly recognizing the terrible plight of humanity, point to the assurance of victory over sin and death through Jesus Christ.

Pietism has often been accused of teaching a theological hedonism.[3] The goal is human happiness; the means is faith in Jesus Christ. Here we see a link with mysticism, which seeks the satisfaction of human desire through union with God. Ritschl may have a point that the Pietist movement represented the penetration of Catholic themes in the churches of the Reformation. But we must also insist that the other-worldly stance of Pietism was held in remarkable balance with the this-worldly stance of Reformation faith. The mystical vision of God is subordinated to the earthly vision of an ever-expanding kingdom of God on earth. It should be kept in mind that most of the Pietists and Puritans were postmillennial, that is, they envisaged a millennial kingdom in earthly history that advances through the preaching of the gospel. Christ in the glory of his second advent comes not before but after the millennium. Pietism retained the spiritual foundations of faith—uniting the goal of personal conversion with a profound recognition of the ethical fruits of our faith. Both of the hymns discussed in this section reflect emphases in Pietism and mysticism, though "One Thing Needful" is perhaps more mystical than evangelical. Both hymns can profitably be sung by any evangelical congregation. In addition they would both enrich any Catholic or Orthodox book of hymns.

One Thing Needful, Greatest Blessing

EINS IST NOT

Rev. R. A. John, 1916   Joachim Neander, 1680

1. One thing need-ful, great-est bless-ing, Teach me, Sav-iour, while I pray;
2. Oft my soul, in dark-ness grop-ing, Sought Thy peace in earth-ly scene;
3. Keep me, then, O Sav-iour, teach-ing Truth di-vine un-to my soul;

Fear and doubt, my heart op-press-ing, In Thy mer-cy drive a-way.
Blind-ly fear-ing, blind-ly hop-ing, Prone on earth-ly hope to lean.
That, be-yond the earth-born reach-ing, I may grasp the heav'n-ly goal.

The joys of this world, though in splen-dor they glit-ter,
But ev-er and ev-er in an-guish and sor-row
Re-plen-ish my soul from Thy heav-en-ly meas-ure

Will soon turn to ash-es, will soon be-come bit-ter;
I bur-ied the hopes of to-day and the mor-row;
And add to my earth-ly joys heav-en-ly pleas-ure,

The pleas-ure of pleas-ures that nev-er can die
For all that can bring me the soul's pure de-light
That ev-er my soul shall ex-ul-tant-ly sing:

From Thee on-ly com-eth, O Sav-iour on high.
Must come from a-bove, from the land of Thy light.
"Christ on-ly can save and Christ on-ly is King!"

In Thy Service, Lord of Mercy

EINS IST NOT

Rev. Ewald Kockritz, 1916

Joachim Neander, 1680
Harmonized by Dr. Otto Kade, 1869

1. In Thy serv-ice, Lord of mer-cy, We would find our chief de-light;
2. 'Tis not thro' some spe-cial mer-it That sal-va-tion we re-ceive,
3. Lord, by all Thy lov-ing ef-forts Thou didst an ex-am-ple give

Show us then some place to la-bor In Thy king-dom, Lord of Light.
But be-cause our sad con-di-tion Caused Thee for man-kind to grieve,
To be fol-lowed by Thy serv-ants, Show-ing how they are to live:

In hearts that are hope-less sin's tor-rents are rag-ing, The for-ces of
Constrained Thee Thy glo-ry of heav-en-ly splen-dor For our re-
Then strengthen our pur-pose, that we res-o-lute-ly Per-form Thy good

dark-ness their war still are wag-ing; The world lies in sor-row, a
demp-tion to free-ly sur-ren-der; To serve the whole world in its
will and ful-fil ev-'ry du-ty; And serv-ing Thee dai-ly, what-

lost hu-man race, Which naught can re-store but the pow'r of Thy grace.
ter-ri-ble plight; To drive out the dark-ness and give it Thy light.
ev-er the task, We find Thy ap-prov-al, 'tis all that we ask.

NOTES

Preface

[1]William Johnson Everett, *The Politics of Worship* (Cleveland, Ohio: Pilgrim, 1999).

Chapter 1: Introduction

[1]See Dietrich Bonhoeffer, *Letters and Papers from Prison,* trans. Reginald Fuller et al., ed. Eberhard Bethge, enlarged ed. (New York: Macmillan, 1972), pp. 279-82.

[2]There is an affinity between my typology and that of Reinhold Niebuhr, who contrasts what he calls the classical, modern and Christian views. See Niebuhr, *The Nature and Destiny of Man* (New York: Charles Scribner's Sons, 1951), 1:1-25.

[3]Heiler differentiates between several types of prayer including primitive, ritual, philosophical, mystical and prophetic. He gives most attention to the gulf between mystical and prophetic religion. He associates the latter with evangelical Protestantism, though not exclusively so. According to Heiler the principal difference between mysticism and prophetism revolves around the question of God. Is God personal (as in prophetism) or suprapersonal or impersonal (as in mysticism)? See Friedrich Heiler, *Prayer,* trans. Samuel McComb (New York: Oxford University Press, 1958).

[4]Anders Nygren, *Agape and Eros,* trans. Philip S. Watson (1932-1939; Philadelphia: Westminster Press, 1953).

[5]Brunner is especially hard on mysticism in his critique of Schleiermacher, which comprised his doctoral thesis: *Die Mystik und das Wort* (Tübingen: J.C.B. Mohr, 1928).

[6]See Emil Brunner, *Die Mystik und das Wort;* and Brunner, *Truth as Encounter* (Philadelphia: Westminster Press, 1964).

[7]Vladimir Lossky, *The Vision of God,* trans. Asheleigh Moorhouse (Crestwood, N.Y.: St. Vladimir's Seminary Press, 1983), p. 67.

[8]Hans Küng, *Christianity,* trans. John Bowden (New York: Continuum, 1995), p. 452.

[9]Simon Tugwell, *Did You Receive the Spirit?* (New York: Paulist, 1972), p. 60.

[10]See Kenneth E. Kirk, *The Vision of God: The Christian Doctrine of the "Summum Bonum,"* 2nd ed. (1932; reprint, London: Longmans, Green, 1941).

[11]Ibid., p. xxvi.

[12]Ibid., p. 470.

[13]Ibid.

[14]Henry Trevor Hughes, *Prophetic Prayer* (London: Epworth Press, 1947), p. 2.

[15]Emil Brunner, *The Word and the World* (1931; reprint, Lexington, Ky.: American Theological Library Association, 1965), p. 77. Brunner is here condemning not spirituality as such but the supposed divine mandate to leave behind earthly cares and concerns in the pursuit of Christian perfection.

[16]See David C. Steinmetz, "Luther and Loyola," in *Interpretation* 47, no. 1 (January 1993): 5-14.

[17]R. H. Coats, *Types of English Piety* (Edinburgh: T & T Clark, 1912).

[18]See note 4.

[19]Cited by Alan P. F. Sell, "P. T. Forsyth as Unsystematic Systematician," in *Justice the True and Only Mercy,* ed. Trevor Hart (Edinburgh: T & T Clark, 1995), p. 129.

[20]Brunner, *The Word and the World,* p. 90.

[21]F. T. H. Fletcher, *Pascal and the Mystical Tradition* (New York: Philosophical Library, 1954), p. 71.

[22]See Nadejda Gorodetzky, *Saint Tikhon of Zadonsk* (Crestwood, N.Y.: St. Vladimir's Seminary Press, 1976), pp. 69, 123.

[23]Ibid., p. 173.

[24]Ibid., p. 189.

[25]Ibid., p. 174.

[26]Ibid., pp. 111-12.

[27]On Karl Barth's interaction with Pietism, see Barth, *Protestant Theology in the Nineteenth Century* (Valley Forge, Penn.: Judson Press, 1973), pp. 508-18; 643-53; and Eberhard Busch, *Karl Barth and the Pietists,* trans. Daniel W. Bloesch (Downers Grove, Ill.: InterVarsity Press, 2004).

[28]See Teresa of Ávila, *The Interior Castle,* trans. and ed. Kieran Kavanaugh and Otilio Rodriguez (New York: Paulist, 1979). See esp. pp. 12-29; 35-47. She also shares this insight: "In my opinion we shall never completely know ourselves if we don't strive to know God. By gazing at His grandeur, we get in touch with our own lowliness" (p. 43).

[29]"Self-Reliance," in *Selected Writings of Ralph Waldo Emerson,* ed. William H. Gilman (New York: New American Library, 1965), p. 273.

[30]Cited in Alister E. McGrath, *Spirituality in an Age of Change: Rediscovering the Spirit of the Reformers* (Grand Rapids: Zondervan, 1994), p. 148.

[31]Arthur Cushman McGiffert, *Protestant Thought Before Kant* (New York: Charles Scribner's Sons, 1919), p. 40.

[32]Owen Chadwick, *John Cassian: A Study in Primitive Monasticism* (Cambridge: Cambridge University Press, 1950), pp. 77-78.

[33]Clement of Rome *Letter to the Corinthians* 32. In *The Early Christian Fathers,* ed. and trans. Henry Bettenson (1956; reprint, New York: Oxford University Press, 1991), p. 30.

[34]John H. Leith, *The Reformed Imperative* (Philadelphia: Westminster Press, 1988), p. 130.

[35]See *Provocations: Spiritual Writings of Kierkegaard,* ed. Charles E. Moore (Farmington, Penn.: Plough Publishing House, 1999), p. 334.

Chapter 2: In Quest of Spirituality

[1]Martin Buber, *The Eclipse of God* (New York: Harper Torchbooks, 1957), pp. 83, 86.

[2]See Søren Kierkegaard, *Concluding Unscientific Postscript,* trans. David F. Swenson (Princeton, N.J.: Princeton University Press, 1944), pp. 493-508.

[3]Søren Kierkegaard, *Philosophical Fragments,* trans. David Swenson; introduction by Niels Thulstrup, trans. Howard V. Hong (Princeton, N.J.: Princeton University Press, 1962), pp. 17-22, 28-45.

[4]Kierkegaard, *Concluding Unscientific Postscript,* pp. 256, 387, 447-48.

[5]See H. V. Martin, *The Wings of Faith* (New York: Philosophical Library, 1951), pp. 52-58.

[6]Karl Barth, *The Epistle to the Romans,* trans. Edwyn C. Hoskyns (1933; reprint, New York: Oxford University Press, 1975), p. 136.

[7]Karl Barth, *The Word of God and the Word of Man,* trans. Douglas Horton (1928; reprint, Gloucester, Mass.: Peter Smith, 1978), p. 69. Emphasis in original.

[8]Jacques Ellul, *The Humiliation of the Word,* trans. Joyce Main Hanks (Grand Rapids: Eerdmans, 1985), pp. 69-71. Ellul here acknowledges his indebtedness to Paul Ricoeur, who first articulated this distinction.

[9]Ibid., p. 69.

[10]Ibid., p. 192.

[11]See note 8.

[12]Barth, *Word of God and Word of Man,* p 70.

[13]See Francis A. Schaeffer, *True Spirituality* (Wheaton, Ill.: Tyndale House, 1971).

[14]See Charles S. Braden, *Spirits in Rebellion: The Rise and Development of New Thought* (Dallas: Southern Methodist University Press, 1963).

[15]Harold Bloom, *The American Religion* (New York: Simon & Schuster, 1992).

[16]See Merlin Carothers, *Praise Works!* (Plainfield, N.J.: Logos International, 1973), p. 48. The author also advises against asking God for mercy, since God has already answered all our prayers through his Son (p. 72).

[17]See my discussion in Bloesch, *The Holy Spirit: Works & Gifts* (Downers Grove, Ill.: InterVarsity Press, 2000), pp. 188-89.

[18]See Brian D. McLaren, *A Generous Orthodoxy* (Grand Rapids: Zondervan, 2004); Tony Jones, *The Sacred Way* (Grand Rapids: Zondervan, 2005); and Jason Byassee, "Emerging Model: A Visit to Jacob's Well," *The Christian Century* 123, no. 19 (September 19, 2006): 20-24. For an appraisal that sees promise in the Emerging Church movement by a respected Fuller theologian, see Ray S. Anderson, *An Emergent Theology for Emerging Churches* (Downers Grove, Ill.: InterVarsity

Press, 2006). For a cogent analysis of some disturbing trends in this spiritual movement, see D. A. Carson, *Becoming Conversant with the Emerging Church* (Grand Rapids: Zondervan, 2005). For a critique of Carson see David G. Dunbar, David M. Mills, Anthony Smith and Phillip Luke Sinitiere, "The Emergent Church Conversation," *Reformation & Revival Journal* 14, no. 4 (2005): 135-73.

[19]Carl Gustav Jung, *Psychology and Religion* (New Haven: Yale University Press, 1938), p. 113. On Jung's occultism and its affinities with the Germanic Faith movement, see Richard C. Noll, *The Jung Cult: Origins of a Charismatic Movement* (Princeton, N.J.: Princeton University Press, 1994).

Chapter 3: Types of Spirituality

[1]See chapter 4, pp. 49-70.

[2]Cf. Bernard McGinn, *The Foundations of Mysticism: Origins to the Fifth Century* (1991; reprint, New York: Crossroad, 1999), pp. 23-61; Andrew Louth, *The Origins of the Christian Mystical Tradition* (Oxford: Clarendon, 1981); and Père A.-J. Festugière, *Contemplation et vie contemplative selon Platon,* 3rd ed. (Paris: J. Vrin, 1967).

[3]See Aldous Huxley, *The Perennial Philosophy* (New York: Harper & Bros., 1945).

[4]Cf. *The Cloud of Unknowing,* trans. Clifton Wolters (1961; reprint, Baltimore: Penguin, 1967).

[5]See Rudolf Otto, *The Idea of the Holy,* trans. John W. Harvey (New York: Oxford University Press, 1958).

[6]See Anders Nygren, *Agape and Eros,* trans. Philip S. Watson (1932-1939; Philadelphia: Westminster Press, 1953), pp. 220-32; 516-18; 563-637.

[7]Especially instructive is Benedict Ashley's *Spiritual Direction in the Dominican Tradition* (Mahwah, N.J.: Paulist, 1995). Ashley trenchantly shows the imprint of mysticism upon the spirituality of a major religious order in the church. Ashley favors a philosophical underpinning for theology.

[8]Schleiermacher's postmodernism is more evident in his *Speeches on Religion (Reden)* than in his dogmatics, *The Christian Faith*. Even here a this-worldly mysticism lurks in the background.

[9]See Friedrich Heiler, *Prayer,* trans. Samuel McComb (New York: Oxford University Press, 1958), pp. 227-85.

[10]For a perceptive analysis of philosophical personalism, see Gary Dorrien, *The Making of American Liberal Theology: Idealism, Realism and Modernity, 1900-1950* (Louisville, Ky.: Westminster John Knox, 2003), pp. 286-355.

[11]Cited in Fred Berthold Jr., *The Fear of God* (New York: Harper & Bros., 1959), p. 43.

[12]See Luther, *A Commentary on St. Paul's Epistle to the Galatians,* ed. Philip S. Watson (Westwood, N.J.: Fleming H. Revell, n.d.), p. 372. For Luther the true self is "excentrically" located as opposed to being "inwardly" located. George Lind-

beck, "A Question of Compatibility: A Lutheran Reflects on Trent," in *Justification by Faith,* ed. H. George Anderson, T. Austin Murphy, Joseph A. Burgess (Minneapolis: Augsburg, 1985), p. 237.

[13]John Calvin, *Institutes of the Christian Religion,* ed. John T. McNeill, trans. Ford Lewis Battles, 2 vols. (Philadelphia: Westminster Press, 1960), 3.11.23 (1:753).

[14]Karl Barth, *Church Dogmatics,* ed. G. W. Bromiley and T. F. Torrance, trans. G. T. Thomson and Harold Knight (Edinburgh: T & T Clark, 1956), 1(2): 393.

[15]See my earlier discussion in Bloesch, *God the Almighty* (Downers Grove: InterVarsity Press, 1995), pp. 219-21.

[16]See Max Weber, *The Protestant Ethic and the Spirit of Capitalism,* trans. Talcott Parsons (New York: Charles Scribner's Sons, 1958), pp. 93-183.

[17]See Bloesch, *The Struggle of Prayer* (1980; reprint, Colorado Springs: Helmers & Howard, 1988), pp. 78-80, 114, 135.

[18]This does not imply that terms like divinization and deification are never permissible in Christian discourse, only that we must take care to preserve the unfathomable difference between the infinite God and finite humanity.

[19]See *The Cloud of Unknowing,* pp. 58, 64, 137. Also see Paul Tillich, *A History of Christian Thought,* ed. Carl E. Braaten (New York: Harper & Row, 1968), p. 93.

[20]John Calvin *Institutes* 3.2.7 (1:551).

[21]Quoted in Stephan A. Hoeller, *The Gnostic Jung* (Wheaton, Ill.: Theosophical Publishing House, 1982), p. 194.

[22]Cited in Karl Barth, *The Epistle to the Romans,* trans. Edwyn C. Hoskyns (New York: Oxford University Press, 1975), p. 39.

[23]See my previous discussion in Bloesch, *The Church: Sacraments, Worship, Ministry, Mission* (Downers Grove, Ill.: InterVarsity Press, 2002), pp. 190-93.

[24]Quoted in Reinhold Niebuhr, *Christian Realism and Political Problems* (New York: Charles Scribner's Sons, 1953), p. 123.

[25]Thinkers who are classified as radical Pietists or spiritualists include Jacob Boehme, Gottfried Arnold and Friedrich Christoph Oetinger.

[26]On Wesley's reservations on mysticism see Robert G. Tuttle, *Mysticism in the Wesleyan Tradition* (Grand Rapids: Zondervan, 1989). For my further discussion of Wesley see pp. 137-38.

[27]See my earlier discussion in chapter 1, p. 21.

[28]See appendix D in this book, pp. 151-55.

[29]The openness of God theology is a logical development of the rationalist current in modern evangelicalism. See my critique in Bloesch, *God the Almighty,* pp. 254-60.

Chapter 4: Classical Mysticism

[1]While Christian mysticism in this study is included in classical mysticism, the latter also embodies non-Christian elements, such as Neoplatonism.

[2]Quoted in Paul Elmer More, *The Catholic Faith* (Princeton, N.J.: Princeton Uni-

166 SPIRITUALITY OLD AND NEW

versity Press, 1931), p. 206.

[3]Ibid., p. 239. Angela of Foligno is referring to an inner seeing that transcends human perceptivity.

[4]Thomas Aquinas allowed for analogical knowledge of God that presupposes a correspondence between our thoughts and God's thoughts.

[5]Plotinus *Enneads*. Cited in David Manning White, ed., *The Search for God* (New York: Macmillan, 1983), p. 75.

[6]Raymond Bernard Blakney, ed. and trans. *Meister Eckhart* (New York: Harper & Bros., 1941), p. 248. Note that not all of this material can be attributed to Eckhart.

[7]More, *The Catholic Faith,* p. 284.

[8]See Paul Tillich, *A History of Christian Thought,* ed. Carl E. Braaten (New York: Harper & Row, 1968), p. 92.

[9]Plotinus *Enneads,* quoted in White, *Search for God,* p. 44.

[10]*The Theologia Germanica of Martin Luther,* trans. and ed. Bengt Hoffman (New York: Paulist, 1980), p. 70.

[11]George A. Maloney, *The Breath of the Mystic* (Denville, N.J.: Dimension Books, 1974), pp. 21-23.

[12]See Tillich, *A History of Christian Thought,* pp. 201-3.

[13]John Ruysbroeck, *The Adornment of The Spiritual Marriage,* trans. C. A. Wynschenk Dom (London: John M. Watkins, 1951), p. 103.

[14]Paul Tillich, *Systematic Theology* (Chicago: University of Chicago Press, 1963), 3:420-21.

[15]Hans Denck, *On the Law of God,* quoted in White, *Search for God,* p. 114.

[16]Madame Guyon, *A Method of Prayer,* trans. Dugald Macfadyen (London: James Clarke, 1902), p. 103. Also see N. V. Hope, "Madame Guyon," and R. G. Clouse, "Quietism," in *Evangelical Dictionary of Theology,* ed. Walter A. Elwell, 2nd ed. (Grand Rapids: Baker, 2001), pp. 531, 976-77.

[17]More, *The Catholic Faith,* p. 207.

[18]For Plato, true love is *seeing* the perfection of God in contrast to following Christ into the darkness of the world in discipleship. See Irving Singer, *The Nature of Love* (1966; 2nd ed., Chicago: University of Chicago Press, 1984), 1:73.

[19]Quoted in Martin Buber, *Ecstatic Confessions,* ed. Paul Mendes-Flohr, trans. Esther Cameron (San Francisco: Harper & Row, 1985), p. 109.

[20]Here we see the close relation between mysticism and asceticism in the Greek tradition.

[21]See Tillich, *History of Christian Thought,* p. 94.

[22]*The Way of a Pilgrim,* trans. Helen Bacovcin (New York: Doubleday Image, 1978), p. 182.

[23]Albert the Great, *Of Cleaving to God* (Oxford: Blackfriars, 1947), pp. 26-27. The author is quoting from *De spiritu et anima,* a work attributed to Augustine but now known to be by Alcher of Clairvaux. See *New Catholic Encyclopedia,* 2nd ed. (Detroit: Thomson/Gale, 2003), 1:239-40.

[24]See *The Cloud of Unknowing*, trans. and ed. Clifton Wolters (1961; reprint, Baltimore: Penguin, 1967).

[25]See Jaroslav Pelikan, *The Christian Tradition* (Chicago: University of Chicago Press, 1971), 1:206.

[26]See Richard of St. Victor, *Of the Four Degrees of Passionate Charity*, in *Richard of Saint Victor: Selected Writings on Contemplation*, ed. and trans. Clare Kirchberger (London: Faber & Faber, 1957), pp. 224, 230-32.

[27]See Thomas Spidlik, ed., *Drinking from the Hidden Fountain: A Patristic Breviary*, trans. Paul Drake (Kalamazoo, Mich.: Cistercian Publications, 1994), p. 365.

[28]Teresa of Ávila, *Life*, 12.5. In Patrick Grant, ed., *A Dazzling Darkness* (Grand Rapids: Eerdmans, 1985), p. 296.

[29]See Maloney, *Breath of the Mystic*, pp. 175-98.

[30]See John Climacus, *The Ladder of Divine Ascent*, trans. Colm Luibheid and Norman Russell (New York: Paulist, 1982), pp. 48-52.

[31]Cited by Benjamin Drewery, "Martin Luther," in *A History of Christian Doctrine*, ed. Hubert Cunliffe-Jones, with Benjamin Drewery (Philadelphia: Fortress, 1980), p. 321.

[32]Kenneth Leech, *Experiencing God* (San Francisco: Harper & Row, 1985), p. 129.

[33]"On the Perfection of Life," 4.3, in *The Works of Bonaventure*, trans. José de Vinck (Paterson, N.J.: St. Anthony Guild Press, 1960), 1:230.

[34]Teresa of Ávila, *The Way of Perfection*, trans. E. Allison Peers (New York: Doubleday Image, 1964), p. 184.

[35]Thomas Merton, *Seeds of Contemplation* (Norfolk, Conn.: New Directions Books, 1949), p. 42.

[36]Biblical Christianity allows for periodic withdrawal from the cares of family, property, etc., but not permanent withdrawal (cf. 1 Cor 7:5).

[37]See the discussion in Anders Nygren, *Agape and Eros*, trans. Philip S. Watson (1932-1939; Philadelphia: Westminster Press, 1953), pp. 503-12.

[38]Thomas à Kempis, *The Imitation of Christ*, trans. Leo Sherley-Price (Harmondsworth, U.K.: Penguin, 1959), pp. 80-81.

[39]Ibid., p. 171.

[40]Origen *Commentary on the Song of Songs*. Cited in *The Affirmation of God*, ed. David Manning White (New York: Macmillan, 1984), p. 131.

[41]John Climacus, *Ladder of Divine Ascent*, p. 87.

[42]*The Letters of St. Jerome*, trans. Charles Christopher Mierow; ed. Thomas Comerford Lawler (Westminster, Md.: Newman, 1963), 1:62.

[43]See *The Book of the Blessed Angela of Foligno*, in Angela of Foligno, *Complete Works*, trans. Paul Lachance (New York: Paulist, 1993), pp. 126, 143.

[44]*The Homilies of Saint Jerome*, trans. Sister Marie Liguori Ewald (Washington, D.C.: Catholic University of America Press, 1964), 1:123.

[45]Thomas, *Imitation of Christ*, pp. 80-81.

[46]Thomas Merton, *The Monastic Journey* (Mission, Kans.: Sheed, Andrews, and McMeel, 1977), p. 34.

[47]Edmund Colledge and Bernard McGinn, trans. and ed., *Meister Eckhart* (New York: Paulist, 1981), pp. 60-61. The older distinction between Mary and Martha also finds its way into Eckhart; see p. 285.

[48]See Gerald Heard, *A Preface to Prayer* (New York: Harper & Bros., 1944), pp. 48, 55-56.

[49]Eckhart's emphasis was on transcending humanity in order to reach divinity. Cf. Blakney, *Meister Eckhart,* pp. 198-201.

[50]Geert Grote in *Devotio Moderna: Basic Writings,* trans. and ed. John Van Engen, preface by Heiko A. Oberman (New York: Paulist, 1988), p. 113.

[51]Plotinus *Enneads,* cited in White, *Search for God,* p. 112.

[52]Quoted by Jaroslav Pelikan in his "The Predicament of the Christian Historians: A Case Study," *Reformed Review* 52, no. 3 (Spring 1999): 208. See Augustine *Soliloquies* 2.7.

[53]See my more extensive treatment of the biblical-classical synthesis in Bloesch, *God the Almighty* (Downers Grove, Ill.: InterVarsity Press, 1995), pp. 205-40.

[54]Angelus Silesius *The Cherubinic Wanderer,* in *The Fire and the Cloud: An Anthology of Catholic Spirituality,* ed. David A. Fleming (New York: Paulist, 1978), p. 287. Here is another version: "How often have I prayed, 'Lord do your will'. . . . But see: He does no willing—motionless He is and still." *The Book of Angelus Silesius,* trans. Frederick Franck (New York: Vintage Books, 1976), p. 93.

[55]Gregory of Nyssa, *The Lord's Prayer, The Beatitudes,* trans. and ed. Hilda C. Graef (Westminster, Md.: Newman, 1954), p. 31.

[56]Emil Brunner, *The Word and the World* (1931; reprint, Lexington, Ky.: American Theological Library Association, 1965), p. 60.

[57]See Simone Weil, *Gravity and Grace,* trans. Arthur Wills (New York: G. P. Putnam's Sons, 1952), p. 119.

[58]Simone Weil, *The Need for Roots* (New York: Harper & Row, 1952), p. 289.

[59]Arthur Cushman McGiffert, *Protestant Thought Before Kant* (New York: Charles Scribner's Sons, 1919), p. 182.

[60]For a strong endorsement of Edwards as an evangelical and biblical theologian see Robert W. Jenson, *America's Theologian: A Recommendation of Jonathan Edwards* (New York: Oxford University Press, 1988). Also see Gerald R. McDermott, *Jonathan Edwards Confronts the Gods* (New York: Oxford University Press, 2000); and George M. Marsden, *Jonathan Edwards: A Life* (New Haven, Conn.: Yale University Press, 2003). For an acerbic though also telling critique of Jonathan Edwards's doctrine of justification, see George Hunsinger, "An American Tragedy: Jonathan Edwards on Justification," *Modern Reformation* 13, no. 4 (July/August 2004): 18-21. Hunsinger objects to Edwards's attempt to make a place for "inherent holiness" in the Christian; yet this concept is fully in accord

with biblical and Reformation faith so long as it is subordinated to the extrinsic holiness epitomized in the life, death and resurrection of Jesus Christ.

[61]Søren Kierkegaard, *Philosophical Fragments*, 2nd ed., trans. and ed. David F. Swenson, Niels Thulstrup and Howard V. Hong (Princeton, N.J.: Princeton University Press, 1962).

[62]For my earlier discussion see Bloesch, *God the Almighty*, pp. 219-21.

[63]See Irving Singer, *The Nature of Love* (Chicago: University of Chicago Press, 1984), 2:168.

[64]Nygren, *Agape and Eros*.

[65]See Bernard of Clairvaux, *The Love of God and Spiritual Friendship*, ed. James M. Houston, abridged ed. (Portland, Ore.: Multnomah Press, 1983), pp. 154-63.

[66]*The Cloud of Unknowing*, pp. 51-52.

[67]Teresa of Ávila, *The Interior Castle*, trans. K. Kavanaugh and O. Rodriguez (New York: Paulist, 1979), 5.3.7-12, pp. 100-102.

[68]More, *The Catholic Faith*, pp. 279-80. While the mystics of the church generally regarded the contemplative life more highly than the active life, their spiritual heirs were sometimes numbered among the founders of hospitals, schools for the retarded, homes for the disabled and other ventures in creative benevolence.

[69]Evelyn Underhill, *Mysticism* (1911; reprint, Oxford: Oneworld Publications, 1993), p. 89.

[70]Richard of St. Victor, *Of the Four Degrees of Passionate Charity*, pp. 224, 230-32.

[71]See Pelikan, *Christian Tradition*, 1:206.

[72]Cf. Paul Tillich, *Sermons*, in White, *Search for God*, p. 138.

[73]Charles W. Kegley and Robert W. Bretall, eds., *The Theology of Paul Tillich* (New York: Macmillan, 1952), pp. 216-27.

[74]See my earlier discussion in Bloesch, *God the Almighty*, pp. 221-24.

[75]Augustine *On the Trinity*, chap. 8. See *Augustine of Hippo: Selected Writings*, ed. and trans. Mary T. Clark (New York: Paulist, 1984), p. 328.

[76]In contrast to Judaism, Jesus does not promise blessings on all who live in a particular way but announces blessings on all who hear the gospel and believe it. Such persons will see their desires fulfilled, but only because God's blessing has already fallen upon them. According to the biblical scholar Robert Tannehill, "When Jesus speaks the beatitudes, he is announcing to these people the happy news that they have been chosen by God to share in God's kingdom, which will end their hunger and exclusion." Robert C. Tannehill, *Luke* (Nashville: Abingdon, 1996), p. 115. Eduard Schweizer says that in the original form of the beatitudes (Lk 6:20-21), "Jesus proclaims blessings on all who are poor, who hunger, who weep, without the addition of any conditions that men must first fulfill." Eduard Schweizer, *The Good News According to Matthew*, trans. David E. Green (Atlanta: John Knox Press, 1975), p. 81. According to Robert Gundry, "'Blessed' means 'to be congratulated' in a deeply religious sense and with more emphasis on divine approval than on human happiness." Robert H. Gundry, *Matthew*

(Grand Rapids: Eerdmans, 1982), p. 68.

[77]In Craufurd Tait Ramage, *Great Thoughts from Classic Authors* (New York: John B. Alden, 1891), p. 445.

[78]*The Triple Way, or Love Enkindled,* in *Works of Bonaventure,* 1:63.

[79]See John W. Bailey, "The First and Second Letters to the Thessalonians," in *Interpreter's Bible* (Nashville: Abingdon, 1955), 11:324.

[80]Angelus Silesius, *The Cherubinic Wanderer,* trans. Maria Shrady (New York: Paulist, 1986), pp. 94, 117.

[81]See Oscar Cullmann, *Immortality of the Soul or Resurrection of the Dead?* (London: Epworth Press, 1958).

[82]Quoted in Matthew Fox, *Creation Spirituality* (San Francisco: Harper & Row, 1991), p. 99.

[83]Quoted in Reinhold Niebuhr, *An Interpretation of Christian Ethics* (New York: Harper & Bros., 1935), p. 71.

[84]Plotinus *Enneads,* in White, *Search for God,* p. 128.

[85]*The Oxford Book of Prayer* (1985; reprint, Oxford: Oxford University Press, 1990), p. 329. See *Plato,* ed. and trans. W. R. M. Lamb (London: William Heinemann, 1961), 5:207.

[86]*Philo of Alexandria,* ed. and trans. David Winston (New York: Paulist, 1981), p. 147.

[87]Geert Grote in *Devotio Moderna,* p. 113.

[88]John of the Cross *A Spiritual Canticle Between the Soul and Christ* 3. Quoted in Grant, *A Dazzling Darkness,* p. 248. Also see *The Collected Works of St. John of the Cross,* trans. Kieran Kavanaugh and Otilio Rodriguez (Washington, D.C.: Institute of Carmelite Studies, 1973), p. 428.

[89]Quoted in Matthew Fox, *One River, Many Wells* (New York: Jeremy P. Tarcher/ Putnam, 2000), p. 164.

[90]Gregory of Nyssa, *The Life of Moses,* trans. and ed. Abraham J. Malherbe and Everett Ferguson (New York: Paulist, 1978), p. 93.

[91]Aldous Huxley, "Reflections on the Lord's Prayer," in *Vedanta for the Western World,* ed. Christopher Isherwood (New York: Viking, 1945), p. 312. It should be noted that Huxley and his mystical fraternity have not overcome an anthropocentric orientation; God is supremely important but as a means toward human self-realization.

Appendix A: Christian Mysticism and Gnosticism

[1]See Hans Jonas, *The Gnostic Religion,* 2nd rev. ed. (Boston: Beacon, 1963); Elaine Pagels, *The Gnostic Gospels* (New York: Random House, Vintage Books, 1981); *Beyond Belief: The Secret Gospel of Thomas* (New York: Random House, 2003); Kurt Rudolf, *Gnosis,* trans. Robert McLachlan Wilson (San Francisco: Harper & Row, 1983); Alastair H. B. Logan, *Gnostic Truth and Christian Heresy* (Peabody, Mass.: Hendrickson, 1996); and Karen L. King, *What Is Gnosticism?*

(Cambridge, Mass.: Harvard University Press, 2003).

[2]See my earlier discussion of the relation of mysticism and Gnosticism in Bloesch, *The Holy Spirit: Works & Gifts* (Downers Grove, Ill.: InterVarsity Press, 2000), pp. 91-97.

[3]Note that a minority of Christian Gnostics did hold that Jesus really suffered and died (see Pagels, *Gnostic Gospels,* pp. 108-9), but they envisaged this trauma as a martyrdom rather than an ontological conversion of the world to Jesus Christ (as in Karl Barth).

[4]Russell E. Saltzman, "Modern Marcionites," *Forum Letter* 30, no. 2 (February 2001): 3.

[5]Sermon 30, in Matthew Fox, *Breakthrough: Meister Eckhart's Creation Spirituality in New Translation* (New York: Doubleday Image Books, 1980), p. 423.

[6]Fox, *Breakthrough,* p. 132.

[7]Another major difference between Plotinus and the Gnostics was that the latter posited a redeemer figure who would descend from the Pleroma to show people the way to salvation. For Plotinus salvation is basically a matter of self-liberation. See Karl Jaspers, *The Great Philosophers,* trans. Ralph Manheim (New York: Harcourt, Brace & World, 1966), 2:80-91.

[8]John Hellman, *Simone Weil: An Introduction to Her Thought* (Waterloo, Ont.: Wilfrid Laurier University Press, 1982), p. 70.

[9]Simone Weil, *Notebooks,* trans. Arthur Wills (1956; reprint, London: Routledge & Kegan Paul, 1976), 2:616.

[10]Nicolas Berdyaev, *Truth and Revelation,* trans. R. M. French (New York: Collier Books, 1962), pp. 83-85.

[11]Carl A. Raschke, *The Interruption of Eternity* (Chicago: Nelson-Hall, 1980), p. 69.

[12]See Gerald Heard, *Is God in History?* (New York: Harper & Bros., 1950); *Is God Evident?* (New York: Harper & Bros., 1948); *The Creed of Christ* (New York: Harper & Bros., 1940); *The Code of Christ* (New York: Harper & Bros., 1941); *Training for the Life of the Spirit* (New York: Harper & Bros., 1941); and *The Ascent of Humanity* (New York: Harcourt, Brace & Co., 1929). For the seminal contribution of Gerald Heard to modern spirituality, see Leigh Eric Schmidt, *Restless Souls: The Making of American Spirituality* (San Francisco: HarperSanFrancisco, 2005), pp. 260-64. This book is also an important resource for Ralph Waldo Emerson, Rufus Jones, Douglas Steere and Walt Whitman.

[13]Augustine *True Religion* 29.72. Quoted by John Paul II in *Fides et Ratio* (Washington, D.C.: United States Catholic Conference, 1998), p. 26. See also John P. Kenney, *The Mysticism of Saint Augustine: Rereading the Confessions* (New York: Routledge, 2005). The author makes a credible case that Augustine in his overall theology rises above mysticism.

[14]See Philip J. Lee, *Against the Protestant Gnostics* (New York: Oxford University Press, 1987). pp. 19-33.

[15]Jonas, *Gnostic Religion,* pp. 326-27.

[16]For Tillich's criticisms of neo-orthodoxy see Paul Tillich, *A History of Christian Thought,* ed. Carl E. Braaten (New York: Harper & Row, 1968), pp. 34, 41-42.

Chapter 5: Biblical Personalism

[1]Emil Brunner, *The Word and The World* (1931; reprint, Lexington, Ky.: American Theological Library Association, 1965), pp. 23, 26.

[2]A. J. Heschel, "The Concept of Man in Jewish Thought," in *The Concept of Man,* ed. S. Radhakrishnan and P. T. Raju, 2nd ed. (Lincoln, Nebr.: Johnsen Publishing, 1972), pp. 138-39.

[3]See Søren Kierkegaard, *Eighteen Upbuilding Discourses,* ed. and trans. Howard V. Hong and Edna H. Hong (Princeton, N.J.: Princeton University Press, 1990), p. 393.

[4]W. Herrmann, *The Communion of the Christian with God,* ed. Robert T. Voelkel (Philadelphia: Fortress, 1971), pp. 116-17. A quite different orientation toward life and the world appears in the "Christian hedonism" of John Piper, in which personal happiness becomes the supreme end in life and is to be found in union with God. See Piper, *Desiring God: Meditations of a Christian Hedonist* (Portland, Ore.: Multnomah Press, 1986). This new kind of hedonism, which goes back to the Pietists and Puritans and ultimately to the mystics, is based on the biblical truth that God wills the best for his people, who are then permitted and encouraged to will the best for themselves. Yet we must keep in mind another side of the Christian life—that sometimes we as Christians are called to forego personal happiness and security in order to magnify and glorify God, whose counsel exceeds and at times contradicts human wisdom. Piper to his credit does not confuse Christianity with the religion of self-esteem, but he nonetheless makes a place for an enduring egocentric element in religion and therefore does not sufficiently challenge motifs of self-aggrandizement that are so ubiquitous in our culture. Piper's book merits serious consideration by all those immersed in the study of spirituality.

[5]Cited by Benjamin Drewery, "Martin Luther," in *A History of Christian Doctrine,* ed. Hubert Cunliffe-Jones with Benjamin Drewery (Philadelphia: Fortress, 1980), p. 321.

[6]C. S. Lewis, *The Four Loves* (New York: Harcourt, Brace & World, 1960), p. 175.

[7]Here we see how the love of God presupposes the doctrine of the Trinity. God's love is other-regarding even within himself, since he exists as a fellowship of persons.

[8]Robert Jenson, *America's Theologian: A Recommendation of Jonathan Edwards* (New York: Oxford University Press, 1988), p. 194.

[9]Ibid. See my earlier discussion of Edwards on pp. 61-62.

[10]See Søren Kierkegaard, *Philosophical Fragments,* 2nd ed., trans. and ed. David Swenson, Niels Thulstrup and Howard V. Hong (Princeton, N.J.: Princeton University Press, 1962).

[11]Cf. Ted Peters, *The Cosmic Self* (San Francisco: Harper, 1991), pp. 191-93.

[12]In Owen Chadwick, introduction to *John Cassian: Conferences,* trans. Colm Luibheid (New York: Paulist, 1985), p 15.

[13]Roland H. Bainton, *Here I Stand: A Life of Martin Luther* (Nashville: Abingdon, 1950), p. 219.

[14]See Niels Thulstrup, "Commentator's Introduction," in Kierkegaard, *Philosophical Fragments,* pp. xlv-xcvii.

[15]On my earlier treatment of natural theology, see Bloesch, *A Theology of Word & Spirit* (Downers Grove, Ill.: InterVarsity Press, 1992), pp. 143-83.

[16]Emil Brunner, *The Theology of Crisis* (New York: Charles Scribner's Sons, 1929), p. 32 (italics in original).

[17]In *The Search for God,* ed. David Manning White (New York: Macmillan, 1983), p. 19.

[18]See Francis A. Schaeffer, *He Is There and He Is Not Silent* (Wheaton, Ill.: Tyndale House, 1972).

[19]This action of the Spirit can be called a mediated immediacy. The Spirit works in conjunction with the Word rather than apart from the Word.

[20]*The Tabletalk of Martin Luther,* ed. Thomas S. Kepler (New York: World, 1952), p. 143.

[21]Brunner, *The Word and The World,* pp. 75-76.

[22]See Bloesch, *A Theology of Word & Spirit.*

[23]See Louis Bouyer, *The Spirit and Forms of Protestantism,* trans. A. V. Littledale (Westminster, Md.: Newman, 1956).

[24]See Philip Schaff, *History of the Christian Church* (1910; reprint, Grand Rapids: Eerdmans, 1981), 3:1016-28.

[25]Martin Luther, *The Bondage of the Will,* trans. J. I. Packer and O. R. Johnston (Old Tappan, N.J.: Fleming H. Revell, 1957).

[26]See Peter T. Forsyth, *The Work of Christ* (London: Independent Press, 1910), pp. 80-81.

[27]*Luther's Works,* ed. Hilton C. Oswald (St. Louis: Concordia, 1972), 25:90.

[28]See Augustus M. Toplady, "Rock of Ages," in *The Hymnal for Worship & Celebration* (Waco, Tex.: Word Music, 1986), no. 204.

[29]For my earlier discussion see Bloesch, *God the Almighty* (Downers Grove, Ill.: InterVarsity Press, 1995), pp. 219-21. Also see chapter 4 on mysticism in this volume, pp. 49-70.

[30]Emil Brunner, *God and Man,* trans. David Cairns (London: Student Christian Movement Press, 1936), p. 121.

[31]See Anders Nygren, *Agape and Eros,* trans. Philip S. Watson (1932-1939; Philadelphia: Westminster Press, 1953), pp. 61-159.

[32]Note that Kierkegaard described the neighbor whom we are to love as "the ugly."

[33]Martin Luther, *The Heidelberg Disputation* (1518). For another translation see

Luther's Works, ed. Harold J. Grimm (Philadelphia: Muhlenberg, 1957), 31:57.

[34]See Nygren, *Agape and Eros,* pp. 731-32.

[35]The Catholic Quietists also tried to overcome a preoccupation with self. But contrary to the teaching of Reformation theology, they cultivated an indifference to salvation rather than agonizing over the salvation of others.

[36]See "Reply to Sadolet," in *Calvin: Theological Treatises,* trans. and ed. J. K. S. Reid (Philadelphia: Westminster Press, 1954), p. 228.

[37]*What Luther Says,* ed. Ewald M. Plass (St. Louis: Concordia, 1959), 2:828.

[38]*Luther: Lectures on Romans,* trans. and ed. Wilhelm Pauck (Philadelphia: Westminster Press, 1961), p. 262.

[39]For Augustine's synthesis of eros and agape in *caritas,* see Nygren, *Agape and Eros,* pp. 449-562.

[40]See Dietrich Bonhoeffer, "*Ecce Homo!,*" in *Ethics,* ed. Eberhard Bethge (New York: Macmillan, 1955), 1.3.70.

[41]People in these circles sometimes hold up the goal of rising above the "zoo level" or "animal level" within us in order to be in communion with God. See Gerald Heard, *The Code of Christ* (New York: Harper & Bros., 1941), p. 61.

[42]Jacques Ellul, *Living Faith,* trans. Peter Heinegg (New York: Harper & Row, 1983), p. 277.

[43]See Jacques Ellul, *The Political Illusion,* trans. Konrad Kellen (New York: Alfred A. Knopf, 1967).

[44]The other alternatives that Niebuhr examines are "Christ of Culture" and "Christ and Culture in Paradox." See H. Richard Niebuhr, *Christ and Culture* (New York: Harper & Brothers, 1951).

[45]See Bloesch, *Freedom for Obedience* (San Francisco: Harper & Row, 1987), pp. 233-44; and Bloesch, *The Church* (Downers Grove, Ill.: InterVarsity Press, 2002), pp. 69-81.

[46]See Max Thurian's discussion of Calvin's position in Thurian, *Marriage and Celibacy,* trans. Norma Emerton (London: SCM Press, 1959), pp. 21-31, 57, 60, 62, 71-72, 78-80, 83, 85, 88-90, 92-93.

[47]In addition to centers of mission and evangelism, I see a place for retreat houses and religious communities devoted to prayer and inner, personal renewal. See Bloesch, *Centers of Christian Renewal* (Philadelphia: United Church Press, 1964); and *Wellsprings of Renewal* (Grand Rapids: Eerdmans, 1974).

[48]See Bloesch, *The Struggle of Prayer* (1980; reprint, Colorado Springs: Helmers & Howard, 1988). Also see Bloesch, "Prayer," in *Evangelical Dictionary of Theology,* 2nd ed., ed. Walter A. Elwell (Grand Rapids: Baker, 2001), pp. 946-48.

[49]See Richard J. Foster, *Prayer: Finding the Heart's True Home* (San Francisco: HarperSanFrancisco, 1992), see esp. pp. 179-81. Also see Foster, *Streams of Living Water* (San Francisco: HarperSanFrancisco, 1998).

[50]John Calvin, *Instruction in Faith (1537),* trans. and ed. Paul T. Fuhrmann (Philadelphia: Westminster Press, 1949), p. 57.

[51]Gerald Heard, ed., *Prayers and Meditations* (New York: Harper, 1949), p. 102.

[52]Teresa of Ávila, *The Way of Perfection*, cited in White, *Search for God*, p. 114.

[53]See Bloesch, *Freedom for Obedience*, pp. 238-44.

[54]Ellul, who stands in the Puritan and Pietist traditions, presents the case for iconoclasm in his *The Humiliation of the Word*, trans. Joyce Main Hanks (Grand Rapids: Eerdmans, 1985).

[55]I am thinking of groups like the Brethren of the Common Life, the radical Quakers, the Theosophical Society and the Rosicrucians.

[56]See also Heard, *Code of Christ*, p. 168.

[57]See H. Richard Niebuhr, *The Kingdom of God in America* (Chicago: Willett, Clark & Co., 1937), pp. 17-44.

[58]*New Jerusalem Bible*, notes on Ps 27:8, p. 839.

[59]See A. J. Lewis, *Zinzendorf: The Ecumenical Pioneer* (Philadelphia: Westminster Press, 1962), pp. 78-97.

[60]Richard Collier, *The General Next to God* (New York: Dutton, 1965), p. 209.

[61]See *Christianity Today* 11, no. 3 (November 11, 1966): 63.

[62]See D. T. Niles, *That They May Have Life* (New York: Harper & Row, 1951), p. 96.

[63]Gerald Heard, "Notes on Brother Lawrence's Practice of the Presence of God—II," in *Vedanta for the Western World*, ed. Christopher Isherwood (New York: Viking, 1945), p. 416.

[64]*Luther's Works*, trans. Jaroslav Pelikan (Saint Louis: Concordia, 1963), 26:387.

[65]In Karl Barth and Christoph Blumhardt, *Action in Waiting* (Rifton, N.Y.: Plough Publishing House, 1969), p. 7.

[66]*Provocations: Spiritual Writings of Kierkegaard*, ed. Charles Moore (Farmington, Penn.: Plough Publishing House, 1999), p. 334.

[67]Rudolf Bultmann, *Jesus and the Word* (New York: Charles Scribner's Sons, 1934), p. 47.

[68]Hans Urs von Balthasar, *The Theology of Karl Barth*, trans. Edward T. Oakes (San Francisco: Ignatius Press, 1992), p. 325.

[69]Quoted in Finbarr Flanagan, *Faith & Renewal* 15, no. 6 (May/June 1991): 16-21.

[70]Balthasar, *Two Sisters in the Spirit*, trans. Donald Nichols and Anne Elizabeth Englund (San Francisco: Ignatius Press, 1992), p. 278.

Chapter 6: The New Spirituality

[1]Sam Keen, *To a Dancing God* (New York: Harper & Row, 1970), p. 141-60.

[2]Peter Bien, *Kazantzakis: Politics of the Spirit* (Princeton, N.J.: Princeton University Press, 1989), p. 68.

[3]Nikos Kazantzakis, *Zorba the Greek*, trans. Carl Wildman (1952; reprint, New York: Ballantine, 1969), pp. 85-86, 334-35.

[4]Quoted in Michael Horton, *In the Face of God* (Dallas: Word, 1996), p. 53. See Matthew Fox, "A Mystical Cosmology: Toward a Postmodern Spirituality," in *Sacred Interconnections*, ed. David Ray Griffin (Albany: State University of New

York Press, 1990), pp. 15-33.

[5]Quoted in Irving Singer, *The Nature of Love* (Chicago: University of Chicago Press, 1984), 2:179.

[6]Descartes is often considered the father of the Enlightenment, but John Locke is more representative of the Enlightenment in its maturity.

[7]Cited in Paul Tillich, *Perspectives on 19th and 20th Century Protestant Theology* (New York: Harper & Row, 1967), p. 146.

[8]Feodor Dostoevsky, *The Brothers Karamazov*, trans. Constance Garnett (New York: New American Library, 1957), p. 297.

[9]See Langdon Gilkey, *Catholicism Confronts Modernity* (New York: Seabury, 1975), pp. 56-60; and Gilkey, "The God of Nature," in *Chaos and Complexity*, ed. Robert John Russell, Nancey Murphy and Arthur R. Peacocke, 2nd ed. (Berkeley, Calif.: Center for Theology and the Natural Sciences, 1997), pp. 211-20.

[10]Cited by Rudolf Bultmann, "The Idea of God and Modern Man," in *Translating Theology into the Modern Age*, ed. Robert W. Funk (New York: Harper Torchbooks, 1965), p. 93.

[11]Miguel de Unamuno, *The Tragic Sense of Life*, trans. J. E. Crawford Flitch (1921; reprint, London: Macmillan, 1931), p. 207.

[12]Ibid., pp. 181-82.

[13]"Self-Reliance," in *Selected Writings of Ralph Waldo Emerson* (New York: New American Library, 1983), pp. 277-80.

[14]On Rorty's developing secular spirituality see Jason Boffetti, "How Richard Rorty Found Religion," *First Things* no. 143 (May 2004): 24-30.

[15]William James, *The Will to Believe* (New York: Dover Publications, 1956), p. 62. See pp. 106, 109, 177 in *Spirituality Old and New*.

[16]D. H. Lawrence, *The Rainbow* (1915; reprint, New York: The Modern Library, 1943), p. 322.

[17]See Matthew Fox, *Breakthrough: Meister Eckhart's Creation Spirituality in New Translation* (New York: Doubleday Image Books, 1980).

[18]Ibid., p. 46.

[19]See Mechthild of Magdeburg, *The Flowing Light of the Godhead*, trans. Frank Tobin (New York: Paulist, 1998), pp. xxx, 14, 16, 43-44, 52, 58-62.

[20]Henri Bergson, *Creative Evolution*, trans. Arthur Mitchell (New York: Henry Holt, 1911), p. 248.

[21]Frederick Copleston, *History of Philosophy* (New York: Doubleday Image, 1985), 7:81.

[22]Dostoevsky, *Brothers Karamazov*, p. 295. See the discussion in Nicholas Arseniev, *Mysticism and the Eastern Church*, trans. Arthur Chambers (Crestwood, N.Y.: St. Vladimir's Seminary Press, 1979), pp. 118-19.

[23]Matthew Fox, *Original Blessing* (Santa Fe, N.M.: Bear, 1983), p. 284.

[24]André Gide, *Journals* [1947], trans. Justin O'Brien. Quoted in *The International Thesaurus of Quotations*, ed. Rhoda Thomas Tripp (New York: Thomas

Y. Crowell, 1970), p. 249.

[25]Lewis Mumford, *The Conduct of Life* (New York: Harcourt, Brace, 1951), p. 75.

[26]M. Scott Peck, *The Road Less Traveled* (New York: Simon & Schuster, 1978), p. 269. See also M. Scott Peck, *Further Along the Road Less Traveled: The Unending Journey Toward Spiritual Growth* (New York: Simon & Schuster, 1993); and *The Road Less Traveled and Beyond* (New York: Simon & Schuster, 1997).

[27]William James espoused meliorism as opposed to both optimism and pessimism. He believed that humans working with God can improve the world, though imperfection will remain.

[28]Fox, *Breakthrough,* p. 45.

[29]Quoted in Richard J. Niebanck, "On the Battlements of Liberalism," *Forum Letter* 19, no. 8 (August 15, 1990): 8. Also see Larry L. Rasmussen, *Earth Community, Earth Ethics* (Geneva: WCC Publications, 1996).

[30]See Van Wyck Brooks, *The Life of Emerson* (New York: Literary Guild, 1932), p. 90.

[31]Theodore Parker, *Theism, Atheism and the Popular Theology,* ed. Charles W. Wendte (Boston: American Unitarian Association, n.d.), p. 306.

[32]Ibid., p. 237.

[33]Ibid., p. 228. For a cogent appraisal of Parker's impact on American religion, see Dean Grodzins, *American Heretic: Theodore Parker and Transcendentalism* (Chapel Hill: University of North Carolina Press, 2002).

[34]*The Philosophy of Nietzsche* (New York: Modern Library, 1927), pp. 6-7.

[35]Robert A. Segal, *Joseph Campbell: An Introduction,* rev. ed. (New York: Mentor; Penguin, 1990), p. 123. See my discussion on pp. 112, 115, 117, 131, 134, 149. According to Campbell all people are embarked on a mystical quest for the purpose of enriching their own lives. The heroic pursuit of this quest benefits others by showing them the way to self-realization.

[36]John Dewey, *Reconstruction in Philosophy,* 2nd ed. (1948; reprint, Boston: Beacon, 1957), p. 177. An authoritarian bent is apparent in Dewey's assertion that society has the mandate to make sure that its members grow in the right direction (see pp. 161-213). Also see Dewey, *Democracy and Education* (New York: Free Press, 1944), pp. 23-40.

[37]Friedrich Schleiermacher, *On Religion: Speeches to Its Cultured Despisers,* trans. John Oman (New York: Harper & Row, 1958), p. 227.

[38]Friedrich Schleiermacher, *Schleiermacher's Soliloquies,* trans. and ed. Horace Leland Friess (Chicago: Open Court, 1957), p. 18.

[39]Rosemary Haughton, "Liberating the Divine Energy," in *Living with Apocalypse,* ed. Tilden H. Edwards (San Francisco: Harper & Row, 1984), p. 85.

[40]Ivan Illich, *Celebration of Awareness: A Call for Institutional Revolution* (New York: Doubleday, 1970), p. 98.

[41]Gilkey, *Catholicism Confronts Modernity,* p. 5.

[42]Michael M. Uhlmann, "The Supreme Court Rules," *First Things* no. 136 (October 2003): 28-29.

[43] *Philosophy of Nietzsche,* p. 183.

[44] Alan Jones, *Passion for Pilgrimage* (San Francisco: Harper & Row, 1988), p. 71.

[45] Jacques Monod, *Chance and Necessity* (New York: Alfred Knopf, 1971), p. 112.

[46] See Charles S. Peirce, *Chance, Love and Logic* (New York: George Braziller, 1956); and Justus Buchler, ed. *Philosophical Writings of Peirce* (New York: Dover Publications, 1955), pp. 339-40, 352, 364-74. Peirce was not entirely comfortable with the term "tychism," though he accepted it. Peirce had a noticeable influence on such representatives of liberal theology as James Luther Adams and Charles Hartshorne. See George Kimmich Beach, "James Luther Adams's 'Covenant of Being' and Charles Hartshorne's 'Divine Relativity,'" *The Unitarian Universalist Christian* 58 (2003): 57-70.

[47] Gregory A. Boyd, *Satan and the Problem of Evil* (Downers Grove, Ill.: InterVarsity Press, 2001), pp. 386-93.

[48] See John Sanders, *The God Who Risks* (Downers Grove, Ill.: InterVarsity Press, 1998); and Gregory Boyd, *The God of the Possible* (Grand Rapids: Baker, 2000).

[49] From my perspective God knows intellectually what the future holds, but he does not know the future existentially until he experiences it.

[50] Copleston, *History of Philosophy,* 7:132.

[51] Tillich, *Systematic Theology* (Chicago: University of Chicago Press, 1951), 1:266-67.

[52] Alfred North Whitehead, *Process and Reality* (1929; reprint, New York: Social Science Book Store, 1941), p. 31.

[53] See Gordon D. Kaufman, *God-Mystery-Diversity* (Minneapolis: Fortress, 1996), pp. 101-9.

[54] Pierre Teilhard de Chardin, *On Love and Happiness* (San Francisco: Harper & Row, 1984), p. 10.

[55] Paul Tillich, *Political Expectation,* ed. James Luther Adams (1971; reprint, Macon, Ga.: Mercer University Press, 1981), p. 118.

[56] Both Schleiermacher and Tillich envisioned the dawning of a new religion of the Spirit that would supersede historical Christianity. See Schleiermacher, *On Religion,* pp. 210-53; and Paul Tillich, *The Future of Religions* (New York: Harper & Row, 1966), pp. 80-94.

[57] Ralph Waldo Emerson, *Journals,* ed. W. H. Gilman and A. R. Ferguson (Cambridge, Mass.: Harvard University Press, 1963), 3:279.

[58] Simone Weil, *Gravity and Grace,* trans. Arthur Wills (New York: G.P. Putnam's Sons, 1952), p. 67.

[59] Jürgen Moltmann, *The Spirit of Life,* trans. Margaret Kohl (Minneapolis: Fortress, 1992), p. 199.

[60] Schleiermacher, *On Religion,* p. 101.

[61] Charles S. Braden, *These Also Believe* (New York: Macmillan, 1949), pp. 162-67.

[62] Nikos Kazantzakis, *Report to Greco,* trans. P. A. Bien (Oxford: Bruno Cassirer, 1966), p. 306.

[63]Alfred North Whitehead, *Science and the Modern World* (1925; reprint, New York: New American Library, 1949), p. 192.

[64]Gerald Heard, *A Preface to Prayer* (New York: Harper & Bros., 1944), p. 121.

[65]D. H. Lawrence, *Mr. Noon* (Cambridge: Cambridge University Press, 1984), p. 189.

[66]Cited in Fox, *Original Blessing,* p. 58.

[67]Starhawk, *The Spiral Dance,* new ed. (San Francisco: HarperSanFrancisco, 1999), p. 56.

[68]See Luther H. Martin, *Hellenistic Religions* (New York: Oxford University Press, 1987), p. 100; H. J. Rose, *A Handbook of Greek Mythology,* 4th ed. (London: Methuen, 1950), p. 69.

[69]Schleiermacher, *Soliloquies,* p. 94.

[70]See Samuel Wells, *Improvisation: The Drama of Christian Ethics* (Grand Rapids: Brazos, 2004), pp. 42-44. Also see my earlier reflections on heroism on pp. 112, 115, 149.

Appendix B: The New Age Movement

[1]For important books on the New Age movement by traditionalist Christian authors, see John P. Newport, *The New Age Movement and the Biblical Worldview* (Grand Rapids: Eerdmans, 1998); Russell Chandler, *Understanding the New Age* (Dallas: Word, 1988); Ross Clifford and Philip Johnson, *Jesus and the Gods of the New Age* (Oxford: Lion, 2001); Michael Cole, *What Is the New Age?* (London: Hodder & Stoughton, 1990); David Jeremiah with C. C. Carlson, *Invasion of Other Gods: The Seduction of New Age Spirituality* (Dallas: Word, 1995); Douglas Groothuis, *Revealing the New Age Jesus* (Downers Grove, Ill.: InterVarsity Press, 1990); Groothuis, *Unmasking the New Age* (Downers Grove, Ill.: InterVarsity Press, 1986); Ted Peters, *The Cosmic Self* (San Francisco: Harper, 1991); Walter Martin, *The New Age Cult* (Minneapolis: Bethany House, 1989); and Duncan Ferguson, ed. *New Age Spirituality: An Assessment* (Louisville, Ky.: Westminster John Knox, 1993). This last book contains essays supportive of the New Age. For further reading see William Bloom, *The New Age: An Anthology of Essential Writings* (London: Rider, 1991); J. L. Simmons, *The Emerging New Age* (Santa Fe, N.M.: Bear, 1990); J. R. Lewis and J. G. Melton, eds. *Perspectives on the New Age* (Albany: State University of New York Press, 1992); Sarah M. Pike, *New Age and Neopagan Religions in America* (New York: Columbia University Press, 2004); and James R. Lewis and Jesper Aagaard Petersen, eds., *Controversial New Religions* (New York: Oxford University Press, 2005), pp. 225-349.

[2]K. C. Cole, "Master of the Myth," *Newsweek* 112, no. 20 (November 14, 1988): 61. Campbell made this remark in an interview with Bill Moyers on PBS.

[3]R. W. Emerson, *Nature,* in *Selected Writings of Ralph Waldo Emerson,* ed. William H. Gilman (New York: New American Library, 1983), p. 223. See David L. Smith, "The Open Secret of Ralph Waldo Emerson," *Journal of Religion* 70, no. 1 (January 1990): 33.

[4]In Cornel West, "Emerson on Personality (and Race)," in his *The American Evasion of Philosophy* (Madison: University of Wisconsin Press, 1989), pp. 30, 33, 34.

[5]See Vera Stanley Alder, *The Initiation of the World* (1939; 2nd ed., New York: Samuel Weiser, 1968), p. 40; and *When Humanity Comes of Age* (1956; reprint, New York: Samuel Weiser, 1974), p. 95.

[6]Alice Bailey, *Education in the New Age* (1954; reprint, New York: Lucis Publishing, 1974), pp. 14, 71, 118, 140. Also see Texe Marrs, *Dark Secrets of the New Age* (Westchester, Ill.: Crossway, 1987), pp. 119-35, esp. 123; and Marrs, *Ravaged by the New Age* (Austin, Tex.: Living Truth Publishers, 1989).

[7]See Helena Blavatsky, *The Secret Doctrine,* 6 vols. (Wheaton, Ill.: Theosophical Press, 1952).

[8]Walter Martin, *New Age Cult,* p. 132.

[9]See Alder, *When Humanity Comes of Age,* pp. 26-35.

[10]See Carrie Tomko, "Anthroposophy: The Occult Influences of Rudolph Steiner, part II," in *SCP Journal* 26, no. 1 (2002): 60-70. Also see Alan Morrison, "From Old Gnosticism to New Age," part 2 in *SCP Journal* 29, nos. 2-3 (2005): 12-23.

[11]See Peter Jones, *Spirit Wars: Pagan Revival in Christian America* (Mukilteo, Wash.: Wine Press Publishing, 1997), pp. 188-90, 307. Note that Jones is an unswerving critic of the New Age movement.

[12]Spiritual writers like Karen Armstrong belong more properly to the wider movement of the new spirituality than to the New Age, especially in its cultic forms. Yet her increasing openness to Buddhism and Hinduism shows an affinity between her thought and the ethos of the New Age. Like many New Agers she vigorously rejects the world-denying spirituality of the medieval cloister. See Karen Armstrong, *The Spiral Staircase* (New York: Viking, 2001); and *Buddha* (New York: Viking, 2001); and *The Great Transformation* (New York: Alfred A. Knopf, 2006).

[13]See George A. Maloney, *Mysticism and the New Age: Christic Consciousness in the New Creation* (New York: Alba House, 1991); and Ferguson, *New Age Spirituality.* See esp. pp. 35-58.

[14]At the same time, as we have observed (see p. 117 in this chapter), there is an indisputable racist tinge in the New Age movement, and this includes Ralph Waldo Emerson, Joseph Campbell, Helena Blavatsky, Vera Stanley Alder, Alice Bailey and Friedrich Rittelmeyer. On Campbell see Richard Bernstein, "After Death, a Writer is Accused of Anti-Semitism," *New York Times* 139, no. 48046 (November 6, 1989): c 17. On Rittelmeyer see Paul Banwell Means, *Things That Are Caesar's: The Genesis of the German Church Conflict* (New York: Round Table Press, 1935), pp. 114-20. Rittelmeyer confessed his indebtedness to Rudolf Steiner's Anthroposophy. Also see the Canadian psychiatrist Richard Bucke, who at the beginning of the twentieth century advanced the idea of an emerging superrace in his book *Cosmic Consciousness,* now a New Age classic (1901; reprint, New York: Arkana, 1991). Cited in Marrs, *Dark Secrets,* pp. 125-26. An-

other highly influential work from an earlier period—one that signifies a blending of racism, cultural imperialism and occultism—is Houston Stewart Chamberlain's *Foundations of the Nineteenth Century,* 2 vols. (New York: John Lane, 1912). In some of these writers the discovery of national identity is subordinated to the unfolding of a global vision that superior peoples impress upon those who are deemed inferior.

[15]Chandler, *Understanding the New Age,* p. 106.

[16]Quoted in Martin, *New Age Cult,* p. 25.

[17]See David Spangler, "The New Age: The Movement Toward the Divine," in Ferguson, *New Age Spirituality,* pp. 99-101.

[18]Richard Blow, "Moronic Convergence: The Moral and Spiritual Emptiness of New Age," *New Republic* 198, no. 4 (January 25, 1988): 26. Note that this is Blow's interpretation.

[19]Ibid. Note that these are MacLaine's words.

[20]Deepak Chopra, *How to Know God* (New York: Harmony Books, 2000), p. 301. For a friendly critique of both Deepak Chopra and Neal Donald Walsch, see Lois Malcolm, "God as Best Seller," *The Christian Century* 120, no. 19 (September 20, 2003): 31-35.

[21]Spangler, "The New Age," p. 105.

Chapter 7: Worldviews in Collision

[1]See Donald G. Bloesch, *A Theology of Word & Spirit* (Downers Grove, Ill.: InterVarsity Press, 1992).

[2]One must be careful in using this terminology, since "Absolute Subject" can carry implications of the God of idealism, whose knowledge encompasses the world but who does not creatively interact with the world in self-giving love. The biblical God does not only know; he also speaks and acts. He is not so much Being itself as Being in communion.

[3]See James K. A. Smith, "What God Knows: The Debate on 'Open Theism,'" *The Christian Century,* 122, no. 14 (July 12, 2005): 30-32. For my critique of open theism or the openness of God theology see Bloesch, *God the Almighty* (Downers Grove, Ill.: InterVarsity Press, 1995), pp. 254-60.

[4]J. A. T. Robinson presents the case for a new kind of mysticism in his *Exploration into God* (Stanford, Calif.: Stanford University Press, 1967). Among his mentors are Pierre Teilhard de Chardin, William Blake, Nicolas Berdyaev and Meister Eckhart.

[5]See Nicolas Berdyaev, *Truth and Revelation,* trans. R. M. French (New York: Collier, 1992), p. 83.

[6]Louis J. Shein, *The Philosophy of Lev Shestov (1866-1938): A Russian Religious Existentialist* (Lewiston, N.Y.: Edwin Mellen, 1991), p. 62. See Lev Shestov, *Athens and Jerusalem,* trans. Bernard Martin (Athens: Ohio University Press, 1966). Shestov appeals both to the Bible and to humanity's creative aspirations.

[7]Lev Shestov, *Kierkegaard and the Existential Philosophy,* trans. Elinor Hewitt

(Athens: Ohio University Press, 1969), p. 95.

[8]For my previous discussion see Bloesch, *God the Almighty,* pp. 137-52; 219-21.

[9]Dietrich Bonhoeffer, *Letters and Papers from Prison,* ed. Eberhard Bethge, trans. Reginald H. Fuller (New York: Macmillan, 1962), p. 175.

[10]See Bloesch, *The Struggle of Prayer* (San Francisco: Harper & Row, 1980; reprint, Colorado Springs: Helmers & Howard, 1988). Cf. John Calvin, *On Prayer: Conversation with God,* ed. I. John Hesselink (Louisville, Ky.: Westminster John Knox, 2006).

[11]Vernard Eller, ed., *Thy Kingdom Come: A Blumhardt Reader* (Grand Rapids: Eerdmans, 1980), p. 77 (italics in original).

[12]See Jürgen Moltmann, *Religion, Revolution and the Future,* trans. M. Douglas Meeks (New York: Charles Scribner's Sons, 1969), pp. 129-47, 200-220. Also see Dorothee Soelle, *On Earth as in Heaven: A Liberation Spirituality of Sharing,* trans. Marc Batko (Louisville, Ky.: Westminster John Knox, 1993); Daniel L. Migliore, *Called to Freedom: Liberation Theology and the Future of Christian Doctrine* (Philadelphia: Westminster Press, 1980); Gustavo Gutiérrez and Richard Shaull, *Liberation and Change* (Atlanta, Ga.: John Knox Press, 1977); and Robert McAfee Brown, *Spirituality and Liberation* (Philadelphia: Westminster Press, 1988).

[13]See Edward Le Joly, *Servant of Love: Mother Teresa and her Missionaries of Charity* (San Francisco: Harper & Row, 1977). See especially pp. 136-44.

[14]This saying has been attributed to Mother Teresa, but it may well have originated with one of her followers.

Appendix C: An Unresolved Tension

[1]Whereas I am inclined to give precedence to "either/or" even while affirming "both/and," mystics are prone to sacrifice the former for the latter. See Rufus M. Jones, *The Inner Life* (New York: Macmillan, 1916), pp. vii-viii, 82-84.

[2]Warfield writes, "We may be mystics, or we may be Christians. We cannot be both." B. B. Warfield, *Biblical and Theological Studies,* ed. Samuel G. Craig (Philadelphia: Presbyterian & Reformed, 1952), p. 462. See his critique on pp. 445-62. Note that Warfield duly acknowledged a mystical thread in Christian faith. See W. Andrew Hoffecker, *Piety and the Princeton Theologians* (Phillipsburg, N.J.: Presbyterian & Reformed, 1981). For mystical overtones in Calvin's theology, see J. Todd Billings, "United to God Through Christ: Assessing Calvin on the Question of Deification," *Harvard Theological Review* 98, no. 3 (2005): 315-34. Billings does not gloss over the very real differences between Calvin and the mystical tradition of the church, as can be seen in his recognition of Calvin's strong affirmation of the doctrine of forensic justification. From my perspective Calvin, like Luther, indubitably belongs in the category of biblical personalism. For a sympathetic Catholic appraisal of Calvin's spiritual legacy, see Lucien Joseph Richard, *The Spirituality of John Calvin* (Atlanta: John Knox Press, 1974).

[3]See Robert G. Tuttle Jr., *Mysticism in the Wesleyan Tradition* (Grand Rapids: Francis Asbury, 1989).

[4]John Wesley, *The Letters of the Rev. John Wesley,* ed. John Telford, 8 vols. (London: Epworth, 1931), 1:207.

[5]John Wesley, *The Journal of the Rev. John Wesley,* ed. Nehemiah Curnock, 8 vols. (London: Epworth, 1909), 1:420.

Chapter 8: For Christ and His Kingdom

[1]P. T. Forsyth, *The Church, the Gospel and Society* (London: Independent Press, 1962), p. 96.

[2]See Richard Collier, *The General Next to God* (New York: Dutton, 1965), p. 199.

[3]Forsyth, *The Church, the Gospel and Society,* pp. 124-25.

[4]P. T. Forsyth, *The Church and the Sacraments* (London: Independent Press, 1947), p. 4.

[5]See Marguerite Porete, *The Mirror of Simple Souls,* trans. Ellen L. Babinsky (New York: Paulist, 1993), pp. 121, 124, 127, 156, 170; and Michael A. Sells, *Mystical Languages of Unsaying* (Chicago: University of Chicago Press, 1994), pp. 116-45; 180-205.

[6]Heiko A. Oberman, *Luther: Man Between God and the Devil,* trans. Eileen Walliser-Schwarzbart (New York: Doubleday, 1992), p. 309. Note that these are the words of Oberman.

[7]Thomas Merton, *Seeds of Contemplation* (Norfolk, Conn.: New Directions, 1949), pp. 57-58.

[8]Ibid., p. 58.

[9]Margaret Duggan, ed., *Through the Year with Michael Ramsey* (London: Hodder & Stoughton, 1975), p. 164.

[10]Ibid.

[11]Elizabeth Strakosch, ed. and trans., *Signposts to Perfection: A Selection from the Sermons of Johann Tauler* (St. Louis: B. Herder, 1958), p. xxxvii.

[12]Ida Friederike Görres, *Broken Lights,* trans. Barbara Waldstein-Wartenberg (Westminster, Md.: Newman, 1964), p. 164.

[13]Ibid., pp. 148-49.

[14]Ibid., p. 267.

[15]Merton, *Seeds of Contemplation,* p. 47.

[16]See Steven J. Land, *Pentecostal Spirituality: A Passion for the Kingdom* (Sheffield, U.K.: Sheffield Academic Press, 1993). For my earlier discussion of Pentecostalism, see Bloesch, *The Holy Spirit: Works & Gifts* (Downers Grove, Ill.: InterVarsity Press, 2000), pp. 179-221.

[17]Merlin Carothers, *Praise Works!* (Plainfield, N.J.: Logos International, 1973), p. 71.

[18]Karl Barth on Christoph Blumhardt, *Action in Waiting* (Rifton, N.Y.: Plough, 1969), p. 37.

[19]See Bruce Barron, *The Health and Wealth Gospel* (Downers Grove, Ill.: InterVar-

sity Press, 1987); D. R. McConnell, *A Different Gospel* (Peabody, Mass.: Hendrickson, 1988); and Robert M. Bowman Jr., *The Word-Faith Controversy: Understanding the Health and Wealth Gospel* (Grand Rapids: Baker, 2001).

[20]See Charles S. Braden, *Spirits in Rebellion: The Rise and Development of New Thought* (Dallas: Southern Methodist University Press, 1963).

[21]Calvin on Deuteronomy 8, in *Commentaries on the Four Last Books of Moses* (Edinburgh: Calvin Translation Society, 1852), 1:398.

[22]James Denney, *The Christian Doctrine of Reconciliation* (London: James Clarke, 1959), p. 307.

[23]Pentecostal New Testament scholar Gordon Fee scores modern Pentecostalism as well as much church tradition for playing "the Spirit of conversion and ethics" against "the Spirit of signs and wonders." See Gordon D. Fee, *God's Empowering Presence: The Holy Spirit in the Letters of Paul* (Peabody, Mass.: Hendrickson, 1994), pp. 853-65. There is one baptism of the Spirit, one event of being born from above, but this has to be acknowledged and reaffirmed throughout one's life. See the supportive review of this book by George T. Montague, *The Catholic Biblical Quarterly* 57, no. 4 (October 1995): 803-4.

[24]Gregory of Nyssa, *The Lord's Prayer: The Beatitudes,* trans. and ed. Hilda C. Graef (Westminster, Md.: Newman, 1954), p. 31.

[25]See my previous discussion in Bloesch, *Jesus Christ: Savior & Lord* (Downers Grove, Ill.: InterVarsity Press, 1997), pp. 198-209.

Appendix D: Thérèse of Lisieux

[1]John Beevers, trans. and ed., *The Autobiography of Saint Thérèse of Lisieux: The Story of a Soul* (New York: Doubleday, 1989). Also see Ronald Knox, trans., *Autobiography of St. Thérèse of Lisieux* (New York: P. J. Kenedy & Sons, 1958).

[2]Ida Friederike Görres, *The Hidden Face,* trans. Richard and Clara Winston (New York: Pantheon, 1959), pp. 274-75.

[3]Ibid., pp. 278-79.

[4]Beevers, *Autobiography of Saint Thérèse,* p. 49.

[5]Note that she was not totally devoid of mystical experiences, but they occurred rarely.

[6]Beevers, *Autobiography of Saint Thérèse,* p. 136.

[7]Görres, *Hidden Face,* p. 117.

[8]Hans Urs von Balthasar, *Two Sisters in the Spirit* (San Francisco: Ignatius Press, 1992), p. 338.

[9]Knox, *Autobiography of St. Thérèse,* p. 117.

[10]Balthasar, *Two Sisters in the Spirit,* p. 138.

[11]Görres, *Hidden Face,* p. 282.

[12]Ibid., p. 413.

[13]See Dwight Longenecker, "Tough Little Sister: Thérèse of Lisieux—A Saint for All Christians," *Touchstone* 13, no. 7 (September 2000): 22-27.

[14]Ibid., p. 24.

[15]Beevers, *Autobiography of Saint Thérèse,* pp. 55-56.

[16]See my earlier reference on p. 97.

[17]Note that "Christ and his kingdom" is the motto of the famed evangelical school Wheaton College in Wheaton, Illinois.

Appendix E: A Hymn of Pietism

[1]See R. A. John, trans., "One Thing Needful, Greatest Blessing," from hymns compiled by Joachim Neander. From *The Evangelical Hymnal,* ed. David Bruening (St. Louis: Eden Publishing House, 1922), no. 279, pp. 252-53. Note that there have been other translations of this hymn into English.

[2]See Ewald Kockritz, "In Thy Service, Lord of Mercy," in *The Evangelical Hymnal,* no. 322, pp. 288-89.

[3]See chap. 5 n. 4.

Name Index

Subject Index

Scripture Index